Alice Peterson has written two non-fiction books, a personal story called *A Will to Win*, which has been updated and republished as *Another Alice*, and a family memoir based on her grandmother's life in Rhodesia. *By My Side* is her third novel for Quercus. Alice lives in London.

Also by Alice Peterson

ALICE PETERSON

By My Side

Quercus

First published in 2012 by Quercus Editions Ltd
This paperback edition published in 2013 by Quercus Editions Ltd

Quercus
55 Baker Street
7th Floor, South Block
London W1U 8EW

A CIP catalogue record for this book is available
from the British Library

ISBN 978 1 78206 181 6
EBOOK 978 1 78206 182 3

10 9 8 7 6 5 4 3 2 1

Printed and bound in Great Britain by Clays Ltd, St Ives plc

Typeset by Ellipsis Digital Limited, Glasgow

To Sarah Orr

PROLOGUE

'I have a *very* woolly head,' I tell Sean, wishing I hadn't downed that last tequila shot in the early hours of this morning. It seemed such a good idea at the time to have just one more.

Sean wraps an arm around my waist, our bodies warm in bed. 'Well, Miss Brooks, I happen to know a great cure for woolly heads.'

'You do? Don't say raw eggs.'

'Sex.'

'Sex?'

'Yep, sex.' Sean strokes his chin and adopts a serious expression. 'And plenty of it. In fact, I'm going to write you out a prescription right now.'

'That's so *very* kind of you, Doctor Irwin.'

He pretends to write on my bare stomach, his fingers light against my skin.

'Sex at least three times a day.'

I laugh.

'Missionary in the morning, doggy style in the afternoon, and . . .' He pauses as he surveys me.

I roll on to my side, prop myself up with the pillows. 'Please don't stop, Doctor Irwin.'

'Let's have you in your tartan mini skirt and stilettos up against the wall in the evening.' He's signing the pretend prescription now, and handing it to me. 'And the sooner you start, the better.'

'Great. I'll give Johnny Depp a call.'

'Busy. Only works if you do it with someone called Sean. I hear he's amazing in bed too.'

I raise an eyebrow. 'That's not what I've heard.'

Next, he's on top of me, we're both laughing as I wrestle to push him away, we roll over in bed, almost fall on to the floor, we kiss, Sean runs a hand down my bare back . . . pulls me close . . . until I have to wriggle out from underneath him. 'Sorry, need a pee.' I hear a loud sigh as I leave the room.

'Don't be long,' he calls out.

I look at my reflection in the bathroom mirror. Um. Not a pretty sight. Black eye-makeup is smudged; hair could do with a wash. I gulp down some water with a couple of headache tablets and brush my teeth. Sean shouts for some water too. 'Your woolly head is catching!'

Sean and I are both studying medicine at King's College, London. We're in our fourth year and I have just returned from a four-week placement in Paediatrics in the King's

College Hospital. Next term we'll be doing three-week rotations in A&E, Orthopaedics, Rheumatology and Anaesthetics. Sean and I joke about how we're giddy from information overload. We wake up and forget which end of the body we're working on.

We're alone in the flat today. Our other housemate, Sarah, has already returned home for Christmas. She's also reading medicine. I'm heading to my parents' this afternoon. I dread the holidays. A weekend is fine, but Mum and I together for any longer than that is asking for trouble. After five minutes we bicker. 'You should be reading law, not medicine, *Cassandra*,' she says. 'You're so good at arguing.' Then there's my brother, Jamie. He's nineteen, four years younger than me, and similar to my dad in temperament: soft, loveable, kind and impossible to be cross with. On a camping holiday in France, he stole money from my purse so he could go and buy me a present. He's in Madrid at the moment, teaching English as a foreign language. He doesn't want to go to university. He's not sure what he wants to do. That's where I'm lucky. All I've ever wanted is to be a doctor. My parents never had to nag me to do my biology homework. When I was a child I had a fascination with first-aid boxes, and always gave my toys injuries that I could cure with medicine or mouth-to-mouth resuscitation. Dad used to wonder where this passion came from, since no one in our family likes to go anywhere near a needle. Jamie faints at the sight of blood.

'Hurry up, Cass! I'm dying of thirst in here.'

Back in my bedroom, I hand him a glass of water. 'Lazy sod. What's wrong with your legs?'

'Nothing . . . but yours work *so* much better than mine.'

I throw on a pair of skinny jeans, ankle boots and one of Sean's navy jumpers, aware he's watching me. I scoop my long dark blonde hair into a ponytail.

'You're beautiful.'

'Sean Irwin, what do you want?'

'Nothing. Well, some hot sex?'

I smile, wondering what's got into him this morning.

'Where you going? Remember that prescription! Come back to bed,' he groans, stretching his arms.

'We need some milk and bread and stuff. I thought I could make us some brunch, you know, before we head home.' My parents live in Dorset, close to Dorchester. Sean's family live in Dublin. It was Sean's Irish accent that attracted me at once, when he chatted me up in the student union bar – he could have spouted out the telephone directory and I'd still have been entranced. His accent, coupled with a sharp sense of humour that shone from his pale blue eyes, and I was hooked. I grab my wallet, collecting a few bits of loose change on my dressing table. 'How about a big fat bacon butty? I need *grease*. Sean?' I wave a hand in front of him.

'I love you, Cass.'

'What?' I mutter, too shocked to say anything else. We've

been going out for a year, and many times Sean has said, 'I love going out with you' or 'I love the way you make me feel' and when he says, 'I love doing it with you,' I tease him, saying he's such an old romantic.

'I love you,' he repeats.

I kick my boots off and fall back into bed, Sean pulling my jeans off as quickly as I'd put them on.

Outside, the sunlight blinds my eyes. It's freezing cold. Our flat in Pimlico is on a main road, but I've become used to the traffic and the noise; it's almost comforting, like a friend that's always there.

I want to sing and dance and tell the whole world I'm in love.

In a daze I head towards the traffic lights and zebra crossing, which feel too far away today. The road is clear. If I'm quick I could make a run for it now, the idea of bacon and coffee and being in bed again with Sean too tempting to waste time.

'Cass!' I hear him shout.

I turn round, look up to our flat on the third floor and see a bare-chested Sean leaning out of the window, waving my wallet. I'm such an idiot.

'Chuck it down!'

A car races past, and I have to manoeuvre myself out of the way of a couple of joggers on the pavement.

He holds on to the wallet. 'We need sugar too. And fags.'

'Fine. Throw.'

He hesitates. 'I'll come down.'

'Don't. Get on with your packing!' Sean's flight is this afternoon. I jog up and down on the spot. 'Just throw it!'

Sean hurls my wallet towards me. I jump to catch it. It hits the side of my hand and flies over my shoulder and on to the road.

Without thinking I run towards it.

'Careful!' he shouts. I stop. I hear him screaming now.

A car horn blasting.

I don't remember what happens next.

1

Five months later

I hear her coming upstairs. The jangling of her gold bracelets gives her away.

I sense her hovering outside my bedroom door, summoning the strength to enter. The handle moves and in she comes, in a bright red sundress, her vanilla scent overpowering.

'Morning!' She strides across my room in her high heels. I don't think Mum has ever worn a pair of flats. 'The God of height wasn't on my side,' she'd once said.

'What a lovely day!' she says with gusto, opening the curtains to allow the sunshine to stream in. 'I thought we could go out for lunch, just to the pub opposite?' Clocking my hesitancy, she says, 'Or how about a nice drive?'

'Maybe.'

She picks my tracksuit trousers off the floor, hangs them

on the back of my chair. 'Or we could go for a walk . . . maybe see a film?'

I don't move. 'I'm fine, Mum. But you go.'

'Oh, Cass, it's been weeks!' she says, raising her voice for the first time since I returned home from Stoke Mandeville Hospital at the end of April. 'You can't fester inside, day after day.' The telephone rings. 'I'll be back in a minute,' she warns me.

I'm testing her patience, but I don't feel ready to face the world yet. Minutes later she returns, notepad in hand this time. 'That was Sarah,' she says, sitting on the end of my bed. 'I told her you'd call back.'

Sarah's the one Sean and I shared a flat with at King's. She was my clinical partner, which basically means we did everything together. In our third year, when we were pushed out of our safe lecture-room environment and thrown into the world of real-life patients, Sarah and I clung on to one another in fear, scared they might bite. I see us turning up on our first day at hospital, dressed in long pleated skirts, white shirts and navy cardigans. We looked as if we were in school uniform. When I was asked to clerk a patient Sarah came with me, and as we walked down the long airy corridor we were too nervous to talk; all we did was make sure our stethoscopes were placed squarely round our necks. Sarah is in her final term of year four. She told me she was planning to go to Gibraltar during the summer break. At the end of year four we had to organise a two-month placement abroad. I was planning to go to a bush hospital in Africa.

I feel a prod. 'Cass?' Mum says.

'Hmm?'

'Oh, Cassandra, you haven't heard a word I've said.' Impatiently, Mum flicks open her notepad. 'I was saying you have a baseline.' She draws a thick horizontal line across the paper. 'The fact of the matter is –' she takes in a deep breath, as if she's about to plunge herself into ice-cold water – 'this is how it's going to be for the rest of your life. We can't change that, but what we *can* do –' she sketches neat arrows going upwards from this baseline – 'is change how we *manage* it.'

I raise an eyebrow. 'Will you be doing a PowerPoint presentation next?'

She puts the pen down. 'You need to think about your future.'

'What future?' I burst out. Why doesn't she understand? 'Everything I loved . . . everyone I loved . . .' I trail off.

'I've damaged my spinal cord,' I'd said to Sean when he'd visited me in hospital for the first time since the accident. I saw the colour literally drain from his face; he knew exactly what that meant. 'I'm paralysed, Sean, from the waist down.'

Ironically one of his favourite subjects was neurology and spinal cord injury. Sean didn't shed a tear. He looked as if he wanted to punch the living daylights out of the next person who came into the ward. I searched his face, looking for signs that he was going to stick around, but all I could see was anger and helplessness in his eyes. Part of me wanted to ease his pain, tell him he was free to go. I didn't want him to stay with me out of pity.

The other half wanted him to get off that chair and give me a hug, and tell me everything was going to be all right, and that he still loved me.

As I looked at him, all I could think was how could life change so quickly? Only days ago we were dancing, fooling around in bed and making plans for the New Year. He had invited me to Dublin. I was going to meet his parents for the first time.

He stood up, turned his back to me. 'This is my fault.'

Tears came to my eyes. 'No. Don't blame yourself.'

'Visiting hours are over,' said an abrupt Georgina, my assigned nurse, examining my medical notes on her clipboard. 'Off you go, now. She needs her rest. You can see her tomorrow.'

Sean gathered his coat and scarf. He hesitated before kissing my cheek and touching my hand. 'I'm so sorry,' he said. As he reached the door, he looked over his shoulder. 'Will you come tomorrow?' I called out, my voice as fragile as my broken body.

I was in hospital for four months. Sean did visit again, ten days later. He left a letter on my bedside table, telling me not to open it until he'd gone—

'*Cassandra!*'

I shudder when I feel another prod on my shoulder. 'I give up,' she says with resignation. 'What can I do?'

'Why don't you go back to work?' I suggest. Mum runs a successful property-letting company. She founded the business in London, where we'd lived until I was sixteen. Mum agreed to Dad's demands to move out of the city, to Dorset, on the proviso that she could expand her company to the West Country. Her company now deals with properties in the southwest region, covering Somerset, Dorset and Devon.

She looks indignant. 'I *am* working.'

'I mean full-time, in your office?' Mum has an office in Dorchester.

'Not yet. A, I can work from home and B, if I wasn't here, I'd come home in the evening and find you still in bed.' She looks at me, concerned. 'Would you like me to arrange some counselling for you?'

'No! I'm fine, I promise.' I say, praying to be left alone.

'I want you up. Five minutes.' She grabs my dressing gown from the back of the door and throws it at me.

I push the gown away from my face. 'I feel sick, Mum.'

Dad walks in now.

'She won't get up, Michael.'

'Cass can stay in bed a bit longer, can't she?' Dad reasons.

Mum's temper explodes like a pressure cooker. 'Wrapping

her in cotton wool isn't going to help anyone!' she says, 'least of all Cass!' Next thing I know, Dad grabs her by the arm and pulls her out of my room.

'I need your support!' Mum says in protest, shaking her arm free. 'My parents are hopeless, not one single visit. Mum can't even be bothered to pick up the bloody phone.'

'Look, it's going to take time,' Dad says in a low voice. 'The doctors warned us Cass will be abnormally tired in the first year.'

I hear them walking away. I strain to hear what Mum's saying now. Something about me getting out of my bed and doing my exercises. 'She's depressed!' she shouts in exasperation.

I close my eyes, feeling guilty that I'm causing this grief.

Five minutes later Dad stands at my bedroom door, his face creased with anxiety.

'Dad, I'm sorry.'

'Could you try and get up this morning?'

I nod, my lip quivering.

Ten minutes later Mum is back with the shower chair on wheels. 'You haven't undressed yet.'

Slowly I unbutton my pyjama top. My hand is shaking. 'I'm trying.'

'Well, try harder,' comes back the harsh reply, like the smash of a tennis ball into the body of an opponent. I can feel her stare as she waits for me to transfer myself from the edge of the bed across to the shower seat. Finally she wheels me into the bathroom.

'Cass, I shouldn't have snapped earlier but I hate seeing you like this. You have to stop feeling so sorry for yourself.' She turns on the shower and tests the temperature of the water. 'You need to make some kind of plan.'

'I had my heart set on medicine.'

'I know you did. You could go back to King's. Why don't you talk to Doctor Lewis?' She reverses the chair into the right position before putting the brakes on.

Doctor Lewis was my clinical supervisor.

'He's used to dealing with all kinds of problems and I'm sure he'd want to—'

'No,' I cut her off. 'I can't.' Sarah has also tried to convince me to return, but each time I try to imagine it, all I see is disabled accommodation and pity on people's faces. How would I cope bumping into Sean or seeing him with someone else? It's too raw. It's too soon. And even if I did qualify, what would a patient think when they saw me in a wheel-chair? 'It wouldn't be the same, Mum.'

'No, no it wouldn't, but you have to do something. Us Brookses, we're fighters, we don't give up.'

'This didn't happen to you.'

'No, it didn't. It happened to us.' Close to tears, Mum hands me the shampoo bottle. '*Us*, Cass.'

I watch her leaving the room. I wish I could see a way forward, but I don't know where or how to begin. 'It's a terrible thing to come to terms with but you are in the best possible care,' the consultant had said to me from the foot of my bed. 'With lots of physiotherapy we will teach you how to make the most of what you've been left with so you can be independent again.'

But what they can't teach you is how to *care*. My heart can't go to the gym. It's broken.

When I'm dressed I call out for my father. Dad was the first person I saw in the ward when I'd regained consciousness.

'How are we going to tell her?' he'd said.

I wasn't able to turn to see the person he was talking to because there was something hard against my back, stiff like a brace, but I was sure it was Mum by my side. 'What's wrong?' I cried out. I can remember desperately trying to move my feet. 'I can't move!'

Mum was stroking my hair and I felt terrified by the gentleness of her touch and what it was trying to tell me.

I wheel myself to the top of the stairs where my father is waiting for me. 'Good girl,' he says as he bends down, a hand leaning on my armrest. 'Are you ready?' Carefully he lifts me out of my chair and carries me downstairs, saying, 'It's going to get better, Cass. I promise.'

I wish I'd died that morning.

ALICE PETERSON

2

Dad reaches the bottom of the stairs and Jamie emerges from the kitchen saying he'll bring the wheelchair down. He must have been out because he's still in his jacket.

When I'm finally positioned at the kitchen table Dad retreats into his study. He's an architect and has worked from home since I was nine years old. Before Mum and Dad married they had talked about children, making an agreement that they wanted no more than two and one of them had to look after the family, not hire a nanny or au pair. Looking back, I can see why now. Both Mum and Dad don't get on with their parents. Mum says they feel this deep void; neither of them was nurtured or encouraged, even loved. 'They were strangers to me, they still are,' Mum says. So, when I was born, Mum was the full-time stay-at-home mum.

When I was five, and Jamie was still in his highchair, Mum explained to us, over tea, that Dad was taking on her role. Jamie was too young to understand, but I was worried.

Dad couldn't cook. That same year, Mum launched herself into the property business dealing in lettings. I've seen her website. Mum sits on top of the office tree, shoulder-length blonde hair professionally washed and blow-dried, and she's wearing a figure-hugging grey jersey dress, scarlet lipstick, bronzed cheeks and a beaming smile. Underneath are all her minions in smaller boxes.

'All right?' Jamie asks in his deep rumbling voice.

'Fine.'

'I went to the post office, bought those for you.' He gestures to a white plastic bag in the middle of the table. Inside are a couple of glossy magazines, pictures of Hollywood actresses with pearl white teeth gracing the front.

Jamie looks tired, as if he didn't sleep last night. 'Thanks,' I say. 'While you're up, make me a coffee, will you?'

'Yeah, yeah, sure.' He puts the kettle on. The sound of Mum's Hoover coming from next door in the sitting room is like that of an aeroplane's engine at high pitch just before it takes off. I find myself smiling, remembering how I used to turn the Hoover on when I was much younger just so I could shout, 'Bugger!' and 'Fuck!' without Mum or Dad hearing me.

'She's always cleaning, isn't she?' claims Jamie. 'While you were in the hospital –' he rubs his eyes, and for a moment he looks much younger than nineteen – 'oh my God, you should have seen her.' A small smile creeps on to his face.

'Really? More than usual?'

'Shitloads. This one time, right, she spilt a whole load of washing powder over the sink and went ballistic. Dad says she's upset. That we need to give her masses of support.' Jamie shakes his head. 'Nothing I do is right, Cass.'

'Well, I like you being here,' I say, when he hands me my drink and I take a sip. It tastes weak, reminds me of hospital coffee. 'You just need to brush up on your coffee-making skills, that's all.'

'You're just like Mum, you are!' He smiles. 'Any complaints in this hotel, write to the manager.'

Being here with Jamie reminds me of the time when he visited me in the ward. At this stage I had my own private room. I heard Dad and Jamie muttering in the corridor.

Then Jamie knocked on the door tentatively, before walking into my room wearing scuffed trainers and baggy jeans that showed off his Calvin Klein pants. He was carrying a box of After Eight mint chocolates he'd bought from the hospital shop, with the bright orange price sticker still on them. He looked awkward as he glanced at my white surgical stockings. 'Don't look so jealous,' I said. 'I'm sure they'd have some in your size.'

Next he was staring at the catheter bag that hung under the bed, unable to be hidden. I was desperate for him to look away, and thankfully he did. He checked out the room instead, his eyes wandering over the mini television system.

'I'm thirsty,' I said, gesturing to the water jug on my side table.

He hopped off his chair, grateful for the distraction. 'Don't get too used to this,' he said, daring to grin as he poured me a glass.

'Sorry, but you have to be extra nice to me now.' There was another long uncomfortable pause. 'Open the chocolates then,' I said. 'And pass me that magazine, would you?'

'Oh man, this really stinks. I never liked you much before but now you'll be a real nightmare.'

I found myself smiling, and I could see Jamie's shoulders relaxing.

I look at my brother now. He's tall and handsome, like my father, though slighter in build, like Mum and me. He has dark blond hair and blue eyes, an open face, big nose and a wide smile that puts you at ease immediately. He's looking tanned right now. We both have skin that tans easily. Dad called us his 'little gypsies' when we were on family holidays abroad. Jamie's attractive because he has no self-consciousness, despite the attention he receives from the opposite sex. 'Come on, Jamie. Why are you still at home?' I pick up the cereal box. 'You were *loving* Madrid. You'd saved up for months, working in that old people's home.' All the residents fell for Jamie, of course. Morag was his favourite. Every evening she'd ask for half a banana with her meal, with the peel still on, and when Jamie brought it to her on a tray she'd tuck it into the drawer of her bedside table, and never touch it, but Jamie didn't laugh at her or try to get her to explain. When the boss said this banana charade had to stop, Jamie snuck in his own.

He shrugs. 'I can go back any time.'

We hear the Hoover right outside the kitchen now. 'Anyway, I like being here,' he continues, the hesitancy in his voice giving him away. I throw the magazine at him. 'Jamie Brooks, you can't tell a lie, not even if someone paid you a million quid.'

He scratches the back of his head. 'I'll go back when I'm ready. Madrid's not going anywhere.'

I am touched by what he really means.

After Jamie and I have cleared up breakfast he tells me he's meeting a friend in town. 'Want to come?'

'Are you meeting a girl?'

'No.' He blushes. 'Why?'

'You've brushed your hair.' Jamie has thick hair with a life of its own. 'And you're wearing aftershave.' I pinch my nose and laugh. The Hoover stops. Mum rushes into the kitchen, as if to make sure that that laughter was really coming from me.

3

Mum is back at work and I have been at home for six weeks now. Jamie has moved to London and found a job in an IT company, but he visits regularly at weekends. We all need him. When Jamie comes home, he brings with him a ray of sun.

It's strange being here. Everything is familiar yet offers little comfort. It's as if I've been at war and returned the injured soldier. It's taken some time for Mum, Dad, Jamie and me to get used to the sound of wheels in the house. Wheelchair obstacles such as rugs and coffee tables have all been removed. With planning permission, my father has installed ramps in and outside the house. He's adapted the bathroom, building a sliding door and repositioning the sink so that I can wheel myself alongside the bath to get to the loo. He's built some low glass shelves in the kitchen so that I can reach plates and mugs. I still flinch when I see my jackets and coats on silver pegs halfway down the wall, and my pair of wellington boots that remind me of cliff top walks by the sea, hair blowing in the wind.

As I sip my coffee, I hear the sound of hooves. Cautiously I look out of the shuttered windows. It's one of the neighbours, Emily, riding her horse, Gus.

My fantasy to own a pony started when Mum and I saw two policemen riding horses through Hyde Park. I was ten at the time and thought the horses looked magnificent, their coats as shiny as Dad's polished shoes. That night I made a plan.

We lived in a terrace house. Dad could design and build me a stable in the garden. I could ride Smartie, the name I gave my dream horse, in the park, feed him carrots, and in the winter he could come inside and sleep by the fire. I showed Mum my plan, which included lots of pictures, boxes and arrows.

'Cass, darling, our garden is the size of a sandpit and what am I going to do with Smartie when you're at school? Take it to the office?'

'Well, I have thought about this,' I replied, redirecting her to my diagram, showing her how I'd decided that the best option was for Mum to give up work. I'd drawn a picture of Mum in the kitchen, wearing a frilly apron and high heels. Often I'd ask Dad when it was Mum's turn to work from home again. 'You burn our sausages, like, *all* the time.'

Mum looked up from my masterpiece. 'Oh, sweetheart,

I can't give up work.' She ruffled my hair. 'We have a mortgage to pay. Anyway, I love my job.' I started to doodle on my diagram, not wanting Mum to see my tears. 'One day, Cass, when you're a successful hotshot doctor, you'll understand. Not all women are cut out to stay at home.'

'But—'

'No buts! All you need to think about right now is A, getting dressed and B, going to school.'

However, the day did come when I thought I'd won the battle. 'When you get home there will be a surprise for you in the garden,' she said over breakfast. 'It's not a horse, but you'll love him.'

Dad picked me up from school. I was so excited to get home. I'd told all my friends that Mum and Dad had bought me a puppy. 'His name's Henry,' he said, 'and he's very handsome, but he's not *quite* what you're expecting.'

There was a tortoise in our garden.

When I was in my teens, I kept on asking Mum if we could have a dog. I promised I'd walk him or her but Mum kept on saying no. She's asthmatic and allergic to animal hair. 'Anything with fur, Cass, that moves, makes me sneeze and come out in splotches.'

When I was eighteen and had finished my A levels, I travelled to the south of Spain, to a donkey sanctuary, where I volunteered to help out on the farm. There were other abandoned animals too – dogs, cats, rabbits, pigs, chickens, goats, hens and uninvited rats. It was a cheap way to travel, and at last I could be with animals. Every year, until my accident, I'd returned to this sanctuary; it was my fix.

I hear the sound of hooves once more. When Emily glances towards the window I move away quickly, as if she's seen me naked.

I'm on my own this morning. Dad's doing some work for the council, designing a new office block or something. I decide to write an email to my friends Dom and Guy. They were both in hospital at the same time as me. Dom's injury is similar to mine. He's a paraplegic. The consultant had told me I was a T12.

'Rings of bone called vertebrae surround the spinal cord,' he'd explained. 'Together, these bones form the spinal column. The seven vertebrae in the neck are called the cervical vertebrae, the top one being C1, the lowest C7. The twelve vertebrae in the chest are called the thoracic vertebrae, T1 to T12. Below that are the lumbar nerves, L1 to L5, and the sacral nerves, S1 to S5. If the spinal cord is damaged at any level, it means you are paralysed below the level of that injury. The higher the injury, the worse off you are. If you had been unfortunate enough to break your neck, Cass, with a high cervical injury, say C3, you would have no movement in your arms, trunk and legs. You are a T12 complete, meaning the spinal cord has been severed completely and you won't be able to feel or move anything below your waist. An injury like yours, complete and to the thoracic root, only leads to loss of movement in the legs. You are a paraplegic,' he announced as if I had won first prize in a disability competition. 'You're one of the lucky ones.'

When I didn't clap my hands with gratitude, finally he put his notes down. 'I am sorry, Cassandra. In terms of suddenness of onset and extent of impact, nothing compares to spinal cord injury. All I'm trying to say is it could have been a lot worse.'

I send a message to Dom first. 'What are you up to? As weird as this sounds, I miss the hospital, especially you and Guy, even Georgina!' I stop typing, remembering how Georgina would turn me over in bed like a slab of meat to examine my backside for pressure sores.

The thing about hospital was we had structure to our day, and everyone was in the same boat. To my amazement the time went quickly too. The motto was 'keep them busy'. I woke up early to the comforting sound of the breakfast trolley rattling into the ward. Mum turned up later on in the morning, bringing us both a cappuccino or latte from the café because she won't drink instant. By ten o'clock I was in the gym. My physiotherapist, Paul, had given me a tough rehabilitation programme. I had to do hours of stretching on my front and back, lifting weights and doing resistance work with stretch bands. One time, I was so tired that I'd lost my concentration and fallen straight out of my chair. Paul would only put an arm out if I were going to fall awkwardly or catch my skin on something. As I struggled to get back into my seat he told me he wasn't going to help me; the only way I'd learn how to control my balance was by making mistakes. I asked him if he'd been a sergeant major in a former life. 'Thanks,' he said. 'That means I'm doing my job well.'

If I wasn't in the gym I was playing table tennis with Dom or Jamie or I was in the hydrotherapy pool. During my first hydrotherapy session, three weeks after the accident, all I could do was lie in the water supported by floats and armbands, Paul holding my head. It was frightening because I'd realised just how helpless I was. By the end of the four months I could swim lengths, even if it was with a lot of thrashing and flapping. Paul called my style 'Brooks Stroke'. 'You'll be at the Paralympics next,' he'd teased, before adding that the first Paralympics had been held at Stoke Mandeville back in 1948, inspired by a German-born British neurologist. 'A genius called Ludwig Guttmann established the National Spine Injuries Centre here. He realised sport was vital to rehab, so come on, Brooks, another length!'

'I don't know what to do, Dom,' I type. I look outside. It's a lovely summer's day, but the trouble is I want to go out biking or to the beach, play tennis or go for a run – all the things I took for granted. 'This morning Mum and I argued. She suggested I go back to King's. I know she's only trying to help but . . . Do you know what else drives me mad? I'm twenty-three and being told to tidy up my bedroom! How are you? Let me know how you're getting on, and love to Miranda.'

Miranda is Dom's wife. She used to come into the ward with fruit and energy drinks and dark chocolate. Seeing them together made me think of Sean. *I can't do this . . . I'm so sorry, Cass*, he'd written in his letter.

'PS,' I type. 'Tell me a funny joke, Dom.'

'Knock knock . . .' comes the quick response.

'Who's there?'

'Colleen.'

'Colleen who?'

'Colleen up your bedroom!'

I giggle, before replying, 'That's terrible, even for you.'

The first time I'd met Dom was when I'd moved to the rehabilitation ward. It was a mixed ward, most of us young, and Mum was sitting by my bedside, knitting me a pair of socks, as we waited to meet my new physiotherapist. I found it disconcerting because Mum had never even sewn a nametag in a school shirt.

'Good day, I'm Paul Parker,' said a very fit-looking man with a strong Aussie accent.

'All right, Parker!' called out the man from the opposite bed.

'Thank you, Dom,' said Paul, picking up my notes that

were pinned to a clipboard at the end of my bed. 'Para T12 complete,' he muttered.

I wanted to say, 'My name is Cass,' but instead I confided that I'd tried to get up the day before but had fainted.

'Well, the sooner we try again, the sooner you can leave this place.'

'But I want to walk out when I leave,' I said, somehow hoping that I could defy the rules, that there could still be hope.

'Darling, please try to cooperate,' Mum urged.

'Mrs Brooks, do you mind if I see Cassandra on her own?' Paul asked.

Mum picked up her knitting bag, wool trailing out of the back of it as she left. Paul alerted her to the trail. 'We don't want our patients tripping up on the ward,' he joked, helping her gather it back into the bag.

'Ah look,' he said, turning back to me, 'do you want me to help you?'

'Hmm.'

'Speak properly.'

There was no room for weakness in this place.

'Yes.'

'Good. Let's get you into this chair so we can start working on your muscle tone.'

'*Bonne chance!*' shouted the cheerful, nosy man called Dom. His hair was short and showed specks of grey, which gave away his age. I guessed he was in his late thirties, early forties. He looked sporty, as if he were training for the Olympics. The scary man in the next-door bed told him to shut the fuck up, that some people were trying to get some sleep. 'And what's with the French all of a sudden?' he continued.

'Stop being so miserable, Guy,' he replied. 'Come to the gym.'

'Get stuffed.'

'The day goes by much more quickly if you're busy,' he persevered, not taking the slightest offence. He wedged a water bottle into one side of his wheelchair and slipped on a pair of fingerless gloves.

Paul drew the beige flowered curtain around my bed, blocking them both out of sight. 'Right,' he said. 'No nonsense, otherwise you're wasting my time. Are you ready?'

I saluted. 'Yes, sir.'

'Top banana.'

I smiled. 'What did you just say?'

'Top banana. Now, let's start off gently and see how we go.'

As I attempted to sit up I found it hard adjusting to the slightly different position. It felt like I was taking giant steps forward when I knew I was barely moving. 'A bit more,' Paul encouraged, supporting my back. 'Georgina! I need a hand!' he shouted.

When I was finally upright and had transferred myself into the wheelchair, I cried out, 'I'm going to be sick.'

Immediately he tilted the chair back. 'Ah look, don't panic, mate. It will feel strange to begin with,' he said, steadying me. 'Your blood pressure will be low; it takes time to readjust. It's all right, Cass, I'm here, OK.' It felt like I was hanging in midair.

Georgina drew back the curtain and there was my perky fingerless-glove neighbour, still watching, as if it were a soap opera. Finally he stuck his thumb up and raced off in his wheelchair, saying he was going to do a bit of archery. He acted like he was at some kind of holiday camp.

'Don't worry about him,' says Paul. 'He's one of the nice guys.'

Dom turned to me one last time. 'Good luck, Cass. Break a leg!'

And strangely I did find that funny.

Another message appears in my inbox. 'Come to London soon. Don't see your wheelchair as a disability badge, Cass, see it as a way to come and visit me and Guy.'

Both live in West London. Dom's flat is in Hammersmith. Guy lives with his parents in Ladbroke Grove.

'Don't shut yourself away at home. We miss you.'

4

It's late in the evening when my mobile rings. Jamie, who's home for the weekend, hands it to me.

'I've had a terrible day,' Guy says the moment I come on to the line.

'What happened?'

Jamie glances my way, before turning the television off and discreetly leaving the room.

'I met some old work mates.' Guy used to work in the City. 'They asked me if I wanted to meet for a coffee and I thought it'd be good to get out of the house. We met in this bar, they'd sussed out a place with easy access. The boys ordered me an espresso because that's what I used to have, so when the waitress brings it over I drop the cup and coffee spills all over the table. They order me another and I drop that one too, this time the cup breaks. The handle is so fucking delicate, I couldn't hold it properly.'

'Oh God, Guy, I'm so sorry.'

Guy has a higher-level injury than mine. He broke his

neck at C6 and is paralysed from the collarbone down. The nerves on your neck correspond to the movement and strength in your hands and wrists, so as a result his are weak. I can remember his screaming frustration at just trying to brush his teeth. 'It was terrible.' His voice shudders. 'How are you, Cass? When are you coming to London?'

'I'm sorry, Guy,' I say again, understanding there is something else he wants to tell me.

'Oh, Cass, you should have seen the look on their faces, as if I were a cripple. It nearly killed me.'

Later, Dad comes to say goodnight. He has deep circles under his eyes; he has aged ten years since my accident.

'Thanks for doing so much to the house,' I say, thinking of Guy in the downstairs room of his parents' flat where he eats, sleeps . . . He says it's like living in a rabbit hutch. 'It must have been hard work.'

'It was nothing.' He sits on the edge of my bed. 'Do you think you'll sleep tonight?' Dad is aware I'm having recurring nightmares. Sometimes I'm back on the hospital ward; other times I'm running barefoot along a hot tarmac road. Sean is waiting for me at the end. 'Come on!' he's shouting, but just as I'm about to reach him he disappears. When I look down to my feet blood is seeping in between my toes, they're burning like fire.

'I hope so,' I say, unconvinced.

Dad makes himself comfortable. 'What's worrying you?'

I tell him about Guy's day. I can't stop thinking about how traumatic it must have been for him to see the people he used to work with. They head back to the office to resume their normal working day; Guy heads back to his rabbit hutch. This is why I find it hard to talk to Sarah. I can't return to King's.

Dad understands. 'It's tough. All we can do is take one day at a time,' he says gently, before kissing me goodnight. He stands at the door. 'Sweet dreams, OK. No nightmares.'

I close my eyes.

Georgina rushes to my bed. 'It's Cass,' Dom tells her.

'I can feel something,' I insist, lifting the sheets. 'My toes, I think it's my right foot.' At last I feel a tiny connection to my body. 'Georgina?'

'Often you can feel pain below the level of injury in an area you can't move,' she says.

'I've had that,' claims Dom. 'I get terrible pain sometimes, like a hot needle jabbing up and down my spine. It's like biting on foil with a filling.'

'Isn't it good to feel something, Georgina?'

'Yes and no. The problem is pain is hard to treat. Imagine lots of wires inside you, basically your nerves,' she explains. 'Pain goes through one or two and then sparks off as there is no connection. They're alive but don't have anything to do.'

I look at my feet, trying to understand. 'Cass,' she says,

'try and get back to sleep.' My feet are covered again as if laid back in the coffin. Lights are turned off.

'Are you OK, Cass?' Guy asks.

Struggling not to cry I say, 'Not really. You?'

'I'm sorry, Princess. Why us?'

We lie awake in the darkness but I can feel our arms around each other.

'There's no escape is there? Not even in your sleep,' Guy says.

There's no escape. There's no escape. Not even in your sleep—

I scream. Sit up, gasping for breath.

'Cass?' Jamie rushes into my room.

I turn on the bedside light; recover my breath. It was so vivid; their voices as clear as daylight.

'Can I get you anything? Glass of water?' He hiccups. 'Were you having one of your bad dreams again?

I nod. 'Have you been drinking?' I can smell alcohol on his breath.

'No.' He grins.

'Liar liar, pants on fire.' Dad used to say it to us as children.

He walks over to my wheelchair and plonks himself in it. He unclips the brakes and moves forward, crashing into the side of my bed and attempting to steer himself around the small space. 'What does it feel like sitting in this?'

'Horrible. Why?'

'I'm really worried that you must feel like you're this top half –' with one hand he cuts across his own stomach – 'floating above nothing. I'd hate to feel like that, sorry.' He reddens. 'You know what I mean. Dad said I should ask you questions and stuff, about how it feels, not tiptoe round you all the time.' Another hiccup. 'But I'm not very good.'

'I can't describe what it's like,' I admit.

Jamie jumps up from the chair and sits on my bed. 'Shut your eyes,' he demands.

'Why?'

'Do it.'

I shut them.

'If I hit you right here, can you feel anything?'

'Nope.'

'Nothing?'

'Nothing. Can we stop this game now.'

'I'm trying to understand, Cass.'

I open my eyes. 'All right. Do it again, whatever you did before.'

Jamie hits me on the thigh.

'It's slightly different because I saw you doing it,' I say. 'I'm aware of something.'

'What does it feel like?'

'I don't know. It doesn't feel normal but then how do you describe normal?'

'D'you think you'll get back to sleep? Do you have night-mares about the accident?'

I shake my head, telling Jamie I don't dream about that morning in Pimlico. I dream about Dom and Guy. I'm back in hospital with them. Sometimes Sean is in my dreams too. Deep down, however much I pretend to myself that I'm better off without him, I'm hurt by his rejection. Often, late at night, I wonder how I'd feel if it were the other way round. Would I still love him?

'Would you be able to go out with someone in a wheel-chair, Jamie?'

'I don't know. I think so, yeah. You love the person, right, not their legs. I mean it helps if they've got good legs but . . . D'you want to watch a film?' he asks, when he sees my tears. We often do this when he's home. There's a small television in the corner of my room.

'I think we've seen them all now.'

'No,' he insists. 'I bought some new ones.'

Next he's dragging his stripy red and navy duvet into my bedroom, a DVD in his mouth. He slots it into the player and camps on my floor. Jamie keeps on turning to me, making sure I'm all right.

'Thank you, Jamie,' I say, feeling a strong tug of affection for him that I've never felt before. 'And sorry if I boss you around all the time.'

'It's all right. You're my sister. You can boss me around and do whatever, but I'll always love you.'

And it's so clear to me now why Mum loves him so much.
He's her uncomplicated little boy.
He's like Dad.
I don't remember at which part finally I fall asleep.

5

I'm in Dad's study, the walls covered in black-and-white prints of his favourite buildings: the Duomo in Florence, St Paul's Cathedral, the Houses of Parliament, the Savoy Hotel, Notre Dame. The window is open but the room still smells of smoke. A pack of cigarettes is by the telephone, next to a marble ashtray. Since my accident, Dad's taken up the habit again, something Mum pretends to be cross about.

I always feel nostalgic when I'm in this room. It reminds me of my school days, in London, when Dad worked from home and allowed me to do my homework in his study. I loved watching him work at his drawing board. Back then he had longer hair and a beard. We'd listen to his favourite group, The Rolling Stones. After a while he'd open one of his desk drawers and produce a green-and-black pouch of tobacco. He'd smoke a roll-up before spraying a flowery scent across the room. 'Don't tell Mum,' he whispered, blue eyes laughing as he hid the can and his pouch of tobacco back in his secret drawer.

I stop at his desk and pick up the framed photograph of Jamie and me on a beach, standing either side of Dad, holding his hand. I have long fair hair in plaits, a pink spotty costume and chubby legs. Next to this photograph is Mum and Dad's wedding picture. I used to be fascinated by Dad's hair; it was almost as long as Mum's. And he wore hippy sandals. I used to tell him he looked like Jesus.

'I *was* a hippy dude back then, Cass,' he'd say. 'That was the fashion.' Mum's wedding dress was made out of lace; she had designed and made it herself. 'She used to make all my suits too,' Dad said. 'Saved us a blooming fortune.'

Dad must notice me looking at the photograph now. Mum's long blonde hair falls loosely down her shoulders; her dress shows off her small waist.

'She was beautiful,' I say.

'Still is. You're the spitting image, Cass.'

That's a compliment. Like Mum, I have honey-coloured dark blonde hair, deep brown eyes and a wide mouth like Jamie's. Dad used to joke that my smile was as wide as Buckingham Palace.

'Did you want something?' he asks, aware that I didn't come in to look at his old photographs.

'I'm going to London tomorrow.'

'London! Right! London,' he tries to say more calmly.

'I'm meeting Guy and Dom for lunch, and then Sarah later on in the afternoon. Can you give me a lift to the station?'

He taps his fingers against the desk, before picking up his pack of Marlboro Reds. 'Tell you what.' He lights up. 'Why don't I come?' He scratches the back of his head, just as Jamie does.

I raise an eyebrow.

'I promise I'd leave you the minute we arrived,' he suggests. 'I could go and see an exhibition.'

'I'll be fine, Dad.'

His forehead remains crumpled with worry lines.

'Dad, I can't be the only person in a wheelchair on this planet.'

Mum comes in, wearing summer trousers with a cream blouse. 'There you are.' She's just returned from work. She looks at both of us, before slipping off her high heels and rubbing her feet. 'What's wrong?'

'Cass wants to go to London tomorrow,' Dad says as if it's mission impossible.

'That's a great idea.' Mum sits on the arm of Dad's old leather chair. 'You've called the station to get help on to the train?'

'Yep.' Is it going to be like this every time I suggest going out?

'You'll have your mobile switched on all the time?'

I nod. 'All I need is a lift.'

'I'm sure you can take her to the station, can't you?' She turns to Dad, urging him with her eyes. He stubs out his cigarette. 'Cass, why don't I simply drive—'

39

'Dad,' I cut in. 'I have to do this on my own, you know that.' I wheel myself out of the room before he can ask me any more questions to make me doubt myself.

'I'm happy to drive her,' I overhear Dad saying when he thinks I've gone. I stay and listen behind the door.

'That's not the point, Michael.'

'I'm nervous.'

'And I'm not?'

'You don't seem to be.'

'Bollocks!'

'Bollocks? Have you just turned eighteen again?' Dad asks, faint amusement in his tone.

'Bollocks!' she repeats. 'Are we going to be like this every single time she leaves the house? We'll turn grey, we will. We need to have faith.'

He mutters something about losing his faith.

'Cass needs to go.'

'I know . . . I'm on your side.'

'This is a huge step forward, Michael. You need to quit smoking,' she adds.

'I will.' He inhales deeply. 'After Cass has been to London and come home safely.'

'I know it's hard,' Mum admits finally. 'That day, when you took Cass out in the wheelchair for the first time.' I hear her bracelets jangling. 'This will sound silly.'

'Go on.'

'It reminded me of the opera we saw when we were first

married, you know, *Fidelio*, where the prisoners are let out for a day.'

'Why?'

'I don't know. It was your face, so sad and scared of the future.'

I remember how Dad had stopped dead when he first saw me in my wheelchair back at the hospital, six weeks after the accident. I still hated getting into my chair with a passion. However, thanks to Paul, I was beginning to feel encouraged that I was making progress.

'Look!' I had my back brace on, but I was sitting up and it felt good.

'Great.' He didn't take his jacket off or sit down and start doing the crossword, calling out clues as he normally did.

'What's wrong?'

'Nothing. Why don't we get some fresh air?' he'd suggested, jolting my chair forward.

'I can push myself!' I said, wanting him to be proud of my achievement. 'I just need my woolly hat.' I touched my hair. 'And another jumper.'

He skirted the room saying, 'Hat, hat, hat. Jumper, jumper jumper.'

'They're in my drawer.'

He tried to find them, manically tossing everything else aside.

When we were ready to leave Dad had walked behind

me. We passed the nurses' station where I waved goodbye. 'Don't get cold, Cass,' Georgina called out.

'There's Mum,' I said when we were outside. She was walking towards us.

'Bren, I've left something in the car.'

I knew something wasn't right when she handed him the keys.

'Dad?' I called out to him, but he didn't turn round. 'I thought he'd be pleased,' I said.

'He is. This –' she gestured to me sitting up in my chair – 'it's a big day. You're doing so well.' She had looked over my shoulder then, watching my father walk away.

I lean in towards the study door again.

'We can't be scared. If we're scared, what will Cass think? We have to be strong,' Mum says.

'She's my little brown-eyed girl.'

'I know. But this is good, Michael. For weeks she hasn't made any sound about seeing friends, she hasn't even wanted to talk to Sarah. Doesn't that scare you more? Cass having no life of her own?'

'You're right.'

'I'm always right.'

He laughs softly. 'Vodka?'

'Please, and make it strong.'

6

At the station, a porter in a navy cap scurries around me on the platform before pushing my chair up the ramp and into the carriage. I'm aware of people staring as he steers me into my reserved seat, where there is in fact no seat, just a space for my wheelchair.

As the train departs Dad's car is still in the car park even though I'd told him he didn't have to wait. I watch it fade into the distance, and already feel a taste of freedom.

I think about my day ahead. I'm meeting Guy and Dom for lunch at Westfield Shopping Centre in Shepherd's Bush. Dom had said he wouldn't normally be seen dead in a shopping centre but the access makes it an easy option.

I became good friends with Dom soon after I'd moved into the mixed rehabilitation ward. He was open and friendly, often wheeling himself over to my bed to chat. Before his accident he'd worked for a travel firm, tailoring holidays for the retired. 'I know it doesn't sound that cool, organising holidays for old folk, but it's a real niche market,' he'd said with bright eyes. 'We organise loads of guided tours, mainly in Europe.' The travel company have kept him on, no doubt because they love his attitude and energy. Guy was another story altogether. I gathered from Dom that he had worked in the City. Guy sulked, refused to do his exercises and shouted at the nurses, saying his life was fucking over so why should he do his fucking exercises. However, each time he swore he'd apologise to me and I'd smile back, hoping that that was the end of our conversation.

Dom was the only patient in our ward who had the nerve to persevere with Guy. 'We're all in the same boat,' he'd claim, except that wasn't strictly true. Guy's injury at the C6 level is worse and carries with it a lot more complications.

However, Dom is someone who will not give up. Finally Guy broke down when Dom had insisted on singing Monty Python's song, 'Always Look on the Bright Side of Life'.

'Will you stop being so fucking perky all the fucking time!'

There was this long painful silence that was broken when the entire ward laughed, including Guy. After that moment something changed within him; a small light had been switched on. That was also the beginning of Dom's nickname, Perky.

Gradually Guy joined Dom and me for supper in the evenings. Initially Dom and I did all the talking although

I was aware that Guy listened to every word. I could see he had trouble holding his knife and fork so sometimes he ate his baked beans with a large spoon. We talked about our accidents; it's impossible not to since they haunt you day and night. Dom had finished work, got on his motorbike, and the next thing he knew, he was lying face down on the tarmac. 'My back tyre blew. I torture myself thinking, what if I had taken the bend slower? What if, what if?'

I told them about that morning with Sean in our flat in Pimlico. All I was doing was getting some breakfast. I wasn't concentrating; it was one mistake that had cost me this. 'No one else was hurt,' I confided. I also told them about my student days at King's and Sean writing me a letter. Neither said a word. Deep down I could hear Guy thinking he'd have probably left me too, and I sensed Dom felt guilty that Miranda was unflinching in her support. If anything she loved him even more.

'I remember waking up in my car,' Guy said and Dom and I nearly choked on our food. 'I had this pain in my neck.' And after that moment Guy didn't stop talking. He told us that he had been driving back from a party in the early hours of the morning when his car hit a tree. It had taken the ambulance men six hours to get him out of the front seat. They'd had to cut the car's roof off. He had been as dependent as a baby for the first few months in hospital.

His voice was shaking. I felt unnerved by the pain in his

45

dark eyes but I was glad he was talking, and he had Dom to thank for this breakthrough. It was as if, since his accident, his mind and body had shut down completely and finally he was beginning to come out of the coma.

'They don't mince their words in here, do they?' Dom said during one of our evenings.

'Doctors are arseholes,' Guy said. 'Most of them, anyway.'

'I can't see you being like them, Cass,' Dom added. 'I have to say, I was pretty cheesed off when they told me I wouldn't be able to walk again.'

'You posh sod,' said Guy. 'I went fucking mental. Sorry, Princess.'

'Don't worry.' I handed round the jam tarts that Dad had brought in for me.

'I thought if you broke your neck you died,' Guy continued. 'I thought people in wheelchairs were born like that. Fucking hell – sorry, Cass – I had no idea I could end up like a cabbage. The doc says, "You'll never walk again and it's something you're going to have to get used to."' He rocked in his chair. 'Since I've been here all I've been told are the things I can't do. Can't use my hands properly.'

I hid my own.

'Can't dress myself, won't be able to sweat or shiver because I've lost feeling in my sensory nerves too, so I'm at risk of hypothermia. Can't do or feel a thing. Can't even pick my fucking nose.'

He didn't apologise this time.

'The scariest thing though,' Guy continued, making up time for his silence, 'is that when I leave here I'm moving in with my parents. I loved my pad in London. I worked every hour of the day to buy it. It looked over the Thames. Thirty-five and living at home,' he continued, staring at both of us. 'They're hardly young either, you've seen them.' Guy's father is tall and slim with thinning grey hair and I'd watch him with his son, head hung low and unable to say a word. He looked like a wounded animal. Guy's mother did all the talking.

'I left home when I was eighteen to make my millions in the City. Before this I was a stockbroker. At weekends I'd play sport. What am I going to do now? Crochet? Hang on, can't even do that.'

The more Guy talked, the less scared I became of him. While I loved Dom for his optimism, I related to Guy's cynicism. It also didn't matter that both were older than me.

My mobile rings, telling me I have a new message. 'Can't wait to see u Princess. Restaurant better serve baked beans. Guy.'

I smile, thinking about one time when the supper trolley had rattled round the ward.

'Looking forward to your baked beans?' I'd asked him. We were all in our pyjamas, as if at a sleepover party.

'Don't you, like, trump all the time?' Dom asked.

'I was wondering what the smell was,' I said.

Guy looked at me. 'Don't even think about coming between me and my orange friends, Princess.'

'This lady goes to a smart dinner party in London,' started Dom, 'and there's an American guest. Quite early on in the party the hostess unfortunately breaks wind.'

Guy roared with laughter.

'So the gentleman to her left says, "I'm so dreadfully sorry." The dinner continues but a couple of minutes later the hostess breaks wind again. So the gentleman to her right apologises. The American guest watches these incidents with astonishment. And then a couple of minutes later the hostess does yet another trump. The American, now gob-smacked, leans forward and says, "Hey, madam, have that one on me!"'

The ticket conductor enters our carriage, bringing me back to the present. He punches my ticket. As I think about Guy and Dom again, I find I'm grinning all the way to Paddington, realising how much I'm looking forward to seeing them, almost more than Sarah.

Everyone gathers their cases, laptops, newspapers and magazines. I look out of the window, down the entire stretch of platform. I can't see anyone yet. Don't panic, Cass. The station promised that there'd be someone to help at this end. I watch people filing out and marching across to the exit barriers.

Finally the carriage is quiet. The automatic doors open

and I position myself near to the step. Thankfully I can see a solid metal ramp to the right of me, near to the driver's door, and to my relief a couple of men in official uniform walk on to the platform. 'Hello!' I call out.

'All right?' one of them replies, drinking a cup of tea.

'Can you help me, please? I need that ramp.' I point to it. It's on wheels.

Passengers begin to board the train.

The uniformed men continue talking about last night's football results.

'Do you think you could get that ramp?' I ask, not wanting to shout and make a spectacle of myself. 'Or lift me down?'

'You're young? Can't you walk at all?' one of them asks.

I shake my head.

'Sorry, love, don't think we're insured to lift passengers. You know, health and safety and all that.'

Panic racing through me now, I reverse my chair to allow a couple into the carriage, but they stop. 'Can I help you?' the man suggests. He is balding with spectacles and doesn't look as if he could lift a fly. His wife or partner is wearing a colourful sundress with espadrilles.

'It's my first time on a train,' I tell them. 'Not a great start.'

'You take the chair,' the man says to his wife or partner, as he lifts me into his arms. He's surprisingly strong. 'Health and safety my foot,' he mutters under his breath. 'Tony Blair has a lot to answer for.'

*　　*　　*

49

'How was your day?' Mum asks, the moment I arrive home late that night. I sense Dad signalling to her that all is not rosy. 'How was the journey?'

'Fine.'

'Someone helped you?'

I nod. 'I'm tired, Mum. I might go to bed.' I wheel myself into the kitchen first to get a glass of water.

'But you had a good day?' She follows me. 'You enjoyed seeing Dom and Guy? And how was Sarah? It must have been lovely catching up.'

'Yep,' I reply, fighting the urge to cry. I think of today, how in many ways returning to London and seeing Dom and Guy was positive; yet in so many other ways I was haunted by a city where I used to live and study, party, be wild and free, independent and happy, not think twice about hopping on the tube or running to catch a bus. A home where I'd been in love.

In my bedroom I sit, frozen, with a scalpel that I stole from Dad's office. When Sarah and I had greeted one another, immediately it felt odd, almost as if we were going on a first date. Sarah asked me where I would like to sit, and did I need a hand with my jacket? She scurried round the table, taking away a chair to make room for me.

I grip the scalpel.

When we were waiting for our drinks, there was a long awkward silence, so alien to our past friendship. Sarah and I used to be geeks by day. Over cups of black coffee we'd discuss molecules and genetics, science and weird body parts. By night we were party animals at Tutu's, the famous nightclub named after Desmond Tutu, who had studied at King's. We loved to dance. Being with her reminded me of staggering home at three in the morning, empty bottles of vodka in our hands, only to be at hospital by nine a.m. the following day, bleary-eyed and in need of another coffee shot from the machine.

Today, we talked about my train journey to London and the menu, both of us deliberating for ages about what to eat. Sarah asked after my parents. When I asked her to tell me about her forthcoming summer placement in Gibraltar, all she said was that it was no big deal, as long as she managed to get her certificate of attendance by the end. 'But apart from that, Cass, nothing much is going on,' she said, avoiding eye contact. Sarah is the happiest, most enthusiastic person I know. Sean and I would say her bounciness was great most of the time, except first thing on a Monday morning, when we could hear her singing in the shower.

Being with her today was difficult; I felt disconnected in every way and wanted to be back with Guy and Dom, in a safe place where the three of us could laugh and feel at home with each other and the new worlds we now inhabit.

The evening went from bad to worse when Sarah said, 'I don't know how to tell you this.' She was fidgeting with the strap of her handbag. 'Oh, Cass.' She took a large gulp of wine. 'It's Sean.'

I felt sick.

'He's met . . . he's met someone else.' Sarah refilled my wine glass. I sat silent, shocked. Of course he was going to meet someone else but it felt too soon. 'Cass, say something. This is me you're talking to.'

'Who is she?' I asked, numb inside.

'No one you know. She's in the year below.'

That was something.

'Listen, he's a dickhead, and I hate the way he's treated you. I can't even look at him, the way he carries on as if nothing's happened. I feel so guilty, Cass. I don't want to live with him in our final year. I mean, in my final year . . . Oh God, you know what I mean.' Sarah was getting tangled up in her words. 'I really miss you, it's not the same.'

'Don't feel guilty.' I gripped her hand. 'It's not your fault. I miss you too.' It felt like we were saying goodbye.

With the scalpel I cut a long straight line into my thigh, slicing it into my flesh. I watch blood seeping out, vivid against my pale skin. I want to see how deep I can go until I feel something; anything but this numbness. There's a knock on my door and without waiting Dad walks in to say goodnight.

'Cass!' He kneels down beside me and grabs the sharp object from my hand. 'What the hell are you doing!' He rushes out of the room. I hear him flinging open the bathroom cabinet. Pots of pills crash into the sink. 'Bren!' he shouts. Mum runs upstairs and into my room; the sight of blood makes her stagger but quickly she composes herself when Dad returns with the first-aid box. I watch them struggling to help me, their hands trembling. Mum cleans the wound and they lift my leg so they can wrap the bandage around my thigh. 'Scissors,' Mum demands. Dad hands them to her and she tears through the material in a jagged line.

Next she is bandaging my thigh, pulling each layer tighter than the last. 'Stop it! Let me die,' I beg.

Mum lets go of the bandage and leaves the room.

'How can we help you?' Dad asks. 'Tell us what we can do, Cass.'

He only then notices the mess of torn paper, photographs of Sean reduced to nothing but scraps of memories.

It's two hours later, eleven o'clock in the evening. From the top of the stairs I can see Mum and Dad in the kitchen. They are sitting on the window seat. Dad is holding Mum, rocking her in his arms like a child.

Another hour goes by and still I can't sleep. My bedroom door opens. Disorientated, I turn on the light. 'Can I come in?' Mum asks, wearing her ancient blue dressing gown that I remember as a child. Tentatively she sits on my bed. I want to say sorry. I feel ashamed that I let her and Dad down tonight.

'I'll never hear your footsteps again,' she says. 'See your posture. You had such a graceful posture.'

I can't cry; it's buried too deep. Instead I reach out to hold her hand.

'I only shout at you to get out of bed because I feel guilty that you're stuck at home. I want you to have a life away from us.'

'I know.'

'Please don't hurt yourself again, Cass. I love you, you have no idea.' She breathes deeply. 'And the older you get, the more I love you.'

'I'm sorry,' I say, clutching her hand. 'Today was hard, Mum.'

She nods. 'Your father told me about Sean. Don't be too sad. There'll be someone out there much braver and stronger and that person will fall in love with you, because of who you are, a talented beautiful girl.'

'Oh, Mum,' I say, now feeling a well of tears.

'Do you know what else I miss, Cass?'

'No.'

'I can't hug you properly.'

'We could try?'

Mum lifts the covers and lies down next to me. I hold on to her arm, using it as a rail so that I can position myself on to my side.

'That's much better,' she says, her arms wrapped around me. 'No wheelchair in the way.'

'I'm so sorry, Mum, about earlier,' I say, hugging her back.

'It's going to get better, I promise. There has to be something or someone out there, who's going to help us get through this.'

7

It's the end of July. I've been at home for nearly three months.

Jamie is on holiday in Ibiza. Sarah has just left for her two-month placement, four weeks in Dublin and four in Gibraltar. I try not to think that I'd be in Africa, working in a bush hospital. Instead, Mum and I are out on one of our regular Friday drives. Mum always takes the day off on a Friday, and since the sunshine was out, we left earlier than usual this morning, Mum suggesting we stop and have a picnic lunch.

Mum and I have been going on regular drives for the past month, and I've learned a lot about her in the car, things I didn't know, or previously wouldn't have even thought to ask. I've discovered my grandfather Fred, Mum's father, worked in a factory and Granny Pearl wasn't interested in kids, which is why Mum was an only child. Mum and Dad were neighbours (I knew that). Mum described Dad's father, Eric. 'He was a drunk, Cass. All the street would see him staggering home from the pub after work.' The one time I do recall Granddad Eric visiting us in London, all I can remember him doing was loosening his tie and twitching, sweat breaking out on his forehead. It now makes sense that he was gasping for a drink. Granny Pearl hadn't wanted to be involved in our family life. I realise now why Mum and Dad are so close. They didn't have parents in the way that Jamie and I do. They only had each other.

'We promised one another that we'd run away together, move to London the moment we could,' Mum had said. 'We were wild, Cass. I had this mini skirt. You see, back in our day it was all about Twiggy and Mary Quant. Anyway, my father *hated* it. We always had such fisticuffs, Dad and I, our neighbours threatened to call social services half the time!' Mum had laughed, but there was sadness deep inside. 'I was about to go out with your dad to the pictures, and my dad says, "Brenda, you're not walking out in *that* skirt, I can see your knickers!" I walked on. "You come back here, at once!"'

'And did you?' I'd asked, knowing the answer.

'No! Of course not.' She laughed proudly. 'Michael and I, we were so happy,' she went on. 'In our first flat, it was in Shepherd's Bush, we had no television, no proper bed, no nothing, but it didn't bother us because we had our freedom. We were determined to make something of ourselves. There was no way we were ever going back home.'

I learned that Mum took a catering course in west London.

De-boning turkeys, skinning fish and plucking pheasants put her off cooking for life. She quit after a few months because she found a well-paid job working for a Texan called Troy. He was the senior vice-president of an oil company and Mum was his secretary. She'd lied through her teeth in the interview, pretending she could type as if on speed and she was a demon at shorthand. With Dad's help, she faked her references. The cracks began to show when Troy dictated too quickly, so Mum devised this trick to break her pencil and rush out, fill the gaps and then come back, but one day he presented her with ten shiny pencils, all perfectly sharpened. "There you go, ma'am, there's no need for you to rush your pretty little legs out no more,"' Troy had said, winking at her.

While Mum was flirting with Troy, Dad was busy studying at Kingston to become an architect. 'I needed a good job. Your father was penniless. Troy knew I'd been a little liberal with the truth, but he admired my ambition. Sometimes in life you have to take a few risks.'

I look out of the window. 'Where are we going?' We've been driving for well over an hour now.

'No idea! Let's see where the mood takes us.'

'Well, I'm not in any hurry. The television and biscuits can wait.'

Things have been much better at home in the past month. I'm not miserable; nor am I happy. I'm neutral. I've slipped into a routine, and rub along well with Mum and Dad now.

I've been doing some paid admin work for Mum in her office, typing up tenancy agreements and letters. However, there's still this shadow hanging over us of what I'm going to do next. I can't live at home forever.

As Mum drives on, I turn on the stereo and think about my recent London trip to see Dom and Guy. This time someone was waiting on the train platform with a ramp. Guy told us that his father had broken down. 'They're old, you know. Just when they should be retired and happy they're burdened with me. I'm pretty lucky I'm not in some care home for the elderly, you know. That's where a lot of guys like me end up. So, I've decided I'm going to get my arse into gear and do an Open University course, study history. Before I got sucked into the City my dream was to be a teacher. I don't want to do nothing for the rest of my life. I'm better than that. *We're* better than that.' I knew that comment was directed at me.

Dom often tells me that I need to think about my future and maybe I should think about going back to medicine. However, hearing Guy say it was different. I was pleased for him, but also scared. Now that he was making plans, what excuse did I have?

It's getting late in the afternoon and I'm looking at a map. Mum drives down a narrow road in the middle of nowhere. 'Caution! Please drive SLOWLY,' the sign reads. We've been driving for miles and are now definitely lost as Mum parks us in some field. She unlocks the door, saying she's desperate for the loo. I frown at her, thinking she's about to squat behind a tree, but she runs on ahead, and soon is out of sight.

I shut my eyes, feeling sleepy. I think about Sarah again. She promised she'd write to me. We want to form a new friendship, but I sense it's hard for both of us when we're still grieving for our past. Sarah is uncomfortable talking to me about medicine. The only thing she did mention the last time we'd met in London was: 'Cozzi was asking after you.' Mariella Cozzi was my favourite lecturer. She's Italian, in her fifties with amazing legs, dark hair streaked with pink, and always wears heels like Mum. I picture her in the giant lecture room, giving a PowerPoint presentation. 'If people are obese they eat too much, simple as that.' I loved her un-pc remarks. 'Get a grip. Go to the gym. Eat less! Get on a bike! Or if they can't afford that, walking is free!'

Walking is free.

'What a strange place,' Mum says when she returns to the car and puts her seatbelt on. 'Dogs everywhere.' She scratches her arm.

I stir. 'Dogs?'

'Yes, dogs.'

'It's probably a kennel club.'

'Well, they had these funny purple coats on.'

'Coats?'

'Uh-huh. And they were doing all kinds of weird things too.' She turns the key in the ignition.

'Like what?'

'Well, I saw one poking its head into a washing machine and lifting out a pillow-case!' Mum laughs, a laugh that could fill Wembley Stadium.

'Really?'

'I know! I mean, who wants their linen covered in doggy fish breath? No thanks, mister.'

Slowly we drive back down the bumpy track.

'What kind of dogs were they?'

'Labradors, I think.'

'Maybe they're guide dogs?'

'Oh. Perhaps.' She cocks her head. 'Yes, that's probably exactly what they are.' Suspiciously I look over to Mum but her expression is deadpan. 'Right. Home. Your father will be wondering where the heck we are. Have you found us on the map?'

For the next few miles my head is buzzing. I think of Guy about to study history and Dom continuing his life with Miranda, Sarah working abroad and Sean who moved on a long time ago. Why is a voice telling me to turn round?

'Mum?'

'Hmm?'

'Can we go back?'

'Where?'

'To the doggy place.'

She slows down. 'Why?'

I can't answer that exactly. 'Please. Look, clearly it was

a plan to bring me out here, wasn't it?' I throw the map back into the glove box. 'You know exactly where we are.'

'What are you talking about?'

'Doesn't matter! Just turn round!'

Mum pulls over at the next layby and it's not long before we're heading back down the bumpy track.

8

Mum and I are in the reception area. On the walls are framed photographs of yellow, black and chocolate-coloured Labradors with their purple coats on. Some of them have their paws resting on their owners' laps. In other shots, the dogs sit by the wheelchairs, looking noble and proud, the owners wrapping an arm around them. I wheel myself down the line, reading the inscriptions beneath the photographs. 'Rachel and Elvis'. Rachel is wearing a graduation gown and mortarboard and holds a degree certificate that Elvis also touches with one paw.

On another wall, next to the bathroom, is a pinboard with press cuttings and more pictures of dogs reaching for tins and cereal packets in supermarkets. I hear music coming from one of the rooms; it's The Black Eyed Peas. I glance at Mum. There's no way we could have stumbled upon this place by chance, could we? Cautiously I wheel myself towards the door, before it gets flung open by a plump woman wearing jeans, trainers and a T-shirt, who sweeps past Mum and me without seeming to notice us. I peer into the room and my heart melts when I see golden and black puppies with floppy ears, wearing tiny purple bibs. One of the Labrador pups is jumping through a yellow hoop. 'Wait wait . . . back . . . Good boy!' says a busty woman in a purple T-shirt, as the puppy moves backwards through her legs. 'Oh look at them,' I sigh out loud.

'Can I help you?' says a voice. Mum and I turn and see a tall dark-haired man behind us, wearing a purple fleece.

'Hello. We were just looking around,' says Mum, as if we were browsing in a clothes shop.

He shakes his head regretfully. 'We're in the middle of training. I'm afraid we don't like people wandering about unless they've made an appointment.'

'An appointment?' Mum queries.

'Yes. We're a charity. Canine Partners.' He gestures to the logo on his fleece of an abstract person in a wheelchair, a dog by their side. 'We train our dogs to assist anyone with a disability. Are you interested?' He repeats the question and I look up, surprised he's directing it at me. Normally I am addressed via my mother, with comments like, 'Doesn't she look well!'

'I don't know,' I reply. Yes you are. Tell him you are, a voice urges.

His face softens. 'Stuart Harris. Chief Executive.' He shakes Mum's hand. 'How do you do, Mrs . . . ?'

'Brooks.'

'And you are?' he asks when I don't think to say my name.

'Cass,' I mutter.

'Sorry?' He's so tall he has to bend down to hear me. He gives his ear a tap. 'Bit deaf in my old age.'

He can only be about forty-five. 'Cass,' I repeat, my mouth as dry as straw.

'Now look,' Stuart says, leading us away from the door and across to the other side of the reception room. 'This isn't strictly allowed but if you promise to be quiet you can come in and observe the older pups.' Gently he opens the door. 'These little superstars are in their advanced training,' says Stuart proudly. My heart melts again, this time at much bigger but just as bouncy puppies of all different colours, dressed in their purple coats. There are six dogs in this room, each with their own personal trainer.

We position ourselves in the corner, where there's a desk, computer and filing cabinet. It's a simple room, with a grey floor and white walls.

'We have to keep the room pretty basic,' Stuart says. 'We don't want to distract our heroes. What are you doing?' he whispers, watching Mum brushing the cushion on her chair, her gold bracelets causing a distraction.

'Dog hairs,' she says. 'They make me come out in a rash.'

'You're allergic to dogs?' Stuart asks in disbelief.

'Sit down, Mum,' I beg.

She does one final sweep before tentatively planting her

bottom on the chair, as though she were about to sit on a bed of hot spikes.

Stuart leans towards me. 'As you can see, most of our pups are retriever-type breeds but we do select some crosses between poodles, Labradors and retrievers too.' He gestures to a black Labradoodle with bright eyes and curls to die for, picking up a set of keys and handing them back to his trainer, a woman, in a wheelchair. I notice the trainers are mostly young women and they are all dressed in purple T-shirts with jeans.

Stuart tells us the puppies in this room are anything from fourteen to nineteen months old. 'If we're lucky we get our pups from as young as seven or eight weeks. The beauty of starting their training early is they learn quickly. They're like sponges, wanting to absorb everything.'

I watch in fascination as a chocolate Labrador tugs gently at one of the trainer's gloves. 'Clever boy!' she says, when he has it in his mouth. Proudly he drops it on to her lap and then waits for a treat, wagging his tail. Another Labrador is in one corner of the room by a washing machine, touching the door handle and being rewarded by his or her trainer with chopped carrots.

'It's important to reward them all the time,' Stuart says. 'Our dogs aren't robots or slaves. They won't do anything unless they want to, but matched with the right person there's *nothing* they won't do. It's unconditional love.' Mum and I watch one of the puppies closest to us looking at a small white pedal bin. 'What kind of dog is that?' Mum asks.

'A Goldipoo.'

'A whatiepoo?'

'Goldipoo. A cross between a poodle and a retriever. Poodles are extremely intelligent,' he whispers, as if letting us in on a top secret again.

The trainer has this clicking device that she seems to use only when the puppy is doing the right thing. She stops clicking when he tries to open the lid of the bin with his teeth. The puppy rolls over, wants to be tickled, yelps in frustration when he doesn't get any attention. I get the feeling he's been trying to solve this pedal-bin problem for some time. He sits up again, cocks his head to one side. He lifts his paw, close to the pedal now, and is rewarded with a treat and more clicking and praise. He lifts his paw and presses down on the pedal and the lid swings open to a round of applause.

'Wow! Isn't that incredible, Mum!'

'I wish I could train your father like that.'

'Our dogs can learn to do the most amazing things,' Stuart claims. 'They can help dress and undress, operate a pedestrian crossing or a lift button, carry out a range of emergency response procedures . . . but they do so much more than that,' he says, looking directly at me. 'I tell you, Cass, when I see applicants for the first time they're pale, often overweight and frankly depressed. There's something dead in their eyes.' He narrows his own. 'Once they've bonded with a dog – this might sound rather simplistic, but it's like they've been given a second chance.'

I hear a whine, and notice a puppy in the middle of the room, attached by his lead to a small hook in the wall. Perhaps he's bored waiting for his go at the washing machine or pedal bin? He has a bright red collar and when I wave at him, he wags his tail and attempts to move, only to realise he can't get very far. 'One sec,' Stuart says, leaping off his seat to sort him out. 'Ticket! Settle! It's your turn very soon. There we are, good boy.' Stuart returns to Mum and me. 'He's a live wire, that one. Sixteen months and full of mischief.' Ticket's a Labrador, his coat the colour of honeycomb.

Ticket continues to whine and bark. 'You're going to have to forgive me. He's clearly got something to say to you, Cassandra.'

'To me?'

He walks over to Ticket's mat, releases the lead from the hook, and next thing I know, Ticket bounds over to me, jumping up against my legs. I laugh, a wave of pure joy. Stuart apologises for the disruption, but one of the trainers looks over at us, curious.

'Ticket, I'd like you to meet Cass.' Stuart introduces us as if we are about to go on a blind date.

I reach to stroke and tickle him under his chin. 'Hello, Ticket! Aren't you lovely, yes you are, yes you are.' His ears are velvety soft, his coat so smooth, and his eyes light up with playfulness. He jumps up again, giving me another wet kiss.

'Cass, you don't know where his tongue's been,' Mum points out, before receiving a stern look from Stuart.

'Ticket! That's such a great name and you're so hand-some.' I take his face into my hands and kiss him back. I wish I'd brought a bigger bag. Then I could have taken him home. Surely no one would notice one puppy missing?

Stuart stands back. 'It's love at first sight. He makes *your* tail wag, doesn't he, Cass?' I feel a warm glow inside me, but that's quickly destroyed when the trainer takes Ticket away.

'The next stage is trying to match him with the right partner.'

'You mean someone else could get him?' I blurt out.

Stuart looks at me. 'Well, yes, Cass. But you could apply?'

As we leave Stuart hands me an information pack, along with an application form. 'Don't give Ticket to anyone else,' I plead into his ear. 'Please keep him for me.'

And I swear from the corner of my eye I see Mum winking at him.

Mum and I don't talk about the dogs on the way home but I devour the information pack the moment we get back. I learn that the main role of the puppy parent is to train and socialise their dog by taking them out as much as possible from the age of two to fourteen months. They'll go to places that an assistant dog is likely to find itself in, like busy streets, supermarkets, the hospital or workplaces – and they have to try and do this as if they were disabled, so the puppy parent would use the disabled access in a bank or the wide aisle in Tesco's. A puppy is taught to problem solve, which is considered one of the most crucial qualities for an assistant dog.

After leaving the puppy parents, the dogs are brought to Canine Partners to complete their advanced training, which takes a further four to six months. Thanks to generous sponsorship, the dogs are free.

The form asks for information about me: my work, my home life and my disability. If I want a dog, my doctor must provide Canine Partners with my medical records.

The last line is in bold. *Please tell us why you would like a Canine Partner and how you consider you would benefit. This is a very important part of the application and we would like to hear it in your own words.*

I return to the beginning, filling in my name and address. I tick boxes; circle answers. I find myself running out of space and having to write on the back of the sheet too.

'What are you doing?' Mum asks as I finish the last question. She's surprised to find me sitting more or less in the dark without the television on. 'You can't see a thing in here.' She turns on the light by the sitting room sofa.

I stop writing, black ink smudged across my finger. I

can't quite work out whether today was a set-up or not. Surely a dog is the last thing she'd want in the house?

I hand her the application form.

My heart races as I watch her turn over the page to read my last answer. She looks at me, and then back at the form. 'Because I want a bond,' she reads out. 'I want to care about something again.'

'I really want one,' I say. 'I want Ticket.' Still Mum doesn't say a word. 'What do you think?'

'Cass, if it makes you happy you can fill the whole house with dogs.' She smiles as she wipes an eye. 'You don't know how happy it makes me feel that you've even asked.'

I thought I knew Mum, but as she leaves the room I realise I'd barely touched the surface.

9

It's early evening and I should be packing. I leave tomorrow to go on the Canine Partner Residential Training Course, which is held at the training centre in Heyshott, West Sussex. Since visiting Canine Partners three months ago, an occupational therapist, or one of the purple people as Mum and I call them, visited to see if any adaptations needed to be made to the house. I have also completed three assessment days. These days give the trainers a chance to see how we interact with the dogs. When I saw Ticket for the first time since that day when he'd jumped into my lap, my feelings hadn't changed. If anything they'd grown deeper. He'd charged over and sniffed my boring old shoes, my tracksuit and wheelchair as if they were the most exciting things ever, and then he'd covered my hand in kisses. Lindsey, the head trainer, says it's fairly clear from the assessment days which partners are going to get which dogs, but there's always a small element of doubt. Occasionally we might not see what they see. But surely, *surely* I will get Ticket?

I want to bring him home more than I've wanted anything for a long time. However, being away from Mum and Dad is a plunge into darkness.

I'm nervous about so many things, but not being able to go to the loo properly is one of the worst side effects of spinal cord injury, almost worse than not being able to walk. London for the day is manageable but this is a whole fortnight. What if I have an accident?

After being in Stoke Mandeville for a few days, I realised I hadn't gone to the bathroom. I also knew, from my student days, that something else was terribly wrong but it still came as a shock when Georgina explained that when the spinal cord is damaged, you can no longer feel or control your bladder and bowels.

I close my eyes, remembering how Georgina had talked to me about how to manage my bladder and bowel movement.

'What I'll be teaching you is how to use an intermittent catheter,' she said in her usual matter-of-fact way. 'You'll need to be rigid about how much you drink, learn what your limit is. I suggest every three to four hours you'll need to empty your bladder with one of these.' She was holding up something that looked like a drinking straw. 'They're single use and you must keep them sterile. When you're inserting a foreign agent into your bladder there's a risk of infection.'

I shudder, recalling my first lesson with her. I was lying

on the bed with my legs spread apart, inserting the straw-like catheter into my bladder, via the uretha, Georgina towering over me, saying, 'Up a bit. No! Down a bit!' Georgina didn't pick up on how upset and uncomfortable I was, or if she did, she ignored it. All I could think about during that lesson was how unnatural and degrading it was and that I had to do this for ever. I even wished I were a man. At least they could see what they were doing.

'You'll get the hang of it, Cass,' she said. 'Believe me, there'll come a time when you don't even think about it. It'll be as simple as brushing your teeth.'

I remained silent. It was the only time I was truly relieved that my relationship with Sean was over. It was all so unsexy.

'With the bowel,' Georgina continued, 'you might find it's more sluggish so the best way to deal with this is to manage it by making yourself "go" on a regular schedule, say every morning at the same time. It can be a good idea to take some laxatives the night before to help things along but you can minimise this by drinking lots of fluids and eating a high fibre diet and staying as active as possible.'

Georgina ended the lesson saying, 'You're lucky, Cass, because a lot of injured people can't use a catheter independently. No one will know you even have one, so don't look so glum, my dear.'

I open my eyes when I hear footsteps outside my bedroom.

'Cass, supper . . . oh, what are you doing?' Mum looks at the empty suitcase on the floor. 'Why haven't you packed?'

'I'll do it later.'

Mum stands at the door. 'You'll need lots of warm clothes. Winter's here already,' she says, dressed herself in a chunky-knit polo neck with jeans. It's the end of October.

'Um.'

Mum places her hands on her hips. 'Are you scared?'

'No.' She can read me so well now.

She raises an eyebrow.

'Yes,' I say. That knotted feeling in my stomach won't go away.

She perches on the end of my bed. 'OK. What's worrying you most about being away?'

I chew my lip. 'I don't want to have an accident, Mum. I'm nervous.'

'I understand,' Mum says. 'But if you have any kind of problem, you must talk to someone. Also, darling, they'll make sure you have plenty of breaks during the training so you can have something to eat or go to the bathroom. Try not to worry.'

'Um.'

'You can always call home if you need us, too,' she continues. 'But don't ring after nine.' She nudges me. 'You know what your old dad and I are like, falling asleep in front of the TV. Seven thirty isn't a good time either because it's *EastEnders* and it's getting to a juicy part.'

I nudge her back. 'So that leaves me a free slot at eight?'

'Oh, Cass, you know you can call any time. Now, you won't forget to pack your alarm clock, will you? You won't have me knocking at your door.'

Dad runs upstairs with my mobile. 'It's Guy,' he says, handing it to me. Mum leaves, telling me she'll be back in five minutes, otherwise the fish pie will burn.

'Wanted to wish you good luck for tomorrow, Princess.'

I twist a strand of my hair. 'Thanks.'

'What's wrong?'

'It's two weeks, Guy.'

'You survived four months in hospital with Perky and me so you can survive fourteen days with a cute dog.'

I breathe deeply.

'Look, it's all you've been banging on about recently. Ticket this . . . Ticket that. You'll regret it if you don't go.'

He's right. Of course I would.

'You can do it,' he says. 'Besides, Ticket would never forgive you if he gets landed with that Trevor bloke because you couldn't be bothered to show up.' Trevor is one of the other applicants.

I laugh now. 'Since when did you become so wise?'

'Always have been, just hidden it well. So, what are you waiting for? You go get that dog, Princess.'

10

It's the first morning of the training course and I'm having breakfast with the rest of the group. Unlike last night, we're far too nervous to talk or eat because finally we find out which dog we're going to train for the remainder of the course and take home afterwards. Last night Lindsey had warned us again that occasionally it doesn't work out the way we think, but that she'll make sure we are all happy with the dog we're matched with.

Sitting opposite me is Jenny. Jenny is in her fifties and has a rare disease where the brain sends the wrong messages to the muscles. She has short silvery grey hair, wears glasses and loose clothing and looks as if the slightest breeze could blow her over.

Tom sits at the end of the table; he was born with cerebral palsy. It's hard to understand what he says because his speech is badly affected. He desperately wants to communicate but the disease fights against him to make sure no words come out. However, he did manage to tell me that I was as pretty as Michelle Pfeiffer. I could feel myself blush, surprised by how lovely it was to be given such a compliment. Tom is twenty years old and is studying for a broadcasting degree at Leeds University. He wants to be a journalist or radio producer. His small pale hands are contorted and look painful. He writes his essays with a head pointer that fastens around his forehead. 'What . . . do . . . you do?' he'd asked me, when we first met.

'Nothing,' I said, before adding, 'I used to study medicine.' I think of Sarah, now in her final year at King's. Was I wrong to give it all up?

Then there's Alex who lives in London. She doesn't know what's wrong with her. 'Don't you want to give people a right old slap when they ask what's wrong with you? I feel like turning round and asking what's wrong with them, you know? It's like a family tree, yeah, with us cripples in our own little box and the rest of them branching off into who married who and whatever. Well, I don't know what's wrong with me; all I know is it's to do with me nerves.'

Tom started to say something. 'We . . . can . . . put . . . you in . . .' We all listened patiently, hoping that it was going to be worth the wait. ' . . . the miscellaneous file,' he finished and laughed so much that his shoulders heaved up and down and he dropped his ham sandwich on to his boot.

Then there's Trevor. He has had severe osteoarthritis for twenty years and is desperately overweight, largely because severe pain has stopped him from taking even moderate exercise. Today he's wearing a badge on his jacket that reads, 'Proud to be DISABLED!' Trevor loves to talk gadgets. Last night he was telling us about a chopping board that has spikes on its base and an indent to put your cucumber or whatever into, without it rolling across the board and falling on to the floor. 'But it cost me seventy quid!' he exclaimed, before saying sadly, 'I'm afraid we're a captive audience.'

Finally there's Edward. He's in his late twenties and I discovered he was a lance corporal in the Royal Marines. He told me he'd been out to Afghanistan in 2007, but was flown home injured in a mine strike. He lost his left leg above the knee and now has a prosthetic limb. He can walk, 'Very badly,' he'd added, but when he's in pain or has to walk any distance, he slots his crutches on to the back of his wheelchair. That's about as much as I know. He was quiet over supper last night, answering questions as quickly as he could, and he hardly said a word when we all went on our first outing yesterday afternoon. However much Lindsey reinforces that our dogs want companionship, that it's good to laugh and talk to them, he remains reserved, keeping his gaze fixed firmly on the ground.

After breakfast we meet in one of the training rooms. The moment has come. I know I will get Ticket, yet I still feel as anxious as an actress waiting to find out if I've won the Oscar.

We are deathly quiet when Lindsey walks into the room with her clipboard and stands in the middle of our circle. She's sporty and glamorous even in her purple T-shirt and jeans. 'You're as quiet as mice,' she says, flicking a hand through her hair, knowing full well why we aren't talkative.

'It's called panicking,' Trevor mutters. 'I hope you're not going to give my dog to anyone else. I like Pandora.' He nods at all of us in turn, in case we're in any way confused.

'You mustn't get too disappointed,' Lindsey reminds us. 'You might think that one dog is perfect but they might not be perfect for *you*.'

'Yes, yes, you've told us that,' Trevor grumbles.

Lindsey goes on to prolong the agony by warning us that our dogs might find it difficult to begin with being parted from her and their routine at Canine Partners. 'Dogs love stability and they form strong attachments so these two weeks are all about you showing them that you are now their master. OK, we're going to bring the dogs into the room, one by one.' She goes out and returns with Pandora on the lead, groomed and wearing her purple coat. I think Lindsey is enjoying this. She's acting like a judge on *X-Factor*, prolonging the decision of who goes through to the next round. Trevor is breathing heavily as he watches Pandora trotting by Lindsey's side. I am sure he's going to have to undo the top button of his trousers. Pandora sniffs and wags her tail when she's near him. 'That's my girl,' he says, sure she's going to stop and sit by his sandalled feet, but she moves on and is brought tantalisingly close to me. Pandora circles my chair. 'And the person who will have Pandora is . . .' There's a dramatic pause, all we need is a drum roll. 'Trevor,' she says at last.

When Tom is given Leo he gasps with relief as if he's been holding his breath the entire time.

Edward gets Tinkerbell, the pretty chocolate Labrador. When he smiles I am drawn to the warmth in his green eyes.

So far, everyone has been given their first choice, so Ticket has to be mine. I can relax. Priscilla, the Labradoodle, walks in next. She's a cross between a Labrador and a poodle, but the poodle gene is clearly the stronger as her coat has tight little curls.

'You're joking,' Alex says, followed by an uneasy laugh when Priscilla sits by her side. When Lindsey shakes her head Alex cries out, 'I'm not taking no poodle home. They're not proper!'

'Excuse me?' Lindsey says.

'My friends will take the mickey.' Alex crosses her arms in a huff.

Lindsey looks concerned. 'Alex, of course you need to be happy, but . . .'

'I can't have no poodle in Brixton! When I signed up for this, yeah, I thought I'd be taking home a Labrador, not some poodle with curly hair and fancy ways.' Priscilla barks at this insult. 'I want Captain, the Golden Retriever.'

I catch Edward smiling at me. When no one's looking, I smile back.

'Stop being a Poodleist!' Lindsey continues.

'A what?' Alex screws up her face.

'A Poodleist,' she repeats, annoyed now. 'Alex, I understand you're disappointed and I know you did get on well with Captain too, but didn't you see how Priscilla worked for you in the assessment days? When you were in trouble in the lift, she took over. This is what I mean. Sometimes you don't see what we see. The dogs chooses *you* just as much you chose him or her.'

Alex's face softens for a moment. She looks at Priscilla. 'I did like her,' she admits now. 'She really chose me?'

Lindsey nods. 'So can you give her a chance?'

So if Alex didn't get her choice, there's a possibility I won't get mine now. Jenny could get Ticket. I know she likes him too. He trots into the room next.

Please give him to me. He's my boy. Ticket rests his head on my knee.

'He's yours,' Lindsey says, as if there was never any contest.

11

It's the second week of our training course.

So far we've been given lectures each morning on the many different aspects of looking after a dog: grooming, exercising, feeding, playing, taking them to public places and what to expect, dog psychology – their moods and body language – and we have had to learn all the various commands. We also need to be aware of our environment. For example, if living in student accommodation we need to make sure no one has allergies to pets. That was mainly directed at Tom. I looked over to him, admiring his strength. Tom fights for everything; he writes his essays with a head pointer because he can't type with his curled fists. He doesn't rely on equipment like voice liberators to be understood; he battles to be heard. At university he has a full-time carer, just as he has a carer here. When I'd asked if he found the carer's constant presence intrusive, he said no, but then confided to me that one of them had bullied and taunted his weaknesses to such an extent that he'd cried himself to sleep for months, and almost gave up his degree. Yet, he didn't, because the most important thing for him is to live away from home and to get a job when he gradu- ates. The carer was sacked and he is now much happier with his new one. 'I love my mum, but she'd . . . drive . . . me round the . . . bend!' he'd said to me, followed by a shriek of laughter. He has inspired me to put everything into this training course. If Tom can have a dog and look after it, so can I.

In the afternoons we often perform role-plays in one of the training rooms, pretending to be in a supermarket, bank, restaurant, lift or shop. If we're at a pedestrian crossing, we say, 'Up switch,' asking our dog to use his front paw to push the pedestrian button. The props are laid out for us, the shelves stacked high with plastic tins of baked beans, reminding me of Guy. All this preparation is building us up to our final assessment day at the end of the week, when we will be taken out on a Farmers' Market Day. We have been warned that it will be crowded, 'So you're going to have to have all your wits about you,' Lindsey said.

During the training we are watched every second of the day. Lindsey is never far behind us with her clipboard. I am certain she was hiding behind Trevor's bedroom door last night to see if he was acting the same behind closed doors. Did he go from jolly old man to gruff demanding old sod, ordering Pandora to get him his slippers?

'These dogs are not machines,' she reinforces daily. 'You must love them and treat them with respect.'

The hardest part, however, has been learning the commands. If a dog jumps up at you, you don't say, 'Down,' as that's asking them to lie down. You say, 'Off.' There are four positions around a wheelchair: 'Heel' is asking your dog to stand on the left-hand side, 'Behind' is behind, 'Go through' is go in front of the chair and 'Side' is please stand on my right-hand side. It's important to know where the dog should be placed at all times so they're safe. Lindsey told us about one of their dogs on the last course who had been in the wrong place at the wrong time when entering a lift. The doors shut and his paw was broken. There's so much to learn that I'm not having nightmares any more. Instead I wake myself up saying the commands.

Lindsey slots the video into the machine. We have to watch on film how we work with our dogs outside the training room. I'm anxious about seeing myself on screen, but thankfully it's Trevor first. We watch as he throws a tennis ball across the field. 'Play ball,' he calls out to Pandora. Trevor struggles when it begins to rain, grappling with his hood and trying to zip up his anorak. Rain turns into a hailstorm. Trevor is spitting in fury now and making no sense at all. He calls for Pandora, distress in his voice.

'Why did you flip out?' Lindsey asks him, pressing the pause button.

'I forgot my command, went blank! It's not easy remembering them all, especially at my age,' he jokes.

Lindsey places her hands on her hips. 'That's not good enough, Trevor.'

'I know,' he says, cowering in his seat.

'If you panic, so will Pandora. You see here?' She turns to all of us. 'Pandora is stressed out by Trevor losing his cool. Commands can be less formal inside your home, but outside, there are too many risks so you've got to stay calm. Better luck next time, Trevor. All right, Cass next. Are you ready?'

The last time I looked at myself properly in a mirror was during one of my sessions in the gym with Paul at the hospital, over six months ago. I didn't recognise myself. My face was pale from being cooped up in the rehab ward for weeks and my feet looked dead against the footplates.

'It's purely from the point of view of Ticket and his responses to you,' Lindsey says, sensing my apprehension as she presses play on the machine. 'You see here,' she begins gently, 'when you were at the supermarket and Ticket was sitting by the chocolate stand. Now, I don't blame him for that –' she looks at me, hoping for a smile – 'but he's not in a safe place. Do you see? You need to manoeuvre your chair around him, to protect him from another person's trolley.'

I thought I looked better than that. In my head I imagine I'm the same old Cass. Five foot eight and slender, deep brown eyes, OK, not model legs, but good legs, thick dark blonde hair scooped back into a ponytail. Sean loved to sneak up on me when I was studying and blow softly against the nape of my neck. Then he'd wrap his arms around me, I'd turn and we'd kiss . . .

'You positioned yourself nicely there when it was your turn to pay,' she continues. 'But did you see what you didn't do? Cass?'

I open my eyes and the image on the screen is still there. I look like a giant slug in my wheelchair. I hear Lindsey say something about the conveyor belt, that I should have asked the shop assistant to turn it off.

'Cass, what's wrong?'

I reach for my glass of water. 'I didn't think I was that bad . . . I didn't think I looked like that.'

'What do you mean?'

'That ugly.'

Edward offers me a cigarette.

'It's no smoking in here,' Lindsey reminds him.

He lights up. 'Fuck off. Why are you making us do this? Can't you see we don't want to look at ourselves?'

'Well, I don't mind all that much,' Trevor says, hoping to break the tension. 'I mean, I've never been much of a beauty queen, *moi*.'

Jenny and Alex are quiet. Tom is gazing at his feet, humming.

'But it's about the dogs,' Lindsey tries to explain to us

again, 'and their interaction with you. This is an essential part of the training. I know it's difficult but—'

'It's not just about the fucking dogs!' Edward shouts now.

'Edward! Calm down, please.'

'What part of this don't you get? At home I have no mirrors, right? Don't you understand? I hate seeing me.'

Lindsey sits down. 'I know it's hard, but if you want to take Tinkerbell home, you need to put the past behind you. You have a chance at a new life, Edward. It's not the same as your old one, but it could be a good life.'

'Don't fucking patronise me.'

Unfazed, Lindsey says, 'Are you going to take it?'

'It's too late. I don't want this fucking life. I'm in hell. This is hell on wheels,' he says, leaving the room.

Later that evening there's a knock on my door. 'Come in,' I call. Jenny enters, Captain by her side. Ticket immediately jumps up, his tail wagging. They play for a minute until Jenny says, firmly, 'Down, now. Good boy.' Captain lies down by her chair but keeps a close eye on Ticket.

'I was checking to see if you were all right?' she asks in her soft voice.

'Fine, thanks.'

She isn't convinced.

'Really, I'm fine, Jenny. It's Edward I'm worried about.'

She nods. 'I don't like the filming either.'

'You'd never know.'

'I want to do my best for Captain. He didn't ask to be an assistant dog so we have to do this, for our boys.' There's a pause. 'Besides, I was in hospital for twenty years.'

'For two years?'

'No, twenty.'

'You're joking!' is the first stupid thing to tumble out of my mouth, but of course I know she's not.

'I was told I was in the best place,' she continues in a voice so calm, like waves gently rolling on to the shore. 'No one could cope with me being at home. I needed too much care.'

I am out of my depth, struggling to know the right thing to say. 'What kept you going all that time?'

'I put my name down on a housing list. I had the faintest hope that one of these days I'd get out. I couldn't accept that I was going to die in hospital. I had to believe I'd go back into the community. Every day I'd think of people who were worse off than me. I know what you're thinking,' she says, when she registers my incredulous face, 'but I'm glad I didn't give up, and if that doesn't make me a strong person, nothing will.'

'How did you hear about Canine Partners?'

'It was a guardian angel day. My sister was taking me out for a change of scene and we walked past one of the staff rooms where there was a demonstration going on. Lindsey told me to come in and watch. "I have to have one of those," I said to her afterwards. The hospital didn't think anyone in their right *mind* would give me a dog but Lindsey was always positive. I worked so hard to leave that place for this one. My lap,' she says to him, and Captain jumps up, both paws pressed against her knees, and she strokes him affectionately.

I look at her. She has seen nothing but her four walls and yet I think she's seen more than most of us, especially me. 'Is it wonderful to be out?'

She shakes her head. 'Strange too. Technology has moved on so much in the last twenty years, what with Facebook and texting and emails. It was like walking into another time zone!' She pauses. 'Here I am talking all about myself, but I don't know much about you, Cass.'

I tell her, briefly, why I'm in a wheelchair. Each time I tell someone about my accident, it gets a tiny bit easier.

'Lindsey!' we hear Edward calling outside in the corridor. His bedroom is next door to mine. 'Can we talk?'

Jenny and I stop. Wait.

'Do you want to come into my office?' Lindsey asks.

'No, I need to say it now, right here. I'm really sorry. I don't know what happened earlier. I was so angry but—'

'Edward, it's all right.'

'I'm so sorry, I was out of order, I shouldn't have spoken to you like that . . . oh God, this is my last hope and I'm scared. I've blown it, haven't I? I've let you down. You'll take Tinkerbell away from me?'

'Edward, you haven't let me down and I certainly won't be taking Tinkerbell away from you.'

'No?'

'I'll see you in the morning and don't give it another thought, OK, because I'm not going to and nor is Tinkerbell.'

Minutes later there's another knock on the door. 'It's me,' Alex calls. Both Ticket and Captain bark as they jump to their feet, tails wagging, acting like they're hosts letting in the next party guest. Alex walks in with Priscilla. She sits down, leaning her stick against the wall, before she produces from her bag a plastic cup along with a bottle of gin. 'No sniff, Cilla,' she says, pushing her away. 'It ain't food, sweetheart. It's medicine.' She offers both Jenny and me a glass.

Jenny takes a tentative sip. I take a large gulp. And another.

'D'you feel better now?' Alex asks me.

'Yes, much.'

'I envy you, you know.'

'Me? Why?'

'The thing is, you're pretty. Whatever you saw on the screen, I didn't see it,' she says, 'honest to God. I bet you have guys queuing up.'

I laugh, confiding that I haven't been on a date since the accident; that the dating scene terrifies me almost as much as looking in the mirror.

'Edward's dead handsome too. Those beautiful green eyes and dark hair, and he's a real hero and all that, ain't he? Just imagine him in his uniform,' she giggles.

Jenny and I smile. I had noticed Edward was handsome too. It's hard not to.

'But whatever I have, it's degenerative, right, it's like MS and it's only going to get worse. I can't drive now, and that really hurts.'

'Why do you want a dog, Alex?' Jenny asks.

'Well, I love 'em, always have. I thought my doggy days were well 'n' truly over when I got this.' She shrugs her shoulders. 'This sounds stupid, right.'

'Go on,' Jenny and I say at the same time.

'I don't think I'll meet anyone now.' She laughs that painful laugh we are all guilty of; the laugh that attempts to mask the sadness. It makes me think of Guy. 'I've kinda reckoned on being celibate for the rest of me life. I want a friend though. I don't want to be alone no more,' Alex confesses. 'Loneliness, it's a killer. How about both of you?' she rushes on, hoping we don't focus on what she's just said.

'That's not stupid,' I say. 'It's exactly how I feel.'

'I couldn't have put it better myself,' Jenny adds.

'To loneliness, and beating the crap out of it,' I suggest.

We raise our glasses to each other and to Captain, Cilla and Ticket.

12

It's a crisp winter's day in January and sunlight streams through my bedroom window. Ticket and I have been together for nearly three months since the two-week residential training course. He's now twenty-two months old and fully grown, but still a giant puppy at heart. We love having him at home. Without Ticket, we couldn't have got through our first Christmas since my accident. He received so much attention in church, and when it came to present time, he had the best fun opening all of his toys, including a red squeaky Santa given to him by Trevor and Pandora. On New Year's Day Mum, Dad, Jamie and I wrapped up in thousands of layers and took Ticket for a long walk, followed by a pub lunch.

Ticket sits in front of me, his face close to mine as I wipe the sleep dust from his eyes with a moist cotton wool pad. It's hard to keep him still for long, he's always raring to go on to the next thing. He's a bundle of energy, giving our home a pulse again.

The past three months have slipped by. Mum doesn't nag me to get up any more. Ticket's taken her place, whining to be let out. With the strap in his mouth, he pulls my chair over to me, and waits patiently as I transfer myself to it from the bed. Once I'm positioned on the landing, by the stair-lift, Ticket rushes downstairs to bring the old wheelchair that we hired from the Red Cross to the foot of the stairs. Once I'm in that chair, we make our way to the back door that leads into the garden. I can reach the handle, but Ticket jumps up and tugs at the cord without me even saying the command now. Once I'm showered and dressed, Ticket and I do a couple of chores. With Ticket's help, together we bundle my bed sheets or clothes into a basket; with the basket on my lap we head downstairs (the same routine with the wheelchair and stair-lift) and into the utility room. Ticket then takes over, loading the machine. I can almost feel him flexing his muscles as he says, 'Stand back, Cass, this is where I come in.' He can't go so far as setting my lingerie on a delicate wash, or hanging my frilly knickers, bras and socks on the clothesline, but if he could, he would. *Captain is a man in Labrador's clothing,* Jenny had told me recently in a letter, because she still can't fathom computers and email. *In his own funny way, he talks to me, Cass, and seems to know what I'm thinking. He's my friend, my power, he means the world to me.*

If I'm alone and have any kind of accident, Ticket has been trained to alert Mum or Dad, but if they're not around, he can bring the telephone to me. I used to be unable to imagine living independently or doing the most basic things for myself without calling for Mum, but with Ticket I'm catching a glimpse of what it might be like moving back to London. And Ticket's not only helping me. My parents are beginning to have a social life again. 'We know you're in good paws,' Dad says with a wink, before they head out. Dad even suggested to Mum that they go on a winter mini-break to a country hotel with roaring log fires and cooked breakfasts. Mum still sneezes and scratches and says she should buy shares in antihistamine tablets.

Ticket has given me colour in my cheeks and air in my lungs. On our walks, I wrap up warm and pack my bag with beef and chicken treats and his favourite half-chewed lime-green tennis ball. I loop his lead securely to the wheelchair, so I have both arms free to steer myself, and I take us down the long winding Dorset lanes. We say good afternoon to the sheep in the fields; we pass the grand house with the iron gates, and Ticket barks at the peacocks on the lawn.

We often stop at the butcher's. I can't get my wheelchair up the steps so out comes Mr Steel in his navy apron, looking like the butcher in a set of *Happy Family* cards as he asks how many miles we've covered that day. It doesn't matter if I say half a mile or five; he always replies, 'Aye, no rest for the wicked!' Occasionally he brings Ticket a marrow or rump bone, so of course Ticket loves visiting Mr Steel. In fact he loves everything. Whatever we do, Ticket seems to think it's the most exciting adventure ever, even if it's exactly what we did the day before.

We pass many dog walkers and my parents' neighbours, who always want to stop and talk and to my surprise I enjoy making conversation. Even though Ticket's coat says, 'Don't distract me, I'm working' I can see their hands restless at their sides, itching to stroke his soft golden fur. Children pat him all the time and tell me he's 'so cute', which makes me glow like a proud mother.

Ticket and I also visit Mrs Henderson, one of Mum and Dad's elderly neighbours. She lives on her own in a thatched cottage with books on every shelf and a neglected swimming pool in her back garden. She had a proposition for me. She's writing her memoirs but her typing is slow, so would I consider working for her? She'd pay, of course, she added. I'm aiming to save enough money to plan a trip before I move back to London and get a job. I haven't told Sarah my plans. We've barely been in touch. She's living in new accommodation in Pimlico. Thankfully she's stopped trying to persuade me to go back to King's. Going back there is my old life; it would only remind me of my accident. I crave something new.

In secret, I've been online researching and slowly I'm making small steps to begin building a future. When I'm ready, I'll tell Mum and Dad what I'm planning.

13

Mum, Dad, Jamie, Ticket and I drive to Canine Partners for Ticket's graduation day, where we hope to see again all the friends we made on the training course. It's a celebration for everyone who has been involved in the process of forming our partnerships, from the breeders to the puppy parents, occupational therapists, foster parents, sponsors and, of course, the trainers and staff who work for the charity.

We've dressed up for the event. Jamie and my father are looking handsome in jackets and ties. Mum's modelling an elegant suit with fake fur cuffs. I'm wearing a blue jersey dress with leggings and boots and both Mum and I went to the hairdresser's yesterday to have our hair washed and blow-dried. But the most important person looks like a Hollywood star. Last night I gave Ticket a bath and groom and told him he'd give George Clooney a run for his money. I even polished the silver studs on his purple collar until they were sparkling like stars.

Guests mill in the reception area of the training centre,

the atmosphere like a drinks party. I'm eager to show Jamie round, pointing to the purpose-built chalets where my friends and I had stayed on the course. Jamie looks at some of the framed photographs, slowing down when he comes to a shot of a beaming Prince Harry holding a golden puppy.

Guests and dogs gradually begin to make their way into the main training room. Today it's lined with blue plastic chairs and there's a PowerPoint screen at the far end, which reads: 'Partnership Ceremony, February 11, 2011'. Ticket's tail hasn't stopped wagging since we arrived, and he almost pulls me out of my wheelchair when he sees the purple people again, especially Lindsey and Stuart testing the microphone. Today Stuart is wearing a suit with a shiny purple tie with the Canine Partner's logo. Immediately he approaches us, greeting Ticket first.

Amongst my friends, I spot Alex in a stripy shirt and navy woollen pinafore dress, clutching her stick. I introduce her to my family. Cilla is lying down on a dark green doggy paw-print mat, a fancy purple pompom attached to her collar. When she sees Ticket she springs to her feet, almost yanking Alex off her chair. I tell Ticket to calm down, we don't want to spoil Cilla's hairdo.

Alex glances at the screen and the increasing number of guests filing into the room. 'What you gonna say when it's your turn? This is scary, huh?'

'Got any gin under your jumper?' I whisper.

Trevor glides past us in his wheelchair, which seems to

have acquired an army of new gadgets, including a front mirror and what looks like a bright red fly swatter on one of the arms. 'Greetings!' he booms, parking his chair close to us and introducing his wife. I notice he's lost a lot of weight, so much so that I can see the outline of his chin. I realise only now that he must have been quite handsome as a younger man.

As everyone takes their seats, Jenny waves at me from across the room. Captain is sitting on his doggy mat looking like a king at his coronation. The last person I see before the ceremony begins is Edward. He's sitting in the front row. I watch him tenderly stroking Tinkerbell under her chin. As if sensing I am watching, he turns round and smiles.

'Order!' Stuart shouts, telling the dogs to keep quiet too. He taps the microphone, before beginning to describe how none of us would be here today if it weren't for the breeders. 'Our pups are not super-canine puppies, they are just normal pups that widdle and chew flexes and furniture, and do all the things we wish puppies wouldn't do. But with lots of love and fun, patience and hard work, these puppies become the canine partners of the future.' Stuart continues to describe how the charity operates, and that each person plays a unique part. 'We have some very special partnerships to present to you today, so, without further ado, let's start with Pandora and Trevor.'

Up comes an image on the screen of Pandora as a puppy,

her head buried in a flowerpot. Pandora's trainer comes to the front, telling us where Pandora was born and what she was like as a puppy. Stuart then invites Trevor and Pandora to the front. 'Before my beautiful Pandora came into my life, I didn't go out much,' he says. 'Pain wipes out all the pleasure of doing anything and if I'm honest I'd lost my faith, but I've begun to go to church again,' he says, his voice filled with emotion.

Soon there's a photographer taking a shot of Pandora and Trevor with a swarm of people around her. It's like a *This Is Your Life* dog show, Pandora reunited with her breeder, puppy and foster parents, and trainer.

Jenny and Captain are next.

As she tells her story I can sense the disbelief from the audience that she endured twenty years in hospital. 'Captain's speciality seems to be picking out my clothes. He has great style, right down to the colour coordinating of my underwear.' There are lots of laughs. 'Before the days of Captain, when I was taken out by my carer, nobody would look me in the eye. I'm sure they thought, "This old ducky, she's not quite right upstairs!"' Though Jenny smiles, the audience understand the sadness behind what she's said. 'Now I'm seen as a person,' she says, collapsing into tears, years of frustration and pain finally coming out. The audience applaud, encouraging her to continue. 'My condition made my world so small, but Captain has made my world big again.'

Tom is the next in line. Stuart holds the microphone for him. 'Leo is the class mascot,' he says in one go, his speech dramatically improved. 'My . . . other friends ask . . . if they can rent . . . him . . . out, for the night!'

Ticket is getting restless now as Alex walks up to the front, unsteady on her stick. Nervously she begins, 'I used to wake up gloomy, you know, but Cilla jumps up on the bed with me shoes as if to say, "Come on! Let's go!" I'm so clumsy, always dropping me keys and me stick but Cilla brings 'em to me. When I'm stressed she breathes gently against me hand, as if to say, "Mum, it's all right." Cilla gives me a reason for living. She's with me twenty-four seven. I love her. Cheers!' she finishes triumphantly.

Edward is next and as he talks, Tinkerbell gazes up at him, as if there's no one else in the room. They make a handsome couple. Edward is dressed in a stylish grey suit and a striped Royal Marine tie; Tinkerbell is wearing a red-spotted collar and her coat is now adorned with an embroidered black and red Royal Marines Commando badge.

'In 2007 I returned home, injured, from Afghanistan. As you can see –' he coughs – 'I lost my right leg, just above the knee. I knew the risks going into the Marines, but you still don't think it's going to happen to you.' Tinkerbell rubs her nose against his thigh. 'After life in the forces it was tough moving back home and trying to fit into civilian life. I felt boxed in. I'd get up, work on my laptop, take my meds, sleep, have physio. I didn't see much daylight, and it got me down. But thanks to my girl . . .' Tinkerbell can't help jumping on to his lap now, making everyone in the room smile. 'I can't believe how much I love her. She's changed my life,' he says, tears in his eyes. 'I'm not half as scared of my future any more.'

I whisper to Ticket that it's our turn now, looking at the image of him on the screen as a puppy, playing with a tennis ball. Lindsey tells the audience that he was friendly, charming and renowned for his good looks. 'And when I saw him with Cass I knew it was a match made in heaven.' As Ticket and I make our way down the aisle, towards the front, I hear a loud sob, the kind you hear in a cinema when there's one person who can't hold it in any more as the *Titanic* sinks or the hero gasps his last breath in his lover's arms.

It's coming from Mum.

Ticket rests his head against my knee, as I begin, 'I'm not alone any more, am I?' Ticket now jumps up, trying to hug me, wagging his tail. I stroke him fondly. 'I feel stronger day by day, and ready to face the world again. Ticket is so *bouncy*.' Everyone laughs. 'And he's so loving. He's everything . . .' I pause, trying to compose myself. 'He's everything I could want. I couldn't ask—' I look down at him, wagging his tail, and feel a tidal wave of affection overcoming me '—for a better dog.'

Holding back my tears, I thank everyone who gave him

to me. 'But most of all, I need to thank one person. Mum drove us down the bumpy track to Canine Partners, pretending she didn't know where we were.' A silence descends across the hall. No one understands what I mean, except for Stuart. 'I was sworn to secrecy,' he says to the audience.

'It's a long story, but all I'll say is I'm glad you took a risk, Mum. You've taught me that life is about taking chances.' I notice Dad reaching out to grab her hand and whispering something into her ear. Jamie and Dad stand up to clap. And before I know it, most of the audience are on their feet, clapping and cheering for Ticket and me.

14

It's a week after Ticket's graduation day, and Dad and I are chatting in the kitchen as I cook the supper. Ticket is asleep in his basket by the fire. We must have covered a good five miles today. There was a cold wind, the sky overcast, but that didn't stop us. I wore a thousand layers, along with a pair of fluffy blue earmuffs that Alex gave to me as a gift from Cilla. 'When I go down the shops, it's dangerous, 'cos Cilla has expensive taste,' she'd said during the lunch that had followed the speeches.

Edward and I also exchanged contact numbers and addresses, suggesting we meet up. He lives in London, in Richmond.

Mum enters the room and kicks her heels off by the fireplace. 'I've had such a shitty day,' she tells us, collapsing on to a chair and rubbing her aching feet together. 'Spoilt tenant's wife is tired of the house that she's renting for *only* five thousand quid a month and wants to move. So she drags her husband from a meeting to another house that she says she likes more. He agrees, reluctantly. I show them round the new house and she then says, "You know what? I've changed my mind. Let's stay put."'

Dad unscrews the vodka bottle and fetches some ice from the freezer to make Mum a vodka tonic. 'I remember that story about the Japanese man years ago. He was letting one of your properties and was scared by all the frogs in the pond.'

'Oh yes! "I been seeing many big frog,"' she says in a bad Japanese accent, '"maybe more than fifty in pond, and it's kind of fun seeing them jump up and down but we afraid in short time they come out of pond and into house!" Oh thank you,' she says gratefully when Dad hands her the vodka tonic. She asks how my day was, watching as I crack an egg against the side of the bowl. I'm making omelettes with ham and salad for supper.

'When I was a child I had these weird psychosomatic illnesses,' she says. 'I went through this phase, every time I walked I'd kick my right leg out to the side, like a soldier with a leg twitch.' With her drink in one hand she does an impersonation across the kitchen floor. 'I couldn't stop. I did it in the shops, at school, going to church. The only reason Mum did something about it was because she was embarrassed. She had this friend who was into witch doctors and all that crap, and I can remember her doing this strange voodoo dance around me whilst cracking eggs over my head.'

'Weird, Mum. Did it work?'

''Course not! Mum took me to the doctor. He asked me where this strange habit came from and I told him my address.'

'That's a fine answer,' Dad says, raising his glass.

'Anyway, how's your day been?' Mum asks me, glancing at Ticket lying on his back, paws in the air, snoring. 'Clearly busy.' She smiles.

'Good. Actually there's something I want to tell you.'

Mum and Dad are still patiently waiting for my news when Jamie enters the room. Recently he was made redundant, so, unable to afford London rent without a job, he's home making plans to travel back to Madrid this spring, to teach English to businessmen abroad again. 'What's going on?' he asks, sensing the expectant atmosphere. He joins us at the table, where supper has just been laid out.

'I'm going skiing,' I announce.

Dad drops his knife. 'Skiing? But—'

Mum talks over him. 'Where?'

'Colorado.'

'Colorado!' Dad says.

'When?' Mum asks.

'In a couple of weeks.'

'A couple of weeks!'

'Dad, are you going to repeat everything I say?'

'Sorry. It's a lot to take in.'

'Sorry to be thick, right, but how are you going to ski, Cass?' Jamie asks.

'Remember my physio Paul at hospital?'

''Course I remember.'

'Well, he told me about Back Up, and they called me a few months ago to see if I was interested in signing up for a course. I've been doing a lot of research online, it's a spinal cord injury charity, they go canoeing, camping, skiing, kayaking—'

'Hang on! How?' Jamie scratches his head. 'Do they, like, put you on a sledge or something and roll you down the hill?'

'Isn't it dangerous?' Dad asks.

'I was thinking that, Dad.' Dad and Jamie nod in appreciation of one another. They're like two old men sometimes. All they need are their dressing gowns, pipes and slippers.

'It can't be dangerous. It's at the NSCD.'

'The what?'

'National Sports Center for the . . .' I stop. 'Disabled,' I mutter. 'Anyway, Back Up run these trips all the time, Dad. They told me the NSCD provide professional instructors, they have state-of-the-art equipment, plus we'll have a medical team and buddies with us.'

'Buddies?' Dad says.

'They're volunteers for Back Up.' Emma, the CEO, explained to me that they get their course volunteers or buddies mainly from companies. 'They're staff from RBS, Waitrose, Azzuri, that kind of workplace,' she'd said. 'Their HR department basically pay for key staff to come on a course. Others are Back Up staff or family members, not of someone on the course, but perhaps a family member who has seen how much difference it's made to their brother or father, so in turn they want to give something back.'

'Right, volunteers,' Dad repeats.

This conversation isn't flowing the way I'd hoped. I turn my attention to Mum, strangely quiet. 'Back Up was started in nineteen eighty, eighty-six I think, by this guy called Mike Nemesvary. He'd been a professional skier and after his accident his one dream was to get back up the mountain.'

'Um,' mutters Dad.

'You don't need to worry, I promise.'

No one says a word.

'I'm broken already,' I say quietly. 'What more damage can be done?'

Mum, Dad and Jamie don't have an answer to that.

'How about insurance?' Dad asks.

'All sorted.'

'Is it expensive?'

'I've been working for Mrs Henderson, writing her memoirs. I've been saving up for months.'

'Go for it,' Mum finally says. 'I think it's a great idea.'

'Dad?' I turn to him but he's looking at her with a new

admiration across his face. We've both seen a side to her that we now depend on. She has this eternal optimism, something I hadn't been aware of before my accident. Mum throws tantrums and argues much of the time, but she puts one hundred per cent into everything she does, and expects other people to do the same. I'm relieved she makes no allowances for me.

'When did you say you were going?'

'Beginning of March, for a week.'

Mum nods. 'Why didn't you tell us about this before?'

'It was something I had to do on my own,' I confide. 'Ticket and I went to the Back Up office and met the team.' Their office is in London, along Wandsworth High Street in East Putney. I remember that day, returning home on the train, full of information. The Back Up Trust is passionate about transforming lives, wanting to help people with spinal cord injury get the most out of life again. It gives career advice, runs mentoring schemes, organises courses throughout the year, and Paul had strongly encouraged Dom and me to attend one of their wheelchair skill classes when we were at Stoke Mandeville. Back Up supports people like me to become independent again. When I tried to persuade Guy and Dom to come skiing, Dom said he couldn't take time off work so close to Easter. Guy said he was a good skier before his accident; it would kill him doing it on some seat. 'But don't let me stop you,' he'd added. I've never skied before, so this feels like a new challenge.

ALICE PETERSON

'I guess I didn't tell you, Mum, in case I lost my nerve and pulled out at the last minute. But I do have a favour to ask. Will you come shopping with me? I need to buy all the right kit.'

'I'd love to.'

Dad and Jamie nod. Jamie says he's broke so he'll buy me the smallest item of clothing. Maybe some pink goggles.

'You'll be the best-looking girl on the slopes,' Dad says, finally warming up to the idea.

'Oh . . . there's just one more thing.'

'Oh no,' Dad says, as if he can't take any more.

'Can you sponsor my bungee jump off Niagara Falls?'

Dad throws his napkin at me.

'What other thing, Cass?' Mum asks.

He's lying under the table now, his face close to my feet, as if almost sensing my imminent departure. 'Will you look after Ticket for me?'

15

We head for the departure lounge, Mum pulling the luggage trolley and muttering how much she detests airports, almost as much as level crossings. I say nothing. It feels strange not having Ticket by my side. I feel as if I've lost a part of myself. I keep on glancing over my shoulder, as if he might show up any minute. It's odd not hearing the reassuring patter of his paws or seeing that wag of his tail that makes my day first thing in the morning. I wish I could have packed him in my suitcase.

'You promise to call me if anything's wrong?' I say to Mum.

'Promise,' she replies, walking determinedly through the crowds.

'Remember fresh water every day.'

'Uh-huh.'

'And he's due for his worming tablet. I've written it all down.'

'Right. Good.'

'I know this is hard, right, but you have to remain as neutral as you can towards him, Mum. Don't give him too many cuddles.'

'Right,' she repeats, tight-lipped. Mum still coughs and sneezes thanks to Ticket but I can tell she's fallen in love with him too. I see it in her eyes when she watches in awe as he brings me my wheelchair or tugs opens a door for me. She calls him the 'perfect gent'. 'He'd never leave the loo seat up,' she says.

'I mean, you must be nice to him but don't talk or play too much.'

'Unless it has escaped your notice, Cass, I'm a busy woman. I don't have time to play *games* with Ticket.'

'He likes the veggie biscuits, you know, the parsnip ones, and you will take him out for walks, won't you?'

'No, Cass, I'll lock him in the loft and throw away the key.' Mum gives the wheelchair a kick from behind.

'Did you see that woman?' we overhear an old woman say to her companion. 'As if the poor child isn't going through enough.'

Mum and I burst out laughing as we head for Zone F.

I see a group at the check-in desk and a couple are in wheelchairs so I assume we must be in the right place. Who do I approach first? Thankfully one of the organisers walks over to me. 'Hi,' she says loudly over the sound of an announcement that passengers on flight BA3047 need to go to Gate 4. 'Are you with Back Up?'

'Yes.'

'Cool. Name?'

'Cass. Cass Brooks.'

'Great.' She ticks it off as if it were the school register. 'I'm Susi, Group Leader. Nice to have you on board.'

'I'll be off,' Mum says, crouching down to give me a quick kiss. 'Have a wonderful time.'

And she disappears back into the crowd. Don't look back. Don't cry or think about Ticket. I am going to enjoy this. You want to go skiing, Cass. I want to experience new things. Yes I do. I really do. No I don't! Come back, Mum! Oh shit . . . I glance to my left. There are a group of able-bodied young guys standing in a cluster, one of them wearing a cap and hiking boots. He looks as though he's about to climb a mountain. I return his smile before promptly looking away. I never used to be this shy.

'Join the queue here, Cass,' Susi instructs. 'This is Andrew.' Andrew wheels himself towards me. I can tell he is extremely tall, even in a wheelchair. He has fair to reddish hair and is wearing a fleece with baggy combats. As more people in wheelchairs arrive he says, 'I always wonder how the hell we're going to get on to the plane. It's madness.'

One of the flight attendants is pacing up and down, counting us as though we're a flock of sheep. Susi manages to assemble us into some sort of line and we begin to check in, in pairs, like animals going two by two on Noah's Ark. 'They stay in their own chairs until they reach the gates,' she says to the woman in a navy and red uniform, sitting behind the desk, tapping frantically into a keyboard. 'No, none of them can walk,' she says impatiently.

Andrew laughs. 'They always think we can shuffle a few steps. Honestly, Cass, we're never too popular round here.'

'We're trouble on wheels,' I suggest as we edge forward in the queue.

He considers this. 'Trouble on wheels. I like that.'

'Charlie Bell,' says the man sitting next to me, holding out his hand. 'I'm one of the buddies.'

I'm so relieved finally to be sitting in my seat that I don't register his face, only a deep voice, firm handshake and glasses. 'Cass Brooks.'

The flight attendant runs through the safety procedures. The captain apologises for being delayed.

No prizes for guessing why, I think to myself.

'Have you ever been to Colorado?' Charlie asks, twenty minutes after we've taken off.

I turn to face him fully this time, and notice a man with thick, light brown hair and hazel eyes, wearing a pale blue shirt. 'No, never,' I say.

'Have you skied before?' He has a warm, open face.

'No. Have you?'

'Yep. Since I was six. I'm a qualified instructor.'

'Sorry. That was a dumb thing to say. You wouldn't be here, would you, helping us!' I flick the pages of my duty-free magazine, realising I can't talk to men any more. Except for Guy and Dom, but they don't count. They're more like my brothers. 'Why aren't you just skiing? I mean, with friends or something?'

I don't know why, but Charlie finds that funny.

'Last year I made a couple of New Year resolutions,' he confides. 'One of them was to do some volunteer work. I was on one of the Back Up courses last winter, in Sweden.'

I'm impressed.

'Don't be too impressed,' he warns me. 'I wasn't about to do something as altruistic as picking up cigarette butts off the streets. Anyway, I heard about Back Up through one of my best mates, Rich. He knew someone who'd been a buddy and had loved it, and seeing as I can ski, I thought, why not?'

'My summer holidays used to be at a donkey sanctuary,' I tell him.

'Sorry?'

'A donkey sanctuary, in Spain.' I tell him it was voluntary work too. It involved falling out of bed at eight in the morning to feed and muck out the donkeys, before the sanctuary was open to tourists until about two. 'I helped out with the medical rounds, things like checking their hooves and dealing with any skin problems, and then during siesta time I'd head down to the beach.' I shut my eyes, remembering lying on the golden sand in my bikini and shades. I can almost feel the soft breeze against my skin and hair; hear the comforting sound of waves and children playing.

'My favourites were Branson and Feliz.' I sigh nostalgically. 'They were the sanctuary bad-boys.'

'Well, I don't know about you, but I really need a holiday,' he says, taking off his glasses and giving them a wipe.

'I wouldn't exactly call *us* a holiday.'

Again Charlie finds that funny. He has a deep infectious laugh. 'Anything's a holiday after the couple of months I've had.'

'Oh?'

'Long story.'

'Long flight.' I begin to relax.

'Well, work's difficult at the moment. We've lost a couple of major clients this year. Everyone's on tighter budgets.'

I discover Charlie works for a creative design web agency. In an ideal world he'd love to be a full-time photographer, but he doesn't dare change jobs in the recession. 'And I split up from my girlfriend.'

I open my bag of roasted peanuts, feeling my heart skip for a brief second. Not that I fancy him or anything. 'I'm sorry,' I say. 'Had you been going out a long time?'

'Let's not talk about it,' he says, as if he's exhausted that subject. 'Did you know you have to run a marathon to burn off a pack of peanuts?'

I raise an eyebrow. 'Really?'

'Oh sorry, that was a dumb thing to say.'

'Don't worry. Now we're even. You can run, so here . . . finish off mine.'

The drinks trolley comes round. He tells me to ask for a small bottle of red wine, even if I won't drink it. 'Sorry, Charlie, but here's one thing you need to learn about me. I never turn down free booze.'

'So, what do you do?' he asks, as we open our little bottles and pour ourselves a glass.

At that moment the plane hits some turbulence and Charlie splashes red wine down his shirt.

'Oh no!' I gasp. 'Was it an expensive shirt?'

He grins. 'No, but what a waste of wine.'

We've been in the air for four hours and haven't spoken much since the turbulence. I press a button to move my chair back and promptly feel a thump at the back of my seat. I shift uncomfortably. The thump comes again. 'Are you all right?' Charlie asks.

'Fine, thanks.'

I draw in breath, aware of Charlie still watching me. 'Ouch. The woman behind . . . she's kicking me,' I whisper.

Charlie turns round. 'Excuse me, but did you just kick my friend?'

'She didn't ask if she could move her chair back,' comes the snappy reply.

'Really?' He frowns. 'Forgive my ignorance, but perhaps it's more polite to ask someone to move their chair forward again, rather than kicking them in the hopes they'll get the message?'

'Look, it doesn't matter.' I pull at the sleeve of Charlie's shirt. 'I'll put my chair forward again.'

'My friend has spinal cord injury. It hurts her when you kick.'

'Well, why didn't she say so?'

'Well,' he adopts her tone, 'I don't think she expected to be kicked three times. Once is perhaps a mistake. Twice is careless; three times is downright rude.'

I try not to laugh now.

'What?' Charlie asks when he turns back round.

'Nothing,' I say, unable to stop smiling.

'When I get cross it brings out the public schoolboy in me,' he warns me. 'So watch out. If you're naughty I'll drag you into my room and get the cane out.'

Is he flirting with me? It's been such a long time, I can't tell any more.

16

It's the second day and a group of us are outside the hotel, waiting to transfer ourselves from our wheelchairs to our mono skis. We've been taught by the professional instructors the basic rules on the nursery slopes and are tackling an easy blue run today. I'm enjoying getting to know my roommate, Frankie. She's Scottish and breathtakingly pretty, with dark brown hair swept into a ponytail, deep brown eyes that almost match the colour of her hair, and skin as pale and clear as water. She told me she'd had a riding accident when she was seventeen. She's now thirty-two, so has been in a wheelchair almost half her life. 'I lost quite a few mates, they got bored,' she'd confided to me last night when we turned off the lights. 'They were supportive to begin with but then . . . I think they were almost angry when I had to cancel parties or holidays. Except for Ethan.'

I wave when I spot Charlie in his dark shades and salopettes. Susi gathers our group together, and one by one each participant is paired up with a volunteer instructor provided by the NSCD or with a qualified buddy. 'Cass, you're going with . . .' Susi turns over her sheet of paper and scans a list of names.

This is almost as bad as waiting to find out if Ticket was going to be mine.

Charlie stands behind me as I lift my legs into the mono ski, placing my feet against a flat footrest. I then transfer my full body weight across into the chair. 'Well done,' he says, in a way that suggests I've climbed Mount Everest. It feels weird sitting in this. It's basically a small chair that's attached to a ski. The seat has a shock absorber system especially designed for people with spinal cord injury.

'I'm nervous, Charlie. I'm not sure I'll be any good.'

'You'll be fine. Look, I promise you'll be safe, I'll be holding on to you with the reins at all times.' He whips them across his thighs as if he's a cowboy, before kneeling down to strap my feet in properly. 'By the way, like the hat,' he says.

I touch it self-consciously. 'Thanks.' Mum, Ticket and I went shopping along Regent Street. I am wearing a pair of thermal leggings, navy salopettes, boots, an ice blue anorak, white fur hat with earflaps, a pair of gloves and bright pink goggles. This morning, when I caught sight of myself in the mirror, I laughed. I actually looked quite sporty for me. 'You could be in the Olympic team,' Frankie said, dressed in a leopard-print anorak that looked striking with her dark hair.

We all do a few warm-up exercises to loosen our necks and shoulders. Then we make our way to the ski lift.

Charlie attaches the training leads to my chair and we queue in a disorderly line. He crouches down beside me. 'Watch that couple in front. That's how you do it.'

'You won't let go?'

'I won't let you out of my sight, OK.'

We get closer to the starting line; Charlie tells me to stop looking so frightened.

The chair-lift operator slows down the lift. Charlie positions me a few feet in front of it, then guides me backwards on to the seat and a grey safety barrier clamps down. 'See, it wasn't so bad, was it?' he says.

But I'm not allowing myself to relax yet.

'Aren't the views amazing?' Charlie says. 'Wish I had my camera.'

'Um,' I say, staring straight ahead, my body rigid.

'Relax, Brooks.'

'I'm fine, *Bell*.'

As we approach the top of the ski lift we slow down, the safety bar is released and he pushes me forward on to the snow. 'Shit!' I shriek as I slide downhill, towards the fir trees. 'You've let go!'

'I haven't, you're just moving,' he says, trying not to laugh at me.

Today I'm being taught to use my outriggers. These are the equivalent to a normal person's pair of ski poles. They are small with mini skis attached to the bottom, both with a gripper edge. They look more like pick-axes.

With Charlie's encouragement I move gingerly downhill, digging them into the snow to stop going so fast. A skier whizzes past me, the snow making a glorious crunching sound as he swishes along. 'Are you still there, Charlie?' I call out, sunshine and fresh air blasting against my face.

'Right behind you.'

A group of children now fly past me, their ski poles tucked neatly under their arms, bottoms stuck out and going at Olympian speed. They can't be more than seven or eight years old. Distracted, I fall over. Charlie takes my arm and pulls me back up. 'If you go that slowly you will flop over.'

'Flop over? I was going quite fast,' I insist.

'Maybe it feels like it because you're low down? Let's get this right, Cass. Number one rule is only use your arms when you have to. Your outriggers are used for direction. The rest is about mastering control. Effectively you are balancing on one leg.'

Frankie and Ethan, Frankie's buddy and best friend from school, both hurtle past me now, waving. 'They've skied before,' Charlie kindly mentions, placing both hands on my shoulders. 'Let yourself go.'

'I can't,' I say, now distracted by his touch.

'Yes you can. Trust me. Try again?' He releases his hands.

I see one of the Back Up team falling over which makes

me feel better. Charlie and I move again, this time faster but before long I lose my nerve, try to slow down and fall sideways in my seat. I am rubbish. 'Can you help me back up? Ha! Back up!' I seem to find this hilarious and feel almost drunk. It must be the bright sun, my nerves and the cold air.

Charlie grins as he gives me a hand. 'If we're going to be together for the rest of the day, you need to work a lot harder on your jokes.'

After lunch, and strengthened by a mug of hot chocolate, we return to the slopes and Charlie runs through the technique again. 'You can do it,' he says, 'just let go and believe in yourself.'

The sun streams against my face. I push myself forward with my outriggers. I pick up pace and soon my ski chair is like a bullet racing downhill, zipping past fir trees that cast shadows over the snow. 'I haven't fallen over yet!' I shout.

'Steady,' he calls behind me. 'You're doing really well!'

I am beginning to use my upper body, swaying right to left, left to right. I can feel the ski responding to me at last. I spot the village below. This is incredible. I'm skiing! But I need to stop as we're getting close to the bottom. 'Slow down!' Charlie shouts, pulling in the reins. We come to an abrupt halt and I fly out of my chair.

Ouch. I'm lying on the ground, laughing.

Wow.

I have just skied down a mountain. My arm hurts but who cares. 'That was amazing! Can we do it again! Please, Charlie?'

When he recovers his composure he insists on more control next time. 'But you're a quick learner.'

'I have a good teacher.' I smile, glowing from his praise.

'This is bliss.' Frankie groans with pleasure when we're in the Jacuzzi later that evening, easing our aching muscles. 'We skied today,' she continues proudly. 'How did you find it?'

'I'm pretty bruised.' I show her my arms.

'Oh well.' She shrugs. 'With Charlie helping you up each time, I think I'd almost fall over on purpose. "Help, Charlie! Oh, Charlie, you won't let me go, will you?"' she imitates me. I splash her with water and we both laugh. 'He is lovely,' I admit.

She raises an eyebrow. 'I saw you two chatting each other up.'

'We were having fun, that's all,' I say, though my heart dances inside. 'Are you going out with anyone?'

'Ben. He's a chef. I met him on the Internet.'

'Fuck. That's brave to go online.'

'Oh, it's nothing to worry about, as long as you go through a reliable agency. Ben was finding it hard to meet people because his hours are so unsociable, and most of my friends are married or with someone. It's hard meeting new people, especially in your thirties. Everyone does it online these days. You should give it a go.'

'Did you . . .' I stop.

'Did I mention I was in a wheelchair? Yes. If I don't meet anyone, Cass, it won't be because of that. It'll be because I'm independent and know exactly what I want. My last boyfriend asked me to move back to Scotland, but I need to be in London, Cass. I've made my life there. Also Scotland's so inaccessible. Way too many hills and cobbled streets.'

'Way too cold as well,' I suggest.

'Too right.'

'You've never gone out with Ethan?'

'God, no. We know each other too well now. We kissed when we went backpacking across New Zealand and Australia for seven months together. I was nineteen. We were both drunk. I think we needed to get it out of our system.' She smiles as if remembering it. 'Once we got that awkward moment out the way, we became best friends.'

I tell Frankie about Sean. I still feel sad, but to my surprise that gut-wrenching pain is easing; there are no tears when I talk about him this time.

'You know, I respect people who admit they can't handle it. I get the fact that it's not easy, and guys are scared.' She looks me directly in the eye. 'One of these days, Cass, you'll meet Sean again—'

'I hope not.'

'And when you do, I hope you'll tell him he was a coward. A letter,' she repeats. 'The least he could have done was say it to your face. He owed you that much.'

'Dear Perky,' I write on a postcard when I'm back in my room. 'You have got to come skiing next time. I know you'd love it and you'd be much better than me, but I'm getting the hang of it. Everyone is great fun and you'd be able to tell all your jokes to a new audience.'

I sign off and pick up another card.

'Listen, Cass,' Paul had said, after a gruelling workout in the gym. It was towards the end of my four months, when home was on the horizon. 'There's this organisation called Back Up who run all kinds of courses for the spinally injured. You can go skiing, canoeing, camping, skydiving, you name it.'

'I'm not sure.'

'It would help rebuild your confidence, you know, show you what you can still achieve. They're the guys that run the wheelchair classes here. I can get you some info if—'

'I'm not going on some bloody skiing holiday for invalids!' Suddenly exhausted, I slammed my lunch tray on to the table.

His expression remained calm. 'It's not a holiday. It's a course. And you're not an invalid. You're Cass.'

'Dear Paul,' I write, 'you'll be proud. Your whingeing Pom is skiing.'

17

Our group is eating out in one of the restaurants within the hotel complex. We're tired in a happy way after another day's skiing. Charlie took me out this afternoon. I tried to disguise my delirious pleasure when he'd approached me with the news that he was my buddy again. I am still on the training reins and often fall down on the slopes. However, I am no longer gripped with fear every time I look down a steep slope and realise that the only way to get down it is to ski. I'm beginning to master the ski lift too and now that I'm more confident, I can take in the scenery. It is beautiful. The sky is bright blue; looking up into it is like an adrenalin shot in the arm. The snow glistens and the colours of everyone's clothes sparkle like jewels on the mountain.

Charlie took me on a red run this afternoon to show me the views. He took some shots with his flashy camera. He says there's nothing more peaceful or levelling than being out in the mountains. 'They're incredible, don't you think?

They put us in our place,' he said. 'You can never be complacent when you're out here.'

We didn't ski for as long today because he wanted to take me round the Rocky Mountain National Park. We hired a scooter and to keep me safe Charlie had to hold my feet down with his own. As we picked up speed, I found myself laughing out loud from sheer joy at being outside and discovering a new and magical world. The mountain peaks soared above us; they must have been thousands of feet high, and I understood what Charlie had meant earlier. Their grandeur did make me feel small. We must look like mere dots on the landscape. But what I loved most about today was being with him and feeling his arms around me. I haven't allowed myself to think I could meet someone else, but since meeting Charlie, hope has crept into my heart.

It's been fun watching the others ski too. Some wheelchair users are experienced skiers who don't need qualified instructors or buddies with them all the time. Others are more like me; we fall down like skittles but pick ourselves up again with a few more bruises on our arms but strength in our soul.

Over the course of the trip everyone has opened up about their experiences. There's Jeremy. He tells us he was shot in the back in Guatemala by a group of bandits. His life was saved because he was wearing a rucksack and in it was a hardback reference book that protected him from the bullet. The bullet went through the spine but not the organs.

There's Miles who had a rugby accident. Andrew was involved in a car crash when he was seventeen. He was in the back seat, telling his friend, who had only just passed his driving test, to slow down and stop messing with the tape player. Melissa, the mother of the group, apologises. 'All I did was fall off a ladder, gardening. Pruning the climbing rose.' I notice Charlie watching me when I tell everyone my accident was my fault. I wasn't concentrating, stepped out into the road, was hit, but luckily the driver wasn't injured.

I notice, as I did in hospital too, there is a certain hierarchy of people in terms of the level of our injury. Being a T12 I am a mere scratch. My injury pales into insignificance compared to Frankie's. Frankie is a C7, paralysed just under the collarbone. At first they'd thought she had whiplash; it's a classic mistake to miss the C7 fracture on x-ray. She has worked so hard at being independent and says she's lucky in that she has movement in her hands, which is unusual for her level of injury. It makes her able to do much more than she'd imagined.

Most of the other stories we share are about travel. I tell them about my first train journey to London, when a passenger had lifted me out of my chair, and what's funny is we all laugh, especially me. Jeremy, the expert traveller, tells us that one time when he was flying, the plane had to do a crash landing at Nairobi. They missed the next connection and all the passengers were deposited in the departure lounge with a stale apricot Danish pastry. When everyone else was moved into a five-star hotel for the night, he was left behind, in his uncomfortable airport wheelchair.

Andrew tells us about his first night at home after being in hospital. He lives in a council bungalow, and friends had come round to watch the football and drink a few beers. They left him stuck on the sofa with his wheelchair on the other side of the room. 'I had to ring and ask them to come back, luckily the front door wasn't locked.'

Melissa tells us how her husband had taken her to France under false pretences. 'Suddenly I found myself on some religious week, people laying hands on my head, telling me to release the devil inside and I'll be cured. I'll tell you something! The miracle is we are still married!'

We all laugh at that.

The boys talk about the make of their wheelchairs as if they were racing cars and how fast they can go, and the fact that they have two sets of wheels for indoors and outdoors. We're all relieved that heavy wheelchairs made out of steel are a thing of the past. Mine is a lightweight sporty manual model made of titanium with detachable wheels.

At the end of the evening everyone heads back to their room.

'I can open the door myself,' one of the guys says pointedly to Charlie, before barging on ahead of him.

I catch up with Charlie.

'I don't patronise you, do I? Be honest,' he says to me.

'No. Look, just because someone's in a wheelchair doesn't make them an angel. He's probably tired. Don't take it personally.'

We reach my bedroom door. 'Well, this is me. 'Night then,' I say, wishing my bedroom were further away. Why can't it be right at the other end of the building? Or in another place, far away, that would take us all night to reach.

''Night, Brooks.' He leans down to kiss my cheek. I wish somebody could press pause, to keep his face close to mine.

18

Frankie and I are getting ready for a night out.

'Do you think you'll move back to London soon?' she asks, brushing her thick, dark brown hair.

Both Dom and Guy have asked the same. 'We could sit in bars and put the world to rights,' Guy suggested.

I nod. 'But I need to find a job first, and a place to live.'

Frankie works for a corporate events company, but also does a lot of work for a charity that helps those with spinal cord injuries in developing countries like Uganda, India and Tanzania, where there is little support and few services available.

I confide that the idea's daunting.

'The only way you're going to get confidence is by getting out there again,' Frankie says. 'Do you think you could go back to medicine?'

'Love your shoes,' I say, gesturing to her red patent high heels and dodging her question.

She glances at my trainers. 'What size?'

'Six.'

'Fancy that. Me too.'

Frankie opens our wardrobe and tells me to pick out a pair. 'Your suitcase must have weighed a ton,' I exclaim, admiring some silver high heels.

'Tell you what? I've got a silver top that would look fantastic on you too.'

She shows me something scant and lacy.

'I'm fine in this.'

Frankie's face softens. 'You're dressing the way I used to, so no one notices you.' She smiles. 'Off with that top!'

I do as I'm told, throwing my boring old T-shirt across the room.

'And on with this sexy little number! Come on, you need to do some serious flirting with Charlie tonight. We've only got a couple of nights left.'

'I like him,' I admit.

'But you're worried you can't have a boyfriend, right?'

I nod.

'Have you had a relationship since your accident? And Ticket doesn't count,' she says, gesturing to my golden boy in the small oval silver photograph frame on my bedside table.

'I can't imagine, I can't see anyone . . .' I stop, remembering Frankie is in the same position as me. 'Look at the way Sean reacted.'

'Sean's a dickhead.'

'Guys just think you're in a wheelchair, how do you tell them about all the other problems?'

'You tell them when the time's right, maybe not on the first date,' she adds. 'Cass, people get dealt bad hands, but it doesn't mean you have to be alone for the rest of your life.'

'Charlie makes me laugh.' I'm attracted to him in a different way to Sean. Sean was good-looking and knew it and we had our medicine in common. I think in a way that was all we had in common; that and sex. With Charlie, I like the way he looks directly at me when he talks, not over his shoulder, to see if there's anyone more interesting in the room. I'm drawn to the twinkle in his eye that makes him look as if he's about to break into a smile. I like his interest in everyone and what's around him. When I was watching him taking photographs I realised I was falling for him. 'There's this voice in my head,' I tell Frankie, 'that says, "Why would he choose me, with all my baggage, when he could have anyone?"'

'Listen, if you want to meet someone you have to have the courage to be yourself. And believe me, everyone has baggage.'

She senses there's something else I want to ask, something I can't ask Mum or friends, or my consultant.

'You can have sex,' she says.

'But . . . how does it work?' I laugh at myself. This is something I didn't learn at King's. In many ways medicine, as intricate as it is, skims only the surface. 'I mean, how do you feel it?'

'It's different. I feel it in my head. Ben and I have this closeness, a connection that I thought I'd never have. You have to retune, if that makes sense. Remap your body so that different parts get pleasure.'

I twist a strand of hair; coil it round my fingers. 'You're amazing, Frankie.'

'I've been injured for more than half my life, Cass, I'm an old fossil when it comes to this.' She smiles. 'It's still new to you. The first two years are the hardest and most tiring. Your body's trying to adapt. You look beautiful,' she adds, opening the mirrored wardrobe door.

'Yeah. Great.'

'You haven't even looked.'

I wheel myself away. 'Come on, let's go.'

'Cass, you come back here at once!'

'Oh my God, you sound like my mother,' I say, placing myself in front of the mirror again.

'Forget the chair is there,' she says. 'That's what I do. I rub it out so that I can only see me. Stop fidgeting with your hair! Look at yourself. *You*, Cass. You look a million dollars.'

'I look like a Christmas cracker,' I say, a vision of silver.

'Exactly.' She touches my shoulder with affection. 'And ready to be pulled.'

* * *

The restaurant is crowded. I watch Charlie at the far end of the table putting on his glasses to read the dessert menu. Susi, the group leader, is sitting next to him, laughing at something he says. She clearly isn't immune to his charms either. 'Cass, wine?' Frankie asks, pouring some into my glass without waiting for a reply.

During coffee my mobile vibrates and Mum's number flashes on to the screen. She rings every day to make sure I'm still in one piece and to update me on Ticket news. Mum tells me she and Dad took him to the beach and he had a whale of a time playing in the sea.

'I miss him so much,' I tell Frankie when I hang up.

'Oh, come on. He's just a dog.'

'He's not just a dog, Frankie,' I say, my tone surprisingly hard. 'He's the reason I'm here.'

'Sorry, sorry.' She gestures to Charlie approaching. 'Just forget about him for *tonight*.'

'Forget about who?' he says, pulling up a chair and sitting between us.

'The love of her life! Honestly, Cass goes on and on about him all the time, even has a photo of him by her bedside.'

Charlie runs a hand through his hair. 'Who's this?'

'Cass's man,' Frankie continues. 'Catch up, Charlie.'

He turns to me. 'You haven't mentioned him.'

I'm about to tell him we're talking about Ticket. Charlie knows I have a dog. I've told him all about Ticket and Canine

Partners, but Frankie jumps in quickly, saying, 'He's so cute, Charlie. Fair hair, these big brown eyes. You've got him so well trained, Cass.'

'Trained?' Charlie looks confused now. 'Have you met him, Frankie?'

'No,' she says with regret. 'But I'm sure I will soon.'

'Don't go anywhere,' Charlie says, scraping his chair back.

'Frankie, we have to tell him it's Ticket,' I whisper.

'Sure, we can put him out of his misery, but look at the way he reacted,' she says, as we watch Charlie hurry to his end of the table, grab his wine and hurtle back towards us. 'If that doesn't give you confidence, nothing will.'

We've moved from the restaurant to the bar and dance floor.

Charlie holds out a hand and says, 'May I have the first dance?'

Don't say no. Say yes, I tell myself, watching Frankie dance in her chair with Ethan.

An hour later and I'm singing along to the music. Charlie takes me by surprise, lifting me out of my chair and into his arms, spinning me around. I hold on to him tightly, laughing with joy. Why was I so nervous before?

I could happily dance with Charlie all night.

On the last day I ski without any help and Charlie skis

alongside me. I don't feel different to anyone else as we race down the slopes. My wheelchair is a distant memory; something I have left at the foot of the mountain.

Up here, I am in another world.

A magnificent world.

19

It's the beginning of April, three weeks since our skiing trip, and Charlie calls. 'Who was that?' Mum asks after I've hung up and returned to the sitting room, Ticket following closely behind. 'Charlie.'

'Again?' My father lights a cigarette.

'And?' Mum says.

'He's asked me to stay at his parents' place in Gloucestershire.'

'When?'

'This weekend.' Charlie invited me down on Friday afternoon, telling me he was taking the day off work. I can't stop smiling. It feels as if someone has handed me a winning lottery ticket.

Mum and Dad glance at one another. I can tell they'll whisper about this in bed tonight, concluding that Charlie is exactly why I've been in such a good mood lately.

When the train pulls in at the next station the conductor

enters our carriage to punch the tickets of new passengers. The closer we are to Honeybourne, the more anxious I become, my mind plagued with doubts. It's only for a couple of nights, I remind myself. Will he try to kiss me? Or does he see me only as a friend? Maybe I should make the first move? Normally I wouldn't think twice about it, but things are different now. I don't want to screw it up, and if things go wrong, it's not as if I can make a rapid exit.

Will his parents be there? What if it's just the two of us? Do I *want* it to be just the two of us? Where will I sleep? What if Charlie can't even get me up the stairs?

'Relax, Brooks,' I can hear him say.

Since returning from Colorado, I've replayed that evening when we'd danced. Charlie had walked me back to my room in the early hours of the morning, and I think I must have slept with a permanent grin on my face, music ringing in my ears. We spent our final day together on the slopes. Charlie took more photographs. I felt tearful saying goodbye at the airport. We'd only known one another for a week, but somehow Charlie had slipped effortlessly into my life, and I couldn't imagine a world without him any more. I stroke Ticket. 'You'll like him,' I tell him. 'But don't you worry, whatever happens between us, you're still my best man.'

It's close to five o'clock. I look out of the window. It's drizzling.

With only one more station to go, I squirt some perfume

on to my wrist, brush my hair and apply some lipstick. Since the skiing course I have cut my hair and it now falls just below my shoulders. I've been shopping online too. I'm wearing skinny jeans with a pair of black patent high heels that I bought in the sales along with a soft leather biker jacket. Frankie would be proud. Briefly I think of Sarah. She asked if she could come and stay in Dorset over the Easter break. She doesn't know much about Charlie. I make excuses why we haven't been in touch. I live miles away; she's busy studying in her final year. Yet I think we both know the truth: we're letting our friendship slip through our fingers like sand.

As the train approaches the station platform, I see Charlie waiting. He's dressed in jeans, boots and a navy round-neck jumper with the sleeves rolled up. The first hurdle is over; the ramp is positioned and I can, at least, get off the train.

Charlie bends down to kiss my cheek, before stroking Ticket.

'Shake hands, Ticket.' Ticket offers his paw towards Charlie.

'Lovely to meet you,' Charlie says to him. 'How was your journey?' He picks up my suitcase.

'Great.'

'Crikey.' He laughs, pretending to almost drop my case. 'How long are you staying for?' I don't tell him I've packed about ten different outfits, along with many warm jumpers. Even though it's getting warmer, I feel the cold.

'Are you hungry?'

I couldn't eat a thing. 'Yes.'

'I've made us a lasagne for supper. Just to warn you, I'm not a great cook,' he says as we head towards the station car park. 'When I'm on my own I don't eat. There's nothing you can't eat, is there?'

He's gabbling. Maybe he's nervous too?

'I'm a vegetarian.'

'Fuck, no.'

'Only kidding. You know I'm not.'

'Nice day today.'

'It's been raining all day.'

'Oh yeah, terrible day.'

I think we both need to shut up.

'Where are your parents this weekend?' I ask, as Charlie turns down a narrow winding lane.

'With friends. I'm glad you could come down.' He turns to me, one hand on the steering wheel, and says, 'I don't like being in the house on my own. I'm sure it's haunted.'

Ticket barks. 'He's saying you're a scaredy-cat, Bell.'

We turn left through some gates and over an iron grid, into a long driveway with parkland on either side. In front of me are oak and chestnut trees. Charlie tells me they are hundreds of years old. Ticket barks at the sheep.

'Is this all your land?' I ask.

'Yep.'

'Fuck me.'

He raises an eyebrow.

I can't see any sign of a house yet. 'Do your parents live in a palace? Will there be a butler?'

'Watch it, Brooks.'

Finally I see a large imposing house in the distance.

'This was my grandfather's childhood home, my dad's father. Granddad used to take me out on the tractor as a child or I'd help him plant his trees and we'd have these big family parties in the summer, playing rounders with all our cousins.'

'Sounds like fun.'

'How about your family?'

'Oh, there's only Jamie, Mum, Dad and me.'

'Are you close to your grandparents?'

'One of my grandfathers worked on a railway station, he was an alcoholic. He's dead now. The other worked in a factory. I didn't know him. Mum and Dad couldn't wait to leave home. I think they rebelled against their parents, they wanted more from life than staying in their hometown. Mum and Dad didn't even invite them to their wedding. Both my grandmothers are alive, but they're not really interested in getting to know Jamie and me. I can't think why not,' I say with a smile, although it has hurt our family deep inside. Neither Mum nor Dad has had any support after my accident.

'Right,' Charlie says, unsure how to react to a family so alien to his own.

We go over a couple more ramps before turning right into a courtyard. Through a side gate is an expanse of lawn. To think I'd asked Charlie if they had a garden for Ticket to do his business. 'There are no steps at the back of the house, easier to get in this side,' he says, opening the passenger door of his battered VW Golf.

'Thank you,' I say. 'Oh, I need my chair.'

'Oh yes, sorry.' He retrieves it from the back seat, telling me how surprisingly light it is. Ticket jumps out of the car and sniffs the ground with curiosity.

He places my chair and the detachable wheels in front of me, before watching carefully how I assemble it together. 'Show me,' he says.

'All I have to do is slot the wheels on, like this.' I attach one of them and then turn the chair round to do the other side. 'And if I want to take them off –' I point to the press release button in the middle of the wheel. 'I press and hold and it slides off, like that.' Quickly I slot the wheel back on.

'It's neat,' he says, as I transfer myself from the passenger seat into my chair.

As we approach the back door Charlie shakes a keyring with about twenty keys attached to it.

'What are they all for?'

'The garage, cottages, car, tractor . . .'

Finally he finds the right one and we enter. 'Oh my God!' I exclaim, looking at the full-size billiard table right in front of me. I also notice an oil painting of a woman with long dark hair sitting on a sofa in a lilac ballgown. 'Who's she? She's beautiful.'

'My mother.' Charlie walks on with my case. I gaze into the next room, a large drawing room with a grand piano by the window, the top adorned with framed photographs. We cross the stone hall, Ticket's paws padding against the floor. He's keeping even closer by my side than usual and each time I stop, he stops. Ahead of us is an enormous mirror hanging above a squatting Buddha on a marble table.

I look up to the spiralling staircase. Ticket looks up too.

We turn left, past the library (who has a library?) and into the kitchen, a more normal-sized room with a round wooden table at one end.

'Sit down. Sorry, I mean, you are sitting, but . . .'

I smile. 'Don't worry, I know what you mean.'

'Cup of tea?' he asks, before moving one of the chairs round the table to make space for me.

The closeness and ease we had on the slopes somehow seems far away. As Charlie puts a pan of water on the Aga, we don't say anything; all I can hear is the ticking sound of the grandfather clock and Ticket breathing heavily under the table. Anxious that this was a bad idea, I give Ticket's back a reassuring squeeze, wishing Charlie would scrap the tea idea and crack open a bottle of red wine instead.

'I could fit our home into the sitting room alone,' I say when Charlie gives me a guided tour of the house. Around the fireplace is a fender. The coffee table is covered with hardback gardening, antique and history books. The curtains are deep blue velvet. 'It's incredible here.'

'I know. I take it for granted. It's also very cold,' he says, putting some logs on to the fire. Charlie tells me his parents can't justify, nor afford, heating the whole house.

'Do you think you'll live here someday?'

'Maybe.' He sits down next to me. 'One day.'

On the table beside me is a framed photograph of a woman in a mini halter-neck dress, with legs that go on for miles. 'Anna. My sister,' Charlie says. 'She's in New York at the moment.'

She has bright red hair, creamy skin and large sapphire-blue eyes.

I pick up the next frame. 'Who's this?' She has an arm around Charlie. It's clearly windy, her long dark hair blowing in her face; hair caught against her lips.

He leaps up to chuck another log on to the fire. 'Jo. My ex.'

After supper Charlie and I watch television. Ticket lies on the sofa in between us, snoring lightly. It wasn't quite the romantic evening I'd had in mind, especially when Charlie suggests I do something about Ticket's fish breath.

It's eleven o'clock when Charlie and I head upstairs. 'Now hang on, how do I do this?' he asks, and I sense he's been dreading it just as much as me. No wonder neither one of us can relax.

'Well, with Dad, I wrap my legs round his hips and my hands round his neck. It's like a piggyback but on the front, if you see what I mean.'

'Right.'

'I'm sorry, Charlie. Lucky I don't weigh a ton, hey,' I say, positioning myself at the edge of the sofa.

'Trust me, this is a piece of cake. I could take Tyson on.' He flexes his muscles.

When I'm in his arms . . .

'Ticket! Down! Off!'

'He thinks you're in trouble,' suggests Charlie.

'He thinks you're about to have your wicked way with me. Ticket, off! Sorry,' I say to Charlie. 'I doubt you normally have to carry your guests upstairs, do you?'

'Stop saying sorry,' he mutters, carrying me into the hall.

'Sorry. I shouldn't have had that second helping of lasagne.'

'Stop saying sorry,' he repeats, as he tackles the stairs.

I press my lips together, trying hard not to smile. 'Sorry.'

'One more sorry and I'll drop you.'

'You know, this place really should have a lift.'

147

'Cass, shut up!'

Ticket barks, certain I'm in trouble now.

Charlie lays me down on his bed before going back downstairs to fetch the wheelchair. When Charlie is out of the room Ticket jumps up and lies down beside me. 'There's no need to be jealous, I promise you,' I whisper.

I look around Charlie's old bedroom, eyes resting on a black hi-fi system with old-fashioned speakers. His room looks as if it hasn't been touched since he left college. Just like Jamie, he has a map of the world framed over his desk and a stripy navy duvet. He also has what looks like a set of shark's teeth encased in a glass frame.

When he returns, he kicks off his shoes and lies down next to me, Ticket reluctantly making room.

'So . . .' I say, knowing I have to ask the question.

'So,' he repeats.

'Where am I sleeping tonight?'

'In here if you want?'

'Your room? With you?'

'No, with George Clooney.'

'Oh. I'm more of a Johnny Depp kind of girl.'

He smiles. 'Listen, all I was thinking was, well, the spare room has a few steps to get to the loo.'

'Right,' I say, mortified inside. I wish, just wish, I could have a break from this for one night. One night, God. Can't we make a deal?

'But in my room the bathroom's next door so . . .' Charlie

draws in breath, 'if you need me in the middle of the night, you don't have to worry about getting down any steps.'

'Aren't there any other bedrooms with bathrooms?'

'There are, at the other side of the house.'

'The east wing?'

He hits my arm gently.

Ticket sits up and stares into Charlie's eyes. Charlie looks at him curiously. 'What's up with him?'

'He's in a big cold house, Charlie, with a strange man.'

'I'm not strange.'

'Plus, Charlie, you insulted him about his breath.'

'Well, you've got to admit it, it *is* a bit fishy.' It's my turn to hit him on the arm. 'A bit of Colgate could do no harm,' he suggests.

'Block your ears, Ticket. Come to Cass.' Ticket rests his head against my thigh. Next he rolls over, paws upright and I tickle his tummy.

'Anyway, if you want to sleep in here,' Charlie continues, watching Ticket and me with bemusement in his eyes, 'I can camp on the floor.' It makes me think of Jamie and I watching films well into the night. Jamie is in Madrid now. I miss him.

Ticket stretches out even more, Charlie almost falling off the bed. 'Think of Ticket as your bodyguard. Any funny business, Ticket will nip me. Anyway, Cass, you don't need to make this torturous decision yet. What do you want to do now? Are you tired?'

All I want to do is to sink into some warm water. I'm cold and every part of my body aches, especially my shoulders from doing all the transfers. I stretch out my arms and yawn. 'I'd love a bath.'

'Cool. I'll start running it.'

'What?'

'A bath.'

Oh God, I must have said it without thinking. 'Actually, I'm fine.'

'Are you scared of me seeing you without your clothes on?'

'Charlie!'

'Listen, have one if it helps,' he says tentatively. 'You must get uncomfortable.'

Next thing I know, Charlie is opening his chest of drawers and chucking me an old T-shirt, saying he doesn't mind if I get it wet. He heads to the bathroom; I hear water running. When he comes back and sees that I haven't started to undress he scrunches his eyes in a promise that he won't peep.

Ticket follows me into the bathroom. It's an old-fashioned deep bath with silver taps. I see myself stepping into it, lifting my legs to shave, just like I used to. Stepping out and wrapping a warm towel around my body; making a turban for my hair.

Instead I am lifting my bottom from one side to the other to hitch my trousers down. 'Tug, Ticket,' I whisper, 'thank you so much.' Gently he bites on the end of one of my socks, edging backwards as he gives it a little yank. One sock comes off and Ticket quickly moves to the next one, as if it's a race to get me into the bath.

Next I test the temperature of the water. One of the patients in hospital had burnt the soles of her feet because she'd forgotten this rule. There are so many rules; it's like learning to live again.

After transferring myself from my chair to the edge of the bath I hold both sides and lower myself into the scented water. I'd asked for some bubble bath and Charlie had found some in one of the spare rooms. Ticket lies down across the bathmat. I take off my U2 T-shirt; it feels soggy against my skin. Finally I rest my head against the bath, breathe in deeply and allow the tiredness to melt away.

Charlie puts his head round the door. Ticket sits up, alert. 'Everything OK?'

I attempt to cover my body in bubbles. 'Chat to me,' I say.

He pulls the loo seat down and takes some tobacco out of his pocket. He rolls a joint. 'Want one?'

I nod.

He kneels down by the side of the bath. 'How about you, Ticket? Or are you more of a cigar man? Here.' Charlie lights the joint and places it between my lips. I inhale. This time we enjoy the silence.

'So, any more plans to move to London?' Charlie asks, finally breaking it.

'I need to find a job first.'

'Do you know what you want to do?'

'That's half the problem. Give me some ideas, Charlie. I have to do something with my life.' I tell him about my friends, Dom and Guy, both in west London. 'I'd like to live near them.' I also tell him what Frankie had said to me about living at home; how I might lose the confidence to ever make the break if I wait too long. She offered to be my Back Up mentor if I return to London. 'But I can't afford to move until I've found work.'

'Yeah, but you need to be in London to look for work,' Charlie says. 'You need to join some recruitment agencies.' He pauses. 'You wouldn't think about going back to medicine?'

'I don't know.'

'It seems a waste, somehow, a shame to let it go. 'Don't you miss it, Cass? The adrenalin, the buzz, the people?'

'Sometimes.'

There's another long pause. 'Will you think about it?'

I gather some bubbles into my hand and give him a bubbly beard.

'Is that a yes?'

'It's a maybe, Santa.'

I am lying in Charlie Bell's bed. I'm lying in a man's bed.

I haven't been in a man's bed for a long time. Not since Sean. The last bed I shared was with my mother.

Charlie's dressed in his boxers and a T-shirt. He lays his duvet across the floor and lies down. 'Oh fuck, the light.'

'Ticket, up switch,' I say, pointing my head towards it.

'Wow. He's unbelievable,' Charlie says when the room plunges into darkness.

'He is clever. Down, settle, good boy.'

'Are you talking to me now?' Charlie asks. 'This is confusing.'

I laugh. 'How old are you, Charlie?'

'Why? You shouldn't ask such personal questions, especially not in the dark,' he adds. 'Twenty-eight.'

'I had you down at about twenty-six.'

'Thanks. We can stick to your estimate.'

'Charlie?' I say, five minutes later.

'Yes?'

'You can sleep with me if you want? I mean, in the bed.'

'I know what you mean.' I can tell he's smiling. 'It's all right. I'm fine down here.'

I build myself up to say, 'I'd like you to.'

There's another long silence. 'I don't know how Ticket will feel about it,' he says quietly.

Ticket shifts in his basket.

'He trusts you.'

20

I open my eyes and see Charlie, next to me. He must have taken his top off in the night. His shoulders are broad and his chest smooth. One arm is raised above his head. He looks as content as I am. Just as I'm thinking how much I want to kiss him, Ticket jumps up against the side of the bed, before hopping from paw to paw. He attempts to pull my wheelchair towards me but there's not enough space down the side of the bed.

'Charlie.'

'Hmm.'

'Charlie!' I shout now and Ticket jumps up again with an anxious whine.

He sits up immediately, sleepy eyes and hair all messy, as if he's fallen into a bramble bush. 'What? What's wrong?'

'Ticket needs to go out.'

He leaps out of bed, grabs an old dressing gown and puts on some trainers without bothering to tie up the laces.

'Go,' I tell him when Ticket looks anxiously from me to Charlie. 'Good boy, Ticket. Go to Charlie.'

Charlie, Ticket and I spend the afternoon in Chipping Campden, a town close to Charlie's parents' home. We take Ticket for a walk, followed by browsing in bookshops, pottery and jewellery shops. When I sense Charlie can take no more shopping or cream tea I suggest I treat him to a pint of beer and an early pub supper.

We find a table close to the bar and Charlie shows me the photographs he took on our skiing holiday. I've learned that he started taking photographs when he was six. His grandmother gave him an old-fashioned camera for his birthday. When he was at Reading University, he took all the photographs for student union events and magazines. 'I like this one,' he says. I'm in my white fur hat, sitting with Frankie, clutching a mug of hot chocolate. I hadn't even realised he'd taken it. 'That's the whole point,' he claims. 'To keep quiet and out of the way – but always be there.'

'Give me some more hot tips.'

'Hottest tip is this: it's the rule of thirds.' He grabs a papery thin white napkin and asks the barman for a pen. Charlie draws a rectangle that he divides into three and sketches a small figure. 'The focal point of the picture has to be where a line intersects, never in the middle. So if I did a headshot of you, your face should be here.' He places the pen nib a third of the way down the rectangle.

'Why?'

'It frames the picture. Your eye is drawn to the image. It just looks better, trust me.'

'What else?'

'When looking at a photo you have to get the background right. If I took a picture of you here –' he frames my face in his hands – 'I can see a table right behind you with empty beer bottles and crisp packets. Nice. So if I go to the side of you, suddenly the view's a whole lot better. More interesting.' He looks at my profile. It's unnerving. 'The light catches your face here too.'

'Who's the best person you've photographed?'

'The Queen.'

'The Queen!' I repeat, sounding like my father. I really need to leave home.

'My best friend, Rich, his parents run a sheepskin shop in Somerset and she visited. Some people have a way with the camera, they know exactly what to do when they're in front of it.'

'She's had lots of practice.'

'Yeah, but even so, I don't know, she just radiates. She has a wonderful smile. I think she's beautiful.'

It's Sunday. Charlie and I slept in the same bed last night too. Nothing happened. I felt close to him, but he didn't try to kiss me. Confused and wishing he'd stop behaving like such a gentleman, I didn't sleep well. Maybe this attraction is all in my head?

After a lazy breakfast, Charlie and I go for a walk around the grounds of his parents' house. He tells me a little more about his work. He works for a web design and marketing company. He's part of a team of eight 'computer geeks' as he calls them, and they work in a studio in London, Farringdon. He's officially the creative manager. 'Sounds much grander than it is,' he says modestly. 'All I do is design websites and blogs. We do a lot of online marketing too. Everything's changing so fast with social media stuff and businesses have to keep up.' Charlie leads me down a path, past a derelict tennis court that looks as if it hasn't been played on since men had wooden rackets and women wore long dresses. He opens a gate into a grassy field. 'Don't touch, Ticket!' I shout when I see Charlie running on ahead to stop Ticket chasing the sheep. I grab my tin of treats and rattle it urgently, and Ticket bounds towards his liver bites instead.

On our way back to the house we look for Ticket's ball in the garden shed. Ticket sniffs under a tractor.

'Is that your dad's motorbike?' I ask.

Charlie nods.

'Let's have a go.'

'What? Now?'

'No, next Christmas. How fast can this baby go?'

'Cass, it's a dodgy old bike. Dad hasn't driven it for years, and I don't much fancy spending the rest of my Sunday in A&E.'

'Oh God,' I groan. 'I'm so bored.'

'Thanks.'

'Not of you, silly, this.' I gesture to my wheelchair. 'Going skiing was great, so good it's like I need another adrenalin shot, you know. Ticket runs towards me with the ball in his mouth. Charlie grabs it from him, throwing it across the lawn, before saying, 'Shut your eyes, Cass.'

'Why?'

'Shut them.'

I feel one hand under my knees; the other around my back. 'Put your arm around me.'

'What are you doing?'

'Hold on tight. OK, Cass, here's for some explosive fun! Keep your hair on.' He makes the sound of a motorbike and then runs as fast as he can, jolting me in his arms, jogging up and down the lawn.

I burst out laughing. 'Go, Charlie! Faster!'

'And they're coming to the penultimate jump.'

'Thought we were on a motorbike?'

'It's magic. You're on a horse now. Are they going to make it? It's head to head with Aldiniti!'

Ticket barks.

'And they're coming to the last fence. It's nose to nose. Cassandra Brooks looks like she is going to take the gold for her country . . . they're over the final hedge . . .'

'Go!' I squeal, opening my eyes.

But he then decides to put his foot into a rabbit hole and falls forward, both of us crashing down on to the grass. Ticket jumps on to us, covering me with licks. 'Cass! Are you all right?'

I lie flat on my back, spreading my arms. 'No, it hurts.'

Charlie sits up. 'Oh God, I'm an idiot, I'm so sorry.'

'I think it's really serious.' I close my eyes and shudder with pain.

'Where does it hurt?'

'Everywhere.'

'Where? Here?' He presses my ribs.

'Ouch, definitely there.' Ticket's nose rubs against my stomach.

I yelp. 'Especially there,' I say when Charlie touches my back. 'Excruciating.'

'Brooks?'

I sit up and laugh, wiping the grass off my hands.

Charlie pulls out a couple of blades from my tousled hair. 'You nearly had me there.'

'I've had such a great time,' I tell him quietly, returning his gaze. 'I don't want to go home.'

'We don't need to get the Sunday blues yet.' He looks at his watch. It's close to midday. 'We have a couple more hours to play at least.'

'I don't mean that. I don't want to go home.'

Charlie looks at me as if he's had a brainwave. 'Why don't you move in with me?'

'Sorry?'

'Move in with me.'

'With you?'

'Yes! I have a spare room. Why not? I'm on the ground floor, it's a garden flat in Barons Court. There's one pretty shallow step up to the front door, a few steps inside,' he says as if trying to visualize the layout, 'but nothing we couldn't sort out. There's a good pub round the corner, an off-licence, a highly suspicious kebab shop—'

'Slow down!' But I'm enjoying the pace. 'You really want a flatmate?'

'I wouldn't want a stranger, but . . . Come up and take a look at the room. If you hate it or think you can't manage or share a bathroom with me, I won't be offended.'

'We'd have to do it on a business basis. I'd pay for the room.'

'Fine.'

'And I come with Ticket.'

He glances at him. 'If he could work on the breath front.'

I punch his arm, playfully. 'In that case, we'd love to give it a go, wouldn't we, Ticket?'

'That's a yes?'

'It's a yes. Yes!'

Both of us laugh, nervously, knowing this is a big step. We hold each other's gaze, he edges towards me, but pulls away abruptly when Ticket barks and we hear a car driving into the courtyard.

Next I hear two car doors slam, footsteps on gravel and a woman's voice, though it's hard to make out what she's saying.

'Why are they back so early?' Charlie mutters, jumping up and dusting the grass off his jeans. 'Stay here a sec.' As if I can move. He walks towards the side gate that leads to the back of the house. 'Hi, Mum!'

Mum! Mrs Bell? Fuck.

'We tried to call,' she says to Charlie, looking over his shoulder. She must be wondering who I am, sitting here on their lawn. Do I wave? Smile? I feel so stupid. There's no sign of Charlie's dad. He must have taken the luggage inside.

'The beef was too tough last night,' she says to Charlie as they walk towards me. 'You didn't tell me you were bringing a friend down?'

I smile, trying to remain calm and natural. Where's Ticket? I see him sniffing around in the shed.

'Sorry, it was a last-minute thing,' Charlie says.

They now stand over me.

'Mum, this is Cass.'

'Hello!' I say too brightly, overcompensating for the fact that I can't get up. She waits for me to stand but when she sees that I'm clearly not going to she holds out a hand instead. 'How do you do, Cass.'

161

She has a pretty but gaunt face. Her hair is silvery grey and her eyes as blue as the sky. 'Cass came down for the weekend, she's been keeping me company,' he tells her. 'Shall I give you a hand?'

I register the confusion on Mrs Bell's face. 'You have a beautiful home,' I tell her.

'Thank you. Oh! Who's this now?' she says, as Ticket bounds towards us. She dodges out of his way.

'I hope you don't mind, I brought my dog.'

'Er, no.' She doesn't stroke him. 'He's lovely.' Ticket wags his tail, but I can see she's anxious not to get muddy paw prints on to her smart skirt. She continues to look at me expectantly, unable to decide whether I'm rude or just odd with my legs outstretched in front of me, making no attempt to move.

'Ticket, chair.' I point to the shed and he trots off. I hardly dare look at Charlie's mother now. When I do, she's staring down at me, puzzled.

'Ticket is Cass's assistant dog,' Charlie says.

'Oh really?'

'Cass was on the Back Up course,' he continues, hoping that might put her more in the picture. 'Remember?'

'Ah, right.' She twists her sapphire and diamond ring around her finger, slowly.

Ticket pulls the wheelchair across the lawn. I'm praying Mrs Bell will go on ahead, but she stands rooted to the spot, watching.

'Thank you, Ticket,' I say, when the chair's in front of me.

'Here, let me help.' Carefully Charlie places one hand under my knees, the other round my waist.

'Your son is great!' I say, putting my arms around his neck self-consciously. 'Did he tell you how many times I fell over skiing? He saved my life a few times.'

'Well now, how about some lunch?' Mrs Bell suggests when I'm finally in my wheelchair. 'I hope you've left some food in the fridge.'

All I can think about, as we head inside, is the mess Charlie and I had left in the kitchen after our fry-up.

We eat lunch in the dining room. The wallpaper is dark red and the curtains have decorative tiebacks. Charlie's father clamps a hand on his son's shoulder. 'I faked a headache. All I wanted to do was be at home in my old cords and plant a tree this afternoon.'

'Henry, you're an old curmudgeon,' Mrs Bell protests.

Henry is fair, with thinning grey hair and an attractive crookedness to his face, as if one half has been slightly altered so nothing quite lines up. So far, he hasn't commented on my wheelchair, which is a relief.

'Please help yourself,' Mrs Bell says to me.

Charlie catches me looking over to the tall sideboard. 'Why don't I serve everyone?' he suggests.

Mrs Bell stands up. 'Sorry, of course.'

'Mum, don't worry. You sit down. This looks delicious.'

Charlie hands me a plate of ham with coleslaw and knobbly potatoes. There's a silver jug of homemade mayonnaise in the middle of the table, along with various mustards and chutneys.

'Please don't wait,' Mrs Bell says. I gaze at my food, unsure if it's rude to tuck in when no one else has been served yet, even if someone has told you to start. I pick up my knife and fork, but then rest them gently against my plate.

'Where do your parents live, Cass?' Mrs Bell asks.

I tell her about Mum and Dad and what they do, my voice gaining strength when I realise how proud I am of them. 'I considered architecture,' Henry tells me, before going on to say that he used to publish wildlife and nature books but retired three years ago. He now loves painting, but it's just a hobby. 'I'm not very good.'

'Yes you are!' I say. 'There's one of your paintings in Charlie's bedroom, isn't there?'

I'm aware of Mrs Bell staring at me like a hawk. What have I said? 'Of the trees,' I say, trailing off when I realise exactly why she's looking at me.

'Dad has planted almost three thousand trees on the estate in the last thirty years,' Charlie says.

'Did Charlie show you the Wallemi Pine?'

I shake my head.

'Charlie, how could you not show Cass the Wallemi Pine? How about the *Wollemia nobilis*?'

Charlie rolls his eyes. 'No, Dad.'

He shrugs. 'My children aren't the slightest bit interested, Cass. The Wallemi Pine is the botanical equivalent of finding a living dinosaur. It was discovered in Australia, in a chasm that no one had been down. It's so romantic, Cass, dark with these rich purple-tinged leaves. It was given to me for my sixtieth.'

'That must beat cufflinks,' I say, beginning to relax.

He smiles a wonderful lopsided smile. 'You bet! Did you see the tulip trees?'

'Henry, leave the poor girl alone,' Mrs Bell says, wiping the corners of her mouth with her linen napkin. I think she's still picturing me in her son's bedroom.

I turn to him. 'No, I didn't.'

'They have the most extraordinary shaped leaves with these square tops. I tell you what. Why don't we go for a walk after lunch and I can show you?' he suggests, with warmth and charm, and for a split second I see Charlie in him, thirty years later.

'Careful,' Mrs Bell says, as she stands in front of the squatting Buddha, watching Charlie carrying me upstairs. 'Don't hurt yourself.'

'It's fine, Mum,' Charlie says, as if he's now well practised at heaving me around.

Soon he's bringing down my luggage and then carrying me back downstairs, and I'm aware it's hard work. Henry offers to help lift me. 'No, Henry!' Mrs Bell jumps in. 'You're not a spring chicken any more.'

Mrs Bell wants me to sign the visitors' book. 'Oh dear,' she says as she finds the right page. 'We're so antisocial, Cass. We haven't had anyone to stay since January.'

In the left-hand margin I write 1st–3rd April, distracted by the entry above. 'Lovely stay as always! With all my love, Jo.'

I write my name and address. 'You live in Dorset?' she says. 'With your parents?'

'Actually, Cass might move in with me,' Charlie says.

'With you?'

'I have a spare room, so why not?' He sounds defensive, or am I imagining it?

'Yes, you do,' she says with a smile that doesn't reach her eyes.

Charlie drives Ticket and me to the station. 'I don't think your mum's too keen about me moving in,' I tell him, after an unusually long silence between us.

'She'll come round. It's got nothing to do with her any-way. It's not about you either,' he adds. Ah. So he read that reaction too. 'I'm sorry if she was a bit—you know—frosty . . .'

Frosty? I'll say!

'It's not about you,' he repeats. 'It's Jo. She probably thinks that if you move in that rules out any kind of chance of us getting back together. She can't understand why it's over. All she wants is for me to marry and have children. She's *longing* for grandchildren. Anna's never going to settle down, she's wild, always has been. She often tells Mum she'll never tie herself down, she's a free spirit. In many ways Jo became her surrogate daughter.'

'Why did you two break up?'

'I knew it was wrong.'

'Why?' To me, Jo feels like a shadow that follows me down a dark corridor. She is Daphne Du Maurier's Rebecca. I decide that Mrs Bell isn't too far off the brooding Mrs Danvers either.

'I remember this one time,' Charlie says, 'when I was in the garden with Dad. He'd shown me this tree that he and Mum had planted for their silver anniversary. "Twenty-five years of marriage,"' Charlie says in a deep gruff voice, '"and I love your mother more than when I first met her." I loved Jo, but when she talked about marriage and kids, settling down and all that, I knew I wasn't ready. She was seven years older than me, it didn't seem a big deal at the time, but . . . maybe I didn't love her enough,' he reflects. 'I know this sounds stupid, but my best friend, Rich, asked me if I could go to the top of a hill and scream how much I loved her in front of all my friends and family. I couldn't do it, so I knew I couldn't be in that church, saying those vows.'

'That doesn't sound stupid, not at all.' I tell Charlie what Mum had said to me on one of our Friday afternoon drives.

'When Dad proposed on a beach in Norfolk, Mum had jumped up and down with joy.'

I hear her saying to me, 'I shouted "yes" over and over again, Cass. I wanted the whole world to know how much I loved your father.'

We park outside the station and sit quietly for a minute because we're early. 'You haven't changed your mind, about moving in?' Charlie asks.

'No, but . . .' I stop, look out of the window. Is it a really bad idea, me moving in with someone I'm falling for? What if he doesn't feel the same way? Was Charlie about to kiss me, before his parents arrived?

'But what?'

'Nothing,' I say, twisting a strand of hair between my fingers.

'Cass?'

'I was thinking about money and work, that's all.'

'We can sort that out.'

'I want to pay rent, no charity.'

'Good.' He grins, taking off his glasses and rubbing his eyes. 'I need a new lens for my camera.'

After Charlie has helped Ticket and me on to the train, he digs into his pocket and hands me a small box. The conductor blows his whistle. 'Quick, take it,' he says. 'Don't panic, it's not a ring,' he adds, kissing me lightly on the cheek.

I wave as the train pulls away, and soon Charlie is out

of sight. I open the box. Inside are rolled-up joints, lined up like the neat little pencils Mum's boss Troy had presented her when she was working for him. On a scrap piece of paper he's written, 'To have with your bath tonight, love CB. PS Did you notice we have the same initials?'

21

'I'm moving,' I tell Dom on the phone later that evening when I'm back at home, smoking one of Charlie's joints before I have a bath.

'Cass! That's great! Where are you going to live?'

I tell him about Charlie's flat in Barons Court.

'The website designer guy? Your skiing buddy?'

'Yep.'

'The one you fancy?'

I can feel my cheeks burning. Thank God we're not on Skype.

'Come on, Cass, you can tell me.'

'All right, maybe a little.' I laugh. I think I'm stoned. 'Is that crazy, Dom? Me moving in with someone I really like? Am I asking for trouble?'

'Miranda and I were flatmates.' He pauses. 'All I'd say is don't rush things, but you've got to give London a go.'

'We'll meet up all the time?'

'Try and stop me! We're only round the corner. And if it

all goes tits up with Charlie, which it won't, there's always a bed here.'

'Thanks, but I'm not sure what Miranda would have to say about us turning your home into a spinal cord injury unit.'

I hear Mum's footsteps coming towards my bedroom. Quickly I stub out my half-smoked joint. 'Got to go! Call you later. Love you.'

'Love you too.'

Mum opens the door, comes into my bedroom and wrinkles her nose.

Knowing I can't disguise the smell, 'It's just a joint, Mum.' I use the spinal cord injury trump card now. 'Helps me relax.'

She sits down next to me. 'Your father and I wondered if we should get you some pot. Can I?'

'Sure.' I relight it, and watch Mum press it to her lips. I never thought I'd be sharing a joint with my mother but then again nothing surprises me any more. 'You haven't told me about your weekend,' she says, waving the smoke away. 'Oh, this is good,' she adds, 'reminds me of being back in the bedsit with your father.'

'What would you say if I told you I was moving out?'

She hands the joint back to me. 'Are you?'

'I think so.'

'Well, it depends on where and who with.'

'Charlie's offered to rent out his spare bedroom. It's on

the ground floor and he thinks I'd manage. I need to find a job, I can do that . . .'

'But? Has something happened between you?'

'No, no, Mum,' I say, not wanting to have a chat about my love life. 'I might need a couple of months' rent in advance, which I promise to pay back.'

She runs her tongue over her front teeth. 'I'm sure we could come to some arrangement.'

'So you think it's a good idea?'

'I'll worry all the time, but I'd worry more if you stayed here with your old parents.'

Dad comes in. 'What's going on?' He stares at us. 'Are you smoking pot, Brenda?'

She smiles radiantly, the drug clearly working. 'Don't call me Brenda.'

Dad sits down and asks if he can have a puff. I tell him I'm thinking of moving back to London.

'Is he your boyfriend?' Dad asks. 'Will he look after you?' is the next question, followed by, 'Are there steps? Is it easy access? What about your car?'

Earlier in the year I applied for a Motability car. Motability is a national charity that runs a government-funded scheme to provide cars and scooters for people with disability, and I applied for a Volkswagen Polo. They are specialised in adapting cars, and I'll be using hand controls rather than foot pedals to accelerate and brake. The car replaces my monthly disability living allowance.

'Don't worry, Michael! Cass isn't moving out tomorrow.'

He laughs now. 'You know what, Cass? I think it's great.'

'Well, that's settled! You can stick that list back on to the wall, Mum.'

When I was growing up there used to be a framed letter in Jamie's and my bathroom that Mum had written to herself when she was pregnant with me.

'*Dear Me*,' Mum wrote.

> *When I have children I will not stop wearing make-up. If exceptionally busy at least wear mascara.*
>
> *I'll give them a bath at six and then it's my time (glass of wine).*
>
> *If we take them to restaurants they can sleep under the table.*
>
> *When they're eighteen they will be independent – flown from the nest and then life can go back to normal.*

'Life can sort of go back to normal now,' I say to Mum.

'As long as you and Ticket visit us, from time to time.'

We all hold hands.

I look at my parents, realising how much they have helped me reach this position. Six months ago I would have been too scared even to contemplate the idea of moving out. Yet, however much I want to move in with Charlie and build a new life, it's going to take every ounce of strength in me to leave, even with Ticket by my side.

After my bath I dry myself, and then catch my reflection in the inside wardrobe mirror. Rub the chair out, Frankie had said. Tentatively I drop the towel on to the floor. I touch my bare skin, tracing a finger from my collarbone, over my breasts, down to the roundness of my stomach.

As I think of him, I shut my eyes and take myself back to that moment when we were on the lawn, about to kiss.

22

I gaze up to a smart front door. It looks more like a private home than an office, but I'm sure I'm in the right place. 'Have you let them know you're in a chair?' Charlie had asked me last night, over supper. I moved in with him at the beginning of June. It took some time for Charlie to adapt his flat and for one of the purple people at Canine Partners to visit and make sure Ticket was going to be happy in Barons Court. I also had to wait for my Motability car to be ready. The application process takes up to twelve weeks.

'Most places these days have lifts,' Charlie had continued, 'but you don't want to show up and find there are steps.'

'Don't worry, it'll be fine,' I replied, avoiding eye contact.

'I hope you're taking Ticket with you?'

I stare at the five steep stone steps. I hate it when he's right.

What do I do? I have a job interview in – I glance at my

watch – oh Christ, ten minutes, for a PA position in a property firm. It's quite well paid, experience in the property world handy but not essential . . . but what *is* essential is entering the building. It starts to drizzle. People barge past and suddenly I long to be the woman striding along in a stylish navy mackintosh and heels, cup of coffee in one hand, umbrella in the other. I'm not saying she doesn't have any problems, but how I long for a *normal* problem, not how do I get up five steps. Panicking, I dig into my handbag to find my mobile. I wish Ticket were with me. Because I hadn't explained in my application about the wheelchair, I decided to leave him at home, telling myself that if the interview went well and by some miracle they employed me, I'd ask if I could bring him into the office. I am such an idiot! Feeling cold now, and getting wet, I stab at the numbers, but then stop midway. Think rationally, Cass. You have precisely eight minutes now to get inside the building. Charlie is in his office in Farringdon. You're in Mayfair. Not even superman Charlie can get to Half Moon Street in eight minutes and whisk me up the steps and into the reception area. Somehow I have to work this out. I look up to the sky. Oh dear God, please help me.

'Good afternoon. Can I help?' the middle-aged receptionist asks, looking up from her computer. She has auburn hair with a heavy fringe, is wearing glasses and a tight-fitting cream silk blouse.

'I've come for the interview,' I say, now wondering why it hadn't occurred to me that if I do get this job the problem of those five steps isn't going to vanish. Can I always rely on two hot young businessmen being around first thing in the morning to press the buzzer and then carry my wheelchair and me into the building?

The receptionist scans the diary. 'Ms Brooks.'

'Yes, that's me! Sorry I'm late.' Only five minutes late. Not bad considering, I congratulate myself.

'If you'd like to come this way.' She stands up and bustles towards the door.

I wheel myself out of the small reception room and back into the narrow hallway, almost bumping into the wooden banisters. She then stops and turns, as if taking into account my situation for the first time. 'All the offices are upstairs.'

'Right. Is there a lift?' I ask, doing my best to remain composed.

'Yes. Downstairs.' She gestures to a mini flight of stairs to the left. 'Can you walk at all?'

'No. I'm sorry.' I twist a strand of my hair, coiling it round and round my finger. 'And don't do that thing with your hair during the interview,' Charlie had said this morning as he helped himself to some cereal.

'Oh,' she says curtly. 'I see.'

'I'm sorry,' I apologise again. 'I should have mentioned it.'

'That would have been advisable.' Her tone is like a

schoolmistress's. 'It might have saved you, and us, a lot of time.'

'It's just I thought all places had to be legally accessible these days?'

'We're a listed building. It would ruin the aesthetics installing ramps and whatnot.'

'But why stick a lift down there?' I say, raising my voice. 'I mean, don't you think that if I could walk down those steps then I'd be able to walk upstairs too?'

Don't get too cross with the old bat, I can hear Charlie saying in my head. You're going to need her help to get out of the bloody building.

'You're not the first to make that mistake,' Frankie reassures me that night, when we meet in a tapas bar on the Old Brompton Road. After the interview (or lack of it, I should say) I'd called her, asking if she could meet me after work. Back in the reception room the old bat had said to me, spectacles perched on the end of her nose, 'In future I do advise you to alert future employers about your disability.' And then, to make matters worse, Richard Petherick, my potential boss-to-be, had flown down the stairs, paperwork in his hand, asking if his two o'clock interview had arrived. 'Oh,' he'd said, staring at me.

'I know that "oh",' Frankie commiserates.

'I wanted the ground to swallow me up. Richard was nice, actually, very apologetic. He helped me down the steps.'

'Listen, you won't make the same mistake again. Everything goes wrong in a first interview. It's like a first date.'

'OK. So what was your first interview like?'

Frankie smiles.

'That bad?'

She nods. 'After college I didn't know what I wanted to do, right? All I knew was I needed cash to move away from home and pay my rent so I applied for this job in London, in some swanky advertising company. I turned up at the reception and it was all marble floors, glass walls and cupid fountains. Only problem was my interview was on the fifth floor and, believe it or not, there was no lift. "But once you're up there, there's an easy access bathroom and it's all one level," the receptionist said, completely deadpan.'

'So you have to somehow get up five flights to enjoy the mod-con bathroom. It's crazy, Frankie,' I say. 'Doesn't it make you feel like a freak?'

'Not any more. Thing is, Cass, I went on to get a much better job at Oxfam, rehousing asylum seekers. Advertising was never for me. You know what, you really should go back to medicine. At least in hospitals you know there are lifts.'

'And A&E right on the doorstep.' I smile dryly. 'I still can't even think about it though.'

'Fine. Well, next interview just tell them, OK.'

'I will.' I confess that Charlie had said the same too.

'How's it going with him by the way? What's his place like?'

Charlie's flat is off the North End Road, close to Barons Court tube. I call it the white street, since it's all white stucco-fronted houses with pillared entrances. Many of the flats have balconies with colourful window boxes and bay trees. People sit out on their balconies in the sunshine, drinking and playing cards, and there's always music blasting out of windows, especially at weekends.

Everything I need is close by: a dry cleaner's, deli, café, patisserie, and an organic butcher's that I can't afford yet so instead Ticket and I head round the corner to the newsagent's to play the lottery, saying a prayer as I pick my numbers. I have also joined the Charing Cross swimming club, in Hammersmith, recommended by Frankie. 'They have a hoist to lower you into the water and you'll fall in love with Perry. He teaches the kids but will always jump in to save you,' Frankie had said.

'Fantastic,' Frankie says to the swimming, pleased I've taken her advice. 'And Charlie? How's all that going?'

'Good.'

She frowns. 'Expand. Is it going anywhere?'

'I don't think so.' I tell her that living with someone is a quick way to get to know them, warts and all. 'He sees me first thing in the morning now, not pretty,' I say. 'And he hates the way I forget to put the milk back in the fridge.'

'What about his bad habits?' she asks. 'He can't be perfect all the time.'

'He leaves the loo seat up.'

'All men do that.'

'He doesn't wash up. Somehow the plates make a journey from the table to the edge of the sink, but that's where the journey ends. Or the dishes are left "soaking",' I say, using my fingers as inverted commas, 'overnight. He's really untidy too.'

Charlie had confided that his untidiness used to drive Jo mad. She couldn't understand how he could leave the house without at least making his bed or picking up last night's clothes from the floor.

'Seriously, if we were going to get together, the moment's gone.' There's a long pause. 'But don't get me wrong,' I continue, when I see how disappointed she is that there's no gossip. 'He's fantastic. You should have seen how hard he and Dad worked to get the flat right for me.'

Charlie and Dad had to remove the cupboards under both the kitchen and bathroom sinks to allow space for my wheelchair. Charlie's breakfast bar was knocked down and Dad contributed towards a normal-height kitchen table for us. Mirrors in my bedroom and the bathroom were adjusted to my height. Dad and Charlie fixed grab rails around the bath. Thankfully Ticket can turn the light switches on and off, so they didn't need to change them. Frankie's eyes glaze over as I continue reeling out a list of adaptations, including Dad building some low shelves in the kitchen. 'Everyone thought you'd get together,' she cuts in, 'honestly, you two were a hot topic on the slopes.'

As Frankie heads off to the loo, I think about what she has just said. Neither Charlie nor I have mentioned that moment in the garden, when I thought he was about to kiss me. Late at night, when I can't sleep, I do think about that look in his eyes and the touch of his hand on my back. What if we hadn't heard his parents' car in the driveway? What if his mum hadn't turned up? But the following morning, when Charlie knocks on my bedroom door to ask if I'd like a cup of tea, it's as clear as daylight that we're going to be just good friends and flatmates.

Part of me is relieved. Charlie's mother is desperate for him to get back with Jo, and then there's Anna, his sister, whom I've never met – who, according to Charlie, vets all his girlfriends. Apparently Jo had said meeting Anna for the first time was like an interrogation in hell.

'How about the Internet?' Frankie asks when she returns to the table.

I shake my head to online dating. 'I need to concentrate on finding a job first.'

'Right. No dating until you have a job?'

'Definitely not.' What a good delaying tactic, but I don't tell Frankie that.

'Well, we'd better get thinking fast,' she says, raising her glass to mine. 'Before Charlie meets someone else.'

23

Mum calls me most nights, around seven o'clock, when she's returned from work, a drink is in her hand and there's enough time to gossip before *EastEnders*. 'The house seems quiet without you and Ticket,' she says.

It's the middle of August now, and Ticket and I have been living with Charlie for over two months.

'Are you keeping busy? Not getting too depressed?'

'I'm fine, Mum. Busy.'

'Doing your exercises?'

'I swim every other day, Mum.'

'Good. You'll be in the Paralympics next! And how's Charlie?'

Charlie has taken me to a few nightclubs with his friends. Occasionally Dom, Miranda and Frankie come along too, but I haven't seen Guy for weeks. He's had a series of bladder infections that have set him back. He's been screening his calls, understandably low and frustrated. When I spoke to his mum, Angie, she told me that he was struggling to keep up with the history degree that he's studying part-time from home. I feel for him, wishing I could do more to help.

'You're eating properly?' Mum goes on.

'Too much,' I say. 'I'm getting fat.' Charlie and I often eat out at our local Italian. The access is poor, but Charlie insists we eat there because not only is it cheap but they also serve the best spaghetti bolognese. As he carries me up the steps, huffing and puffing to make a point, he says, 'Put on a few pounds, Brooks?'

'Watch it, Bell.'

'No gelato for you.'

It makes me recall how awkward we were that first night, when Charlie had carried me up his parents' staircase. Now we seem like an old married couple who have known one another so long that it doesn't matter if we eat our ice-cream in silence. I didn't feel this sense of ease with Sean. In many ways all we did was jump in and out of bed in between living and breathing for medicine. It was fun, I was happy, and I loved the sex . . . but deep down I'm not sure if I really knew him that well. I'm not sure, in fact, that I knew him at all.

Charlie makes me laugh. When he walks into a room my heart lifts. When I'm with him I feel normal. The chair is an inconvenience, that's all, and a minor one at that.

'I can't wait to meet him,' Mum says. 'Dad said he was charming. You're happy, darling?'

I tell her I'm happy. Ticket is settling in too and getting

used to the traffic, smoke and noise. He loves sniffing all the rubbish left out on the pavements and he's making new friends all the time. The man in the red cap who works in the kebab shop always waves when we walk past. Ticket particularly likes the *Big Issue* man outside our local Sainsbury's, ten minutes from the flat. He also enjoys his walks. He can't wait to get his lead because he knows it might mean chasing squirrels in the park. 'The only good thing about being in a chair,' I say to Ticket when I park my car in a disabled slot inside the gates of Kensington Gardens, close to the Albert Memorial, 'is free parking. And having you, of course.'

'Any news on the job front?' she asks at the end of our conversation, a question I know she dreads hearing the answer to.

The following morning, Ticket picks up the mail and brings it to me. Last week I had an interview for a marketing company in Fulham and they promised they'd let me know shortly. My heart stops when I clutch the pale yellow envelope. I need this job because A, I need the money to pay Charlie rent. B, I want to stop eating baked potatoes and budget cottage cheese. C, I don't want to sign up with any more recruitment agencies. And D, I want Mum and Dad, even Charlie, to stop urging me to go back to medicine.

I open the envelope. I've had three interviews in the past

month. I wore a cream lace jacket that I'd found in Reiss for half price in the summer sales, with navy trousers. I swept my hair into a ponytail so I couldn't do that finger-coiling thing with it. Charlie tells me he knows when I'm going for a job interview because I look like an air hostess. Ticket accompanied me to each interview. I brushed his teeth and groomed his coat. Yet so far the feedback has been:

- I'm afraid you don't have the experience or qualifications.
- You're not quite what we're looking for, but good luck!
- Lovely dog, but . . .

I rip open the envelope, Ticket sitting by my side, watching me. It's as if he senses he was being interviewed too. 'Have we got the job?' he's asking me with those deep brown eyes of his. The moment I read the word, 'Unfortunately,' my heart sinks. 'I'm sorry,' I tell Ticket as he places a paw on my knee. 'They say I wasn't experienced enough. But tell me, how do I get experience if I'm not given the chance?'

Charlie, Ticket and I go out that night to our local Italian. Charlie reassures me that the right job is out there, waiting for me.

'It's hiding very well.'

'If something's too easy, Cass, it's never worth it.'

'Easy would be great. I'm tired,' I tell him, before we argue about who's going to pay the bill.

'Something will come up,' he insists. In so many ways his optimism reminds me of Jamie.

My mobile vibrates. It's Frankie. Just as I launch into why I didn't get the job this time, she stops me. 'What are you doing this Thursday?'

That's three days' time.

'Nothing. Why?'

'Back Up needs a Course Coordinator from the beginning of September.'

24

I reread my presentation. There's something missing. 'What does independence mean to you?' I drum my fingers against my desk, waiting for inspiration.

'They need someone to organise the courses,' Frankie had told me that night, 'recruit buddies, nurses and volunteers, talk to airlines, make sure the accommodation is booked. There's a lot of admin, sorting out insurance and chasing application forms, but it's really challenging too, especially trying to get people interested in signing up.' Having spinal cord injury isn't an advantage, she'd warned me; many people of all different backgrounds have applied. I'll be judged purely on the person I am and on my skills and experience. Frankie did this job in her late twenties and had loved it so much that she'd decided to stay in the events management world. When I'd called Back Up to ask if I could apply for the role, they told me I needed to give a five-minute presentation on what independence means to me at the end of the interview.

'Independence means freedom,' I type. 'To be free and able to make decisions on my own.' Unoriginal, Cass. 'What's going to make my presentation stand out?' I ask Ticket, wishing he could talk to me sometimes. Ticket yawns and stretches. 'Exactly,' I agree, pressing delete and starting all over again.

A couple of hours later there's a knock on the door. Charlie enters. Ticket stirs from under my desk, immediately on guard.

'How are you getting on?' he asks, looking over my shoulder.

'Not great.'

'You've written loads. Want to read it out to me?'

'I'm not done yet.' I reread the last paragraph. It sounds clichéd. I realise I'm much happier in a science lab or lecture room than in front of a computer. It's much easier examining a wounded knee or taking blood than writing a presentation for a job interview. Even our exams were multiple-choice. Rarely did I have to string a sentence together on paper.

'D'you want anything? Cup of tea? Chocolate?'

'Nope. Thanks,' I add, aware of my impatient tone.

He still doesn't take the hint. 'Why don't you take a break?'

'Charlie! I don't have time!' I retrieve my first draft from my virtual waste-paper basket. I think I was on the right lines from the beginning.

I'm aware of Charlie watching me try to decipher what I'd originally typed.

'Look, sometimes it helps giving it a rest, you know, coming back fresh? You've been cooped up in here for hours.'

He makes me sound like a battery hen. 'Charlie, I've *got* to get this job.'

'I know. Just take a break. We can brainstorm it over a glass of wine.'

'No!' I say feeling pressured. 'Look, can you go? I don't always need your help.'

Ticket barks when I raise my voice.

He heads for the door. 'Fine. Sorry. I'll leave you to it.'

Immediately I regret snapping.

He turns. '"What does independence mean?"' he says. 'Isn't it about sometimes allowing people to help you out, rather than always turning them away?'

I clear my throat to read the final paragraph of my presentation. 'Sometimes we think being independent is about doing it on our own. We let pride prevent us from seeing that, with help, we're not giving up.' I pause. 'Oh God, do I sound like the Queen, Charlie?'

He tries not to smile. 'Carry on. And stop fiddling with your hair.'

'Without Ticket, I wouldn't have moved to London. Without Charlie's help, I wouldn't have skied down a mountain, or ever believed I could live in London again. Until I came across Back Up, I thought spinal cord injury meant the end. There will always be things I need to do on my own. I won't hide behind my injury and expect everything to be done for me. But I do now understand that it's stupid being too stubborn. Asking for help when you need it is the key to enabling you to remain independent.' I pause. 'Well?'

He claps. 'You're hired,' he says, impersonating Lord Sugar. 'I particularly liked the Charlie part.'

Charlie and I stay up for a while, chatting and drinking tea in his sitting room. It's a small room with wooden floors, silvery-grey painted walls and two ancient red sofas; his old boarding school trunk is used as a coffee table and the shelves are crammed with design books and old CDs. Charlie's style is the opposite of minimalism. Throughout the flat are photographs, camera equipment, tennis rackets, furniture he's either found on eBay or in antique markets, and pictures – lots of them, some modern, some not. In his bedroom he has a drawing of a nude woman lying on a bed. In the bathroom are prints of birds his father gave to him. Both of them have a love of wild life. When we're out dog walking, he's always stopping to take photographs.

I glance at my presentation, thinking about the stress it caused. 'I don't know how I ever took an exam, Charlie,' I say, sipping my tea. I tell Charlie about our OSCEs.

'Your what skis?'

I laugh. 'Objective Structured Clinical Exams. At the end of each year we had a twenty-station OSCE, each station seven minutes, where we'd be tested on some kind of practical skill.'

'Like what?'

'Oh I don't know. It could be something like, "Take a genito-urinary medicine history".'

'I don't like the sound of that.'

Or, "Examine his knee", "Suture a wound" . . .'

'Ouch.'

'Or "Carry out advanced life support with a defibrillator".'

'Fucking hell.'

'Exactly.'

'You don't miss it, Cass?'

'Sometimes,' I admit. I miss Sarah. I tell Charlie about our friendship at King's, Charlie curious as to why he hasn't met her yet. I explain that I didn't see her over the summer. 'She was revising for her finals and then she went travelling with friends,' I say. I sent her a congratulations card after she'd called with the news that she had passed with a 2:1. I could hear her toning down her excitement. I miss our carefree friendship. Perhaps things can never be the same between us.

'I don't know. Maybe it takes time,' he says.

'What about you, Charlie? Do you love your job?' I ask, changing the subject.

'Love is a strong word. It pays my mortgage. I've always been interested in branding and design but work and bills and demanding clients knock the charm out of it. Still –' he shrugs – 'I do enjoy it, though it can be a little soulless at times.'

'Soulless? What do you mean?'

He takes off his glasses. 'Clients don't understand it's important to market and invest in proper communications and branding. They don't get that if you put the money into your business, you'll get it back. If you do a website on the cheap, you're chucking money down the drain. Your website is the shop window of your business. No one's going to come in if . . . Oh, listen to me. It's boring.'

'No it's not.'

He looks at me. 'You're going to blow them away tomorrow, Cass.'

'You think?'

'I know.'

'Charlie?'

'Hmm?'

'Thank you, and I'm really sorry for snapping earlier.'

'Listen, it's my fault too.' He runs a hand through his hair. 'Sometimes I don't know when to back off. What?' he asks, noticing me gazing at him.

'Why didn't you get a normal flatmate?'

'What?'

'You heard.'

'Normal? Just because they can walk they're *normal*? Christ, Cass, you talk a load of bollocks sometimes.' Without thinking, Charlie lifts my legs and swings them across his lap. 'My last flatmate was called Euan, right. He was Scottish,' Charlie warns me, in a heavy Scots accent. '"Charlie, the rolls you put in the bin the other day are perfectly all right if you just put a wee bit of water on them." Cass, even the ducks would have turned up their noses at them.'

I smile.

'I love having you around,' he says, reinforcing that message by tapping my legs.

'Well, I love being here.'

I don't notice Ticket coming into the room until he drops a pair of knickers on to my lap. 'Ticket!' I grab them, secretly delighted that they are my new lacy pink ones. Ticket jumps up now and nuzzles into my arm. I give him a kiss. 'I love you too,' I reassure him. 'Don't worry, there's no need to be jealous, I love you too.'

'Too?'

Oh fuck. 'You know what I mean.'

Charlie coughs. 'Cass?'

'Yes?'

I wait.

'What? Charlie?'

He leans towards me, grabs my hand to stop me playing with my hair. 'Don't be nervous, tomorrow. Whoever interviews you, think of them naked, and if you don't get the job, set Ticket on them.' I laugh, saying that's not such a bad idea. There's a further pause. 'Right. Bedtime. I'm tired,' he says.

'Me too.' I orchestrate a yawn. 'Ticket and I need an early night.' Reluctantly I transfer myself from the sofa into my chair. As Ticket pulls open the door for me, I look over my shoulder and see Charlie hasn't budged an inch. He's looking right at me. 'If I get this job, I'm cooking you a special meal,' I promise. '*My* treat. Deal?'

'Deal,' he says.

25

As I drive to my interview, I think about Frankie's advice. She told me that they're bound to ask what my motivation is in applying for this role. 'They might also ask you how you'll cope health-wise,' she'd continued, 'with a full-time job. Just say you'll be fine.'

I arrive at their office off Wandsworth High Street. I park outside the main entrance to their building, a four-storey tower block, in one of the dedicated bays for wheelchair users. I look at my watch. It's nine thirty a.m. My interview is at ten. I was so nervous about being late this morning, and paranoid about rush-hour traffic, that I left way too much time. I open my door, lift my wheelchair off the passenger front seat and across my lap before positioning it on the ground right in front of me. As I reach behind for my wheels, I take in a deep calming breath. 'Wish me luck,' I say to Ticket. 'This is our big chance.'

When Ticket and I approach the reception desk Joe, the security guard, greets us with a friendly smile, remembering us from my visit last year when I was researching the idea of going to Colorado. 'You must be here to see Back Up again,' he says. 'How are you, handsome boy,' he adds, stroking Ticket.

Back Up is on the third floor, and Joe presses a button to call for the lift. Inside the lift, I catch a glimpse of myself in the mirror. I'm wearing a navy blazer with a white fitted shirt and trousers. As the lift goes up I tell myself not to be nervous. I can do this. If I get the job, I'm staying in London with Charlie. If I don't . . . Don't even think about it. But the truth is I can't afford to live in London without a job. I can't borrow any more money from Mum and Dad. Keep positive, Cass. Remember what Charlie had said last night. I'm going to blow them away. This could be it – a new life for Ticket and me. I want this so badly. I want to tell Charlie I got the job. I don't want to fail.

'Cassandra,' says a tall elegant woman in her late thirties, shaking my hand. I recognise her from my previous trip to Back Up. She's wearing a cream linen dress and pale pink cardigan 'I'm Charlotte Lamont, the Course Manager. Come this way.'

The office walls are painted white with orange pillars. Charlotte points out two banks of desks either side of us. 'This is where services and fundraising sit,' she says. It's busy and noisy, telephones ringing and people chatting. We head past one group having a meeting on a small round table in the middle of the room. Many look up and turn to admire Ticket, but I sense Ticket knows he's here for an interview and there's no time to play.

Charlotte leads Ticket and me into a meeting room, a bare space with only a table, chairs and a jug of water with glasses and a large window that looks out on to the back of some residential apartments with their double windows. 'It can get quite chilly in here,' Charlotte warns me, making space for my wheelchair on one side of the table, 'so just say if you're not warm enough.'

Seconds later, a woman enters the room. She looks older than Charlotte with fairish to grey hair and glasses, dressed more formally in a grey suit and high heels. She comments on Ticket and the dreary weather considering it's supposed to be our summer, clearly trying to put me at ease. They sit opposite me and open their files. The woman in the suit introduces herself as Sophie. 'I'm the Services Manager and I've been at Back Up for thirteen years.'

'The interview will last an hour,' Charlotte tells me.

I nod. Stop fidgeting. Look them in the eye.

'So, shall we begin?' Charlotte continues.

Before I can answer, my stomach does a giant rumble. I was too nervous to eat a thing for breakfast.

'Why do you think you will be good at this role?' asks Charlotte, ten minutes into the interview.

'I'm organised and efficient. I'm passionate about what Back Up stands for.' I hesitate, unsure what to say next. 'I believe I could make a real difference.'

'Right,' Charlotte says, and it's hard to tell if she's impressed so far or not. I glance at Sophie taking notes. There's an awkward pause. Do they want me to go on? 'I want to tell as many people as I can about Back Up and why they should give your courses a go because I enjoyed Colorado so much. I think my having spinal cord injury is an advantage too. I'd have an insight into what people are going through, how frightening it is to do anything new.'

Sophie puts down her pen and takes off her glasses. 'Back Up attracts people from all walks of life,' she says. 'Whether spinally injured or volunteers. Will you be comfortable dealing with people from all sections of society?'

Shit. What do I say to that?

'Well, um, when I was at King's, working in hospitals I came across people from all different backgrounds and cultures. When I was in Stoke Mandeville for four months I met people I'd never normally meet but we all had our injuries in common. We were in it together, if that makes sense?' Don't gabble. Slow down. 'Spinal cord injury doesn't discriminate.' I catch Sophie and Charlotte glancing at one another. 'SCI can happen to anyone,' I continue, 'the way an illness can. It doesn't matter what your background is.'

It's Charlotte's turn again. 'This role requires supporting people new to their injury to overcome fears related to being away from home or travelling independently. How have you supported someone in their past to overcome their fears?'

'I haven't,' I say. 'But that doesn't mean I can't,' I stress when I see the look on their faces. 'Going to Colorado was a turning point for me, doing something I felt I could never achieve. It opened my eyes about what my life could be despite what's happened. I want to help others have that same opportunity. Medicine is my background. I care for people. I know now I can't fix things, but . . .' I stammer, unsure where I'm heading to on this question. 'I made some good friends in hospital last year. We supported one another, but that probably doesn't count,' I say, registering that neither one of them is taking notes.

'You're newly injured, Cass. Do you think you're ready for this role?' Sophie asks, her voice more gentle.

'Yes,' I say, looking her in the eye. 'I'm ready. Please give me the chance.'

'They asked me why I'd left King's,' I tell Charlie when I call him in the car, before setting off home.

'What did you say?'

'I told them I wanted to go in a new direction, that things had changed since my injury. Oh God, Charlie, I could have done so much better. The other applicants will have way more experience than me.'

'Don't panic. I'm sure you did better than you think,' he says, but I can hear the concern in his voice. 'How did the presentation go?'

'Good, I think.' Ironically that was the easy part.

'When will they let you know?'

'Sophie said they're interviewing until the end of the week. I should know by next Monday.'

As I drive home, I wish I could rewind to this morning and have the interview all over again.

26

The following Monday morning Ticket drops the mail on to my lap. It's half past nine and I'm still in my pyjamas, eating breakfast. Amongst the catalogues is an official-looking letter with the Back Up Trust logo stamped in ink. I delay opening it, gearing myself up for rejection.

'Here goes,' I tell Ticket, unfolding the letter.

Dear Cass. Thank you for applying for the role of Course Coordinator. We enjoyed meeting you . . . I'm waiting for the 'but'. I carry on, . . . *and are delighted to offer . . .*

I scream, waving the letter in the air. 'They're delighted to offer me the job, Ticket!' He jumps on to my lap and licks my face.

I carry on. *Going for a job interview when newly injured shows character in itself and is highly unusual. We admired your honesty and courage.*

'We did it, Ticket! We did it!'

I pick up my mobile and call Charlie.

'I'm guessing you got the job!' he says when he hears me screaming down the telephone.

'Are you in tonight?' I ask him.

'I am now.'

'I'm cooking us a special meal, to celebrate.'

'Can't wait. I'll get the champagne.'

'Time to get dressed,' I tell Ticket, putting on his coat after calling virtually my entire address book to tell them the news. Guy wasn't picking up, so I left him a message. Mum picked up the telephone immediately, as if she'd been waiting all morning for me to call, and she'd screamed, just like me.

'We're off to Sainsbury's to buy some food for tonight. We love going to Sainsbury's, don't we! It's where we meet *Big Issue* man.'

Ticket wags his tail.

Ticket and I first met *Big Issue* man a week after I'd moved in with Charlie. We'd come out of the supermarket and into the pelting rain. I pushed my chair past a man holding up a magazine. 'God bless you,' he called out, when I hadn't given him as much as a smile. Something made me turn round, and when I did, I saw a large man in his forties, rugby build, black, with a shaven head and the kindest brown eyes. I ended up buying a copy, trying not to gasp at the price, and thinking no more of it until I saw him again the following week. This time it wasn't pouring with rain so we had time to talk. I discovered he owned a white cat called Snowy and had two children, but no wife. 'We all sleep in one room, one bed. I kip on the floor. It's important that *they* get a good night's sleep, not me, but it's quite snug as a bug if you know what I mean.' He laughed, but I could see guilt behind those eyes. I bought another magazine immediately. In fact I bought two, one for me and one for Charlie.

We enter the double doors of the supermarket. Ticket wags his tail as he picks up a wire basket, dropping it eagerly into my lap. I steer us towards the fruit and vegetable aisle.

'Up, Ticket, get!' I point to the pot of double cream, on a shelf beyond my reach. Ticket jumps up, paws against the refrigerator and picks up a small pot of fromage frais, turning to me with hope in his eyes. 'No,' I say gently, 'not that one.' I nod my head towards the double cream again. People watch us. 'Look, Mama,' says a fair-haired boy helping his mum push the trolley, 'that doggie's shopping! Look, Mama!'

Being here makes me think of the friends I met on the Canine Partner training course, and the many role-plays we performed in pretend supermarkets. Alex and I send emails occasionally. 'Cilla and I cuddle the whole time, she's like me guardian angel.' Jenny, the one with the softest voice, who lived in hospital for twenty years, wrote to me recently saying how she still gets a thrill from seeing the small things like washing blowing in the wind and hearing the rain outside her bedroom window. Then there's Edward and Tinkerbell. I wonder how he is? I often think of him. In fact, I'm going to call him. I'd like to see him again.

When I reach the checkout the shop assistant seems to find us funny. A lot of people find Ticket and me funny. Maybe I should charge for the entertainment.

'Can he tap in your pin number too?' the assistant asks, breaking into a wide smile.

'Yes,' I reply, just to see his face.

As Ticket and I leave Sainsbury's we notice the *Big Issue* man back in his post, standing close to the entrance and flower stall, wearing faded jeans and a Che Guevara T-shirt. I hand him some of my spare change, but tell him I don't need a *Big Issue* today.

'God bless you and Ticket,' he says, tickling Ticket under his chin. *Big Issue* man is the only man who doesn't pay any attention to the 'Don't distract me, I'm working' message on Ticket's coat. In such a good mood, I decide to tell him about my job.

'That's grand! I hope you're painting the town red tonight?'

I find myself telling him about Charlie and that I'm cooking him a special meal to thank him for his support. Immediately I feel guilty, wondering what *Big Issue* man will feed his kids tonight, so am relieved when he smiles and says, 'Food is the way to a man's heart.'

'Oh no, he's just a friend.'

Big Issue man examines me, stroking his chin. 'Let me ask you one question, right. Was he the first person you wanted to tell about the job?'

'Yes, but—'

'You're in love, girl. Oh, I remember that feeling,' he sighs, before singing Louis Armstrong's 'What A Wonderful World'.

27

'Charlie, there's something I need to tell you,' I say.

'Me too.'

'You go first,' we both say at the same time, before laughing.

We gaze at one another from across the kitchen table, our plates of food barely touched. Charlie encourages me to start.

'You see, the thing is,' I begin.

'I think I know what you're about to say.'

'I've been having these *feelings—*'

'Cass, stop.' He takes my hand. 'I feel the same.'

'You do?'

'I do.' He's now sitting by my side as he takes a strand of my hair and tucks it behind my ear. 'I've loved you since the moment we first met.'

I lean towards him; press a finger over his lips.

We kiss. It's a soft kiss at first, but soon it becomes more intense and then . . .

I feel a nudge against my knee and the vague sound of ringing. I open my eyes, only to see Ticket in front of me, with the mobile in his mouth. It's Charlie. 'I'm on my way home,' he says, 'be with you soon.'

It's eight o'clock. I glance at the kitchen table again. Napkins, steak knives. I've used the best wine glasses. He's bound to be here any minute. Candles? I chew my lip. Is it too obvious? Oh, why not. The wine is chilling and I decide to have a glass while I wait.

I turn on some music. All I need to do when he arrives is cook the steaks. Charlie loves his steak rare. Just as I look at my watch I hear a click in the lock and the familiar sound of his voice.

'To Cass,' Charlie says, raising his glass of champagne towards mine. 'Congratulations.'

Over supper we talk about our day. I tell him half of mine was taken up on the telephone calling friends and Charlotte to accept the job offer. Charlie says he can't compete with my exciting news. 'But I'm always relieved when Monday is over.'

After supper Charlie and I collapse on to the sofa. He smiles when he sees his copy of the *Big Issue* on the coffee table. 'Cass, you're such a softie,' he says.

'I know, I can't help it.' I think of what *Big Issue* man said again. *You're in love, girl.* How do I tell him?

'Can I see the letter? From Back Up?' Charlie asks.

'Really?'

He nods. 'You need to frame it. We should stick it in the bathroom.'

I laugh. 'It's in my bedroom. Hang on.'

'I'm hanging.'

As I wheel myself out of the room, I decide that I'm going to tell him tonight that I love him. I feel so happy. I have a job and the most supportive and wonderful Charlie. I grab the letter off my bedside table. When I return, I hand it to him, watching his every expression as he reads it slowly. 'Oh wow, Cass, that's incredible . . . and very true.' He looks at me. 'You are brave. You haven't hung around feeling sorry for yourself. You've got on with it.'

'I don't have much choice,' I say quietly.

'Yes you do. We make choices all the time. "*Despite your nerves,*"' Charlie reads out, '"*your empathy and strength of character shone through*".' He puts the letter down. 'Cass, I'm really proud of you. You did it.'

Glowing inside, I say, 'I couldn't have done it without you.'

'Yes you could.' He takes my hand. 'You can do anything.'

'Charlie?'

'Yes?'

Tell him, Cass. Be brave. 'Charlie,' I repeat. The buzzer rings.

'Shit,' he says, jumping up and rushing out of the room. 'That'll be Libby.'

Libby? Who's Libby?

Libby looks to be in her late twenties, wearing a pale grey mini skirt and a cream close-fitting jumper that shows off her slender frame. Her long brown hair is sleek; she has a perfect middle parting.

'Lovely to meet you,' she says, shaking my hand in the kitchen. She glances at the empty bottle of champagne on the table. 'I gather you had good news today. Congratulations!'

I want to say, 'Yes, but who the hell are you?' Instead I say, 'Thanks.'

Ticket jumps up to say hello to her.

'Ah, so cute! Aren't you a handsome—' she bends down to take a look at his undercarriage '—boy!'

Charlie opens the fridge and asks if she'd like a drink. 'White wine would be great, honey. So . . .' She turns to me and looks down. 'You're the famous flatmate that Charlie stood me up for tonight! Only joking!' she adds when she sees my face. 'Didn't he tell you? I called to see what he was up to tonight and he told me *all* about you. It's so sweet you wanted to cook him a special meal.'

'Here you go,' Charlie says, handing her a glass of wine.

'Thanks, honey. Can I quickly use your bathroom?'

'Sure. Down the hallway, on the right.'

When she's out of the room Charlie says, 'Sorry, Cass, I meant to tell you she was coming over later,' he whispers, 'but I was so caught up with you and the good news. Fancy another drink?'

'I didn't know . . . didn't know you were seeing someone,' I say, trying to disguise my disappointment.

'It's early days.'

The buzzer rings again. Charlie tells me that will be Rich, who had also called earlier to see if he could come round. Rich is Charlie's best friend from home. He works in film and advertising, and is often abroad, which is why I haven't met him yet. 'He's just got back from the States,' says Charlie, letting him in.

Sitting round the kitchen table, Rich tucks into the leftovers of supper. Charlie, Libby, Rich and I talk briefly about my job that starts in ten days. Rich goes on to describe his trip to Washington and Vancouver. He has returned from filming a documentary about the Second World War, where he was lucky enough to visit some incredible war veterans, men well into their nineties who all had stories to tell. 'What they did . . . well, it makes our lives seem pretty mundane,' he says.

Libby works in Leicester Square for a recruitment company that specialises in media. 'We recruit for the BBC, trade shows, exhibitions, things like that.' I discover Charlie met her a couple of weeks ago; he's designing a new website for their company. Libby explains that her job is all about getting 'hits', in other words, placing people. 'The more people I can find work for—'

'The more commission,' Rich finishes, a note of cynicism in his voice.

'Exactly. Have to earn the pennies. I visit loads of companies to meet the staff, see if I have anyone on my books who would fit in. It's dead in August, though. Roll on September.'

'Tell them what happens when you get a hit,' Charlie says.

Libby laughs. 'Charlie thinks this is so weird! Friday afternoons we have our weekly meeting, OK. If I've placed someone our team manager rings this bell and everyone in the boardroom sings round the table, "Hey, Libby, you're so fine, you're so fine"' – Libby does this little dance, jigging her arms in a circle, and somehow she makes even *that* look sexy – '"You blow my mind, hey, Libby!"'

Why hasn't Charlie mentioned her before? Rich catches me noticing the way his hand brushes across hers.

Charlie and Libby head outside into the garden for a cigarette, leaving Rich and me alone in the kitchen. Rich brings his dirty plate to the sink, thanking me for supper.

They stand close as Charlie lights her cigarette. Libby is clearly into Charlie just as much as he's into her.

'Uh-oh,' Rich says.

'Sorry?' I edge myself away from the French door.

'I've seen that look before.'

'What look? Sorry, Rich. I was admiring . . . um . . . Libby's top.'

'Right. And I was looking at that flying pig.'

'Do you fancy a coffee?' I ask, desperate for him to change the subject.

'Listen, Cass, I love Charlie. I've known him all my life, since I was this high.' He places his hand a couple of feet from the floor. 'His family are like my family.' He pauses. 'But he's complicated.'

'Complicated?'

'He gets close to women and then bottles out. Who knows how long this one will last.'

Maybe he hasn't met the right one, I want to say.

'Jo was lovely. It ended badly, the moment she wanted more. He has a commitment problem. His whole family do.'

'What do you mean?'

'Have you met his sister, Anna?'

'No.'

'Long story.'

'Tell me.'

'I can't.' He glances at Charlie through the window. 'Not now, but one day,' he promises. 'Cass, all I'm saying is don't place your bets on him. I know he thinks the world of you but . . .'

'Listen, Rich, I like him,' I say, partly touched by his concern, but also annoyed with myself that I can't hide my feelings. I stop when I see Charlie kissing her. She has one hand resting against his back jean pocket.

'I didn't even know he'd met someone,' I murmur.

'He can be pretty private. I didn't meet Jo for months.'

'Please don't tell Charlie,' I whisper.

He touches my shoulder in understanding, before walking over to Ticket. Ticket rolls over, allowing Rich to tickle him. I watch them playing; half Rich's white shirt hangs out of his trousers and he has ink on his freckled cheek.

'I don't understand your dog, Cass,' Charlie says, when he enters the kitchen. 'He doesn't let me near him.'

Rich ruffles Ticket's ears. 'Have you been giving my friend a hard time? Well, very wise to be wary of Charlie. I was when I first met him.'

Ticket wags his tail even more, in on the conspiracy.

'Should I be wary?' Libby says, nudging Charlie's arm.

The telephone rings. Libby is in awe when Ticket brings it to me. It's Guy. Never before have I been so relieved to leave the room; Ticket follows me and I shut my bedroom door firmly behind us. 'Sorry I missed your call earlier,' he says. 'That's great about the job! Cass?'

I hear music playing, voices in the kitchen and Libby laughing again.

'Cass? What's wrong?'

'Can I drive over?'

'Tomorrow?'

'No. Right now?'

28

'All men are bastards,' Guy declares. 'He led you on, Cass. Stuff him. Mind you, I was no better than Charlie when I was, you know, not in this.' Guy taps his wheelchair. 'I didn't treat women well, went from one to another as if they were tasters.'

'He hasn't exactly treated me badly, Guy. Maybe I misread the signs.'

'No. You just forget about him, and move on.' With his good arm, he lifts my face towards his, so we are eye-to-eye. 'It might be a lot less complicated too, you know, staying friends. Listen, you're about to start a new job, who knows where that might lead and who you'll meet. And if all else fails, you can marry Ticket.'

'Oh, Guy, I love you.'

'Marry me, then, and Ticket can be our best man.'

We laugh, imagining two wheelchairs down the aisle and Ticket in a morning coat bearing the rings. 'You should get a career as an agony uncle,' I suggest.

'Oh fuck no, that's Dom's job.' Guy and I decide the world needs many more Doms. There are so many people who complain about nothing, their glass is always half empty. 'He saved my sorry arse,' Guy says. 'Both of you did.'

It's one o'clock in the morning when I return to Charlie's. The house is quiet. I let Ticket out into the garden before heading into my bedroom, wondering if Libby is still here. Sleeping in Charlie's bed. I try to put the thought out of my mind.

As I undress, I think about Guy instead. Despite the jokes, he looked tired tonight. After we'd discussed Charlie and relationships, Guy mentioned he'd been rushed into hospital again. One of the biggest fears for people with high-level injuries is autonomic dysreflexia. If the bladder is full it normally spontaneously empties itself, but it can remain firmly shut, which causes a rise in blood pressure and severe pain in the head. It is life-threatening and needs medical attention immediately. I'd learnt about it at King's.

'Oh, Guy, why didn't you say something before?'

He shook his head. 'Because I hate it,' he'd replied. 'I'm bored of it, and I'm bored of myself.'

'But, Guy, you could have died. Please promise me next time you'll call? I can come round, be with you.'

He'd raised a hand to his forehead. 'Scout's honour.'

As I'm getting into bed I notice I've had a couple of missed calls on my mobile and a new voicemail message.

I was so determined to leave quickly after supper that I'd left it behind on my bedside table.

'Hi Cass, it's Edward. Edward Granger, returning your call. Thanks for your message. It was good to hear from you.' He sounds nervous. 'Anyway, Tinkerbell and I would love to see you and Ticket. Give me a call and let's make a plan. Great. Er . . . All the best.'

The following morning I wake up feeling excited about my new job, but that excitement is soon clouded over when I hear voices in the hallway. 'See you tonight, honey?'

'Sure. I'll book a table,' Charlie says.

I hear them kissing.

Thank God I didn't tell him how I feel. What a fool I am! I would have made it so awkward between us. I could have ruined everything. Clearly he only sees me as a friend. Minutes later, I hear him taking a shower. I make a promise to myself to forget about Charlie in that way. As Guy said, keep him as a flatmate. Focus on the new job. I glance at my mobile, remembering Edward had left a message last night.

It's time to move on.

29

It's Friday morning. I'm coming to the end of my first week at Back Up, and I'm about to head to Stoke Mandeville Hospital with Simon, one of my colleagues who works in the Outreach and Support team. I'm here to shadow him and take notes, so that I can explain to anyone with spinal cord injury exactly what is involved in these sessions. Simon has been in a wheelchair for fifteen years, injured in a rugby game. He's now in his late thirties, loves basketball and getting around on his hand bike, and teaches wheelchair skills to patients across the country. Dom and I took part in one of his courses while we were both in the rehab ward.

As we drive out of London, I'm relieved week one is almost behind me. Monday was especially nerve racking. I felt like it was my first day at school. I didn't want to say or do anything wrong. Charlotte, the Course Manager and woman who had interviewed me, showed me round the office, pointing out the accessible kitchen and bathroom and the tables and stools where everyone ate their lunch.

When I was introduced to the team I was so preoccupied to give them a firm handshake and not fidget with my hair that I immediately forgot their names. There are twenty-five staff in total, not including the volunteers. Six staff are wheelchair users, including a partially sighted employee who has a massive screen on her desk. I was shown the computer system and the basics of logging in and out and answering the telephone, along with the long list of extension numbers.

The afternoon was a series of meetings. Jane, Head of Fundraising, gave me an introduction into Back Up fundraising events and how the charity raises its income. Nathan, the PR and Communications Manager, explained to me his role and how I fit into the five-year plan for Back Up. I was given the staff handbook and told I needed to absorb it quickly to understand the ethos of the charity. Louise, from the Outreach and Support team, talked me through the process of calling newly injured people, to try and encourage them to sign up for Back Up courses. By the end of the evening I was so overwhelmed with information that I thought my head might explode. I was also dehydrated from not drinking enough water, as I'd been nervous about going to the bathroom all the time. Ticket and I headed back to the flat and, too exhausted to cook, I ordered takeaway before going straight to bed.

The rest of the week was more meetings and familiarising myself with all the courses Back Up run throughout the year. There are multi-activity courses in Exmoor and the Lake District, and City Challenge Courses in Edinburgh and Belfast, where participants learn wheelchair skills, are given confidence getting around on public transport and overcoming the fear of socialising. There's the skiing in Winter Park, Colorado and Ski Karting in Sweden. Yesterday morning, I spoke to a single woman in her forties, called Samantha, who hadn't been abroad since her injury five years ago. I was trying to reassure her about the travelling and how to manage the cold, explaining that when I went to Colorado, Back Up had brought plenty of snow boots and extra jackets, hand warmers and hot water bottles. 'Though the skiing is so much fun and energetic, you often feel too hot!' I thought of Charlie. 'Also, you meet the best people.' She told me she'd think about it, promising to get back to me at the end of the week. I could sense her reservation, her fear of the unknown. I also sensed she felt isolated and vulnerable. 'I know it's scary, but you have nothing to lose,' I'd said gently. 'Being up in the mountains, it's a different world.'

When Simon and I enter the hospital it brings back memories. I take in a deep breath, praying not to bump into any of the doctors or Georgina. The only person I miss and would like to see again is Paul.

As we wheel ourselves into the sports hall a couple of the patients are playing basketball in their chairs, one aiming and shooting a ball through the net. His arms are covered in tattoos and he's wearing a solid gold chain and tweed cap. Simon tells me his name is Mike and that he was shot by mistake by his best friend. Weirdly it doesn't shock me. It's not easy to shock me these days. A young girl in school uniform wheels herself over to me, saying she was born with spina bifida and that her mum is ordering pizza tonight, because she's allowed takeaway every Friday. It's a treat night. Simon calls her over to join the group.

'You need wheelchair skills,' he says, placing a bottle of water on one side of his chair, wedging it between the spokes. 'It's a big wide world out there and after you've been discharged we don't want any of you lot staying at home with no confidence to be out on the streets. Mounting kerbs, going down steps, it takes practice. No two kerbs are the same. I'm only good now because I've made loads of mistakes and fallen over a zillion times. But once you've mastered the skills it can be fun. You can whip round supermarkets, go up and down escalators, but that takes a lot of practice, so don't do that just yet,' he warns everyone.

As I watch them, it reminds me of my session with Dom. One of the main things we had to learn was back-wheel balancing in preparation for mounting kerbs. Simon had placed a wooden board in the middle of the room to act as one. 'You need to measure the height mentally. Don't use more energy than you have to,' he'd said. 'Timing and technique are more important than strength.'

I can remember the oldest man in our group, Morris, volunteering to go first. Face clenched with determination, he wheeled himself towards the kerb but his back wheels jammed against it with a thud. 'Way too early,' Simon had said. Deflated, Morris joined the back of the queue. Dom and I didn't have much more luck than Morris either, first time round.

'Hello?' I hear someone saying quietly. 'Whingeing Pom?'

I turn. 'Paul! I was thinking about you.'

'Cass! How are you?' He glances at Ticket.

We move out of the hall so we can talk in private and not distract the class.

'Who's this handsome fellow?' he asks, stroking Ticket. I tell him all about Canine Partners. 'And you went skiing,' he says. 'Thanks for the postcard. So, what are you doing here?'

'I work for Back Up.'

'Ah, mate, seriously?'

'Yes.'

'That's terrific. They're a great team.'

'And how are you? How's work?'

'Ah, look, I shouldn't say this, but I will,' he says, his guard finally slipping. 'There are some patients we care about more than others; that's just the way it is. I miss my whingeing Pom.'

'I miss my sergeant major too.'

'Good, glad we got that sorted. Can't be professional all the time, can we?' he says, stroking Ticket again.

I tell him that I keep in touch with Perky and Guy and that I'm living in a ground-floor flat with Charlie. 'It's funny being back here,' I tell him. 'My time here seems like a dream, and then it only feels like yesterday too.'

'I can imagine. But look at you, you're doing great.'

'You did so much for me, Paul. Thank you.'

'I'm glad I helped,' he says with emotion he didn't show at hospital. 'Well, I'd better go. Got a new patient to get up and running, you know what it's like.'

When I return to the sports hall I picture him going to the rehab ward and standing by the bed of the next patient. They won't realise yet how lucky they are to have him on their side.

When Simon and I return to the office late Friday afternoon, I gather my files from my desk, thinking about the night ahead and what I'm going to wear on my first date with Edward. I'm beginning to feel both excited and anxious. We're meeting in a restaurant along Kensington High Street.

As I'm about to leave, my telephone rings. Reluctantly I pick up, praying it's not going to be a long conversation. I want to go home, run a bath and have a glass of wine. 'Hi, Cass. It's Samantha. We spoke earlier this week, about the skiing course in Colorado?'

'Of course,' I say. 'How's it going?'

'Good. I thought about everything you said, and I want to go on this course.'

'That's fantastic!' I'm nodding vigorously at Charlotte, who is approaching my desk.

'You made me realise it's time to live a little,' she says. 'I can't sit cooped up at home forever wishing this had never happened.'

'Well done,' Charlotte says when I hang up. 'It can be hard persuading people. They're often scared.' She touches my shoulder. 'Cass, you have a gift. We saw that in the interview. Keep it up.'

When I return to Charlie's flat, I head straight into the kitchen to feed Ticket, replaying with pride what Charlotte had said to me.

The flat is quiet. I'm relieved Charlie isn't home yet. Normally he works late on a Friday or if Rich is around, they meet for a drink. Maybe he's staying over with Libby tonight. He had asked me a couple of days ago if I'd mind him sleeping over the odd night at her flat in Battersea. 'But if it worries you being in the flat on your own,' he'd said, 'Libby can easily come here.' What could I say? Of course I pretended that I didn't mind being on my own.

Don't think about Charlie, I tell myself, heading into the bathroom to run a bath, before consulting my wardrobe to decide what to wear tonight. Will Edward be smart? Why doesn't Charlie get it? Oh it's so annoying. I pick out my scarlet top. Stop thinking about him! Celebrate the end of your first week and Samantha agreeing to go on a skiing course. Get excited about Edward. Oh why did Libby have to turn up and put a spanner in the works? Is he *really* falling for her?

As I have a bath, I think about Edward and our date and seeing Paul again today. I remember one evening in hospital, after a gruelling session in the gym, when I'd talked to him about Sean. 'This has got to be a turn-off for guys, Paul, and don't patronise me by saying they'll fall in love with me and not the wheelchair. How am I ever going to meet someone? Go on dates? I mean, look at me.'

'I am. I'm looking at a beautiful girl,' he said.

I sighed, half touched and half dissatisfied. 'I wish I could feel something, you know. It's this numbness.' I hit my legs. I felt nothing.

Paul placed one hand behind my neck and his fingers brushed against my skin. 'Can you feel that?'

I nodded, heat rushing to my cheeks.

His fingers pressed against my hair. He was the only person who had dared to touch me since the accident. Jamie, who normally thumped my arm to say hello, would sit as far away from the bed as possible, as if I were a china doll. 'I can feel that,' I said, wanting him to carry on.

He lifted my face to his. 'People come and go in here. Some make it, some don't. I believe you'll have a good life. I know it's different to the one you'd imagined, but there's no reason why you can't fall in love, marry, have kids'—

225

'Hello?' I hear Charlie calling, jolting me back to the present. 'Cass?'

'I'm in the bath!'

I hear Libby saying hello to Ticket. 'How was your day, you handsome young man?'

I close my eyes and sink deeper into the water.

When I'm dressed and about to leave, I make my way into the kitchen to say goodbye to Libby and Charlie, and to ask them if they can let Ticket out into the garden later. Edward had mentioned on the telephone that he wasn't bringing Tinkerbell. She doesn't relax in cafés or restaurants.

Charlie's standing in front of the stove, frying something. The room smells of mince. Libby is drinking a glass of white wine and flicking through the television guide. 'We felt like a quiet night in, didn't we, sweetheart. Work's been manic today,' she says, before admiring my top. 'Red really suits you, with your blonde hair. You look amazing, doesn't she, Charlie?'

He turns. 'You look good. I like your hair down,' he says before carrying on cooking.

'Where are you off to?' Libby asks. 'Hope you've got a hot date?'

'It's not really a date, it's just supper.'

'Cass, honey, it's a date,' says Libby. 'Men don't ask you out on a Friday night if they're not interested, do they, Charlie?'

He doesn't turn this time.

'We'll see,' I say. 'Can you look after Ticket for me? Let him out later?'

'You're not taking him?'

'I think he'd be really bored in the restaurant.'

'You don't want to be a gooseberry, do you,' Libby says to Ticket, tickling him under the chin. 'So come on, who's the lucky man?'

'Libby!' Charlie frowns. 'Stop—'

'I don't mind,' I interrupt him. 'Edward.'

'Where's he taking you?' she asks.

'The Terrace.'

'Blimey, I love that place!' She reaches over to Charlie to stroke his arm. 'Hint hint.' He doesn't react. 'Pricey though.' She rubs her thumb against her index finger. 'I have a good feeling about this. I bet you he'll be asking you home for a *coffee*.'

'Anyway, I'd better go,' I say, beginning to feel uncomfortable. 'See you later.'

Libby smiles. 'I doubt it.'

30

When a waiter escorts me to our table, Edward stands up, kissing me on both cheeks. He's dressed in an open-necked striped shirt and casual jacket, his thick brown hair swept away from his forehead, and his faint line of stubble squares his jawline and makes him look edgy and masculine. I don't normally go for that look, preferring the more clean-shaven appearance, like Charlie, but it looks surprisingly good on Edward.

'Wow, this is great,' I say, gesturing to the disappointingly empty restaurant.

'I wasn't sure what kind of food you're into,' he says, 'but I read a couple of decent reviews so thought what the hell! Let's spoil ourselves.'

The Terrace is a smart restaurant with white linen tablecloths and on each table are gleaming silver cutlery and glass vases filled with fresh lilies and roses. It's old-fashioned in many ways, the waiters dressed in uniform. It's a bit over the top, I decide, and pretty soulless, the atmosphere dead with only two other solitary couples sitting at tables widely spaced apart. But I'm touched that Edward's made such an effort to impress me. 'Shall we order some wine?' he suggests.

'Cool.' I scan the five-page wine list, unable to see any bottles that are under twenty quid. Fuck me. There's a bottle of champagne for two hundred! An awful thought runs through my mind. Is Edward paying for this? I can't assume he is. 'Why don't we go for the house white?' I say, noticing that ordering a bottle is cheaper than buying three glasses. 'It's on page five. The bottom one?' It's still expensive at twenty-eight pounds, but at least it's not a week's salary.

'Sounds good,' he replies, evident relief in his voice.

'So . . .' we both say at the same time, after the waiter has shown us the label on the bottle, uncorked the wine and asked if Edward or I would like to taste, and finally poured us both a glass.

'I was going to say,' Edward begins, 'it feels odd being here, seeing you without our partners in crime.' We talk briefly about the Canine Partner course, both of us wondering how Alex and Cilla are, along with Jenny and Captain. 'How's Ticket?'

'He's grand.'

Grand? Cass, where did that word come from? 'How's Tinkerbell?' I move on quickly, hoping he hasn't registered how nervous I am.

'She's the best. The guys love her at work.' Edward tells me about his job in the security industry. 'Big companies are always terrified of terrorist attacks, so they get in loads of ex-military to advise. Basically I do a lot of consultation work for them.' As he's talking I'm wondering if I can imagine kissing him. He's tall and broad shouldered and I like his thick dark hair and the way a few wayward strands flick across his eyes. There's also a weight to his presence. Maybe that's because I know he's been in the Marines and fought in Afghanistan, but as he talks he appears comfortable in his own skin. He's a different man to the Edward I met on the Canine Partner course; the Edward who had kept his gaze fixed firmly on the ground.

I take a sip of wine, pacing myself since I'm driving. 'Do your friends tease you about her name?'

He laughs, an open easy laugh that reminds me of Charlie. 'Oh yes. I was hoping at the assessment days that there might have been a dog called Hercules . . .'

'Or Goliath?'

He smiles and we catch each other's eye. I'm the first to turn away, muttering how delicious the wine is as I take another sip.

'Tinkerbell's my beautiful girl,' he says. 'I wouldn't trade her for a million Herculeses or Goliaths.'

Over our main course (I suggested we skip starters) Edward tells me he always wanted to be a soldier, ever since he was a child. In the same way that I don't know where my love of medicine came from, he doesn't know why he wanted to be in the forces. His father, who had died when Edward was in his early twenties, was an accountant by trade but had worked in the oil business. His mum was a housewife. 'I joined the Marines when I was eighteen, signed up to the training course. Dad always encouraged me but Mum never liked the idea of it. I'm an only child, you see. Mum hated it even more when my father died. She wanted me to be in an office, safe behind a desk.'

'Nothing is ever safe,' I say. 'And perhaps the more safe we play it, the more dangerous it becomes?'

'Yes,' he says. 'I've never thought about it in that way. We only get one life, Cass. Despite this –' he gestures to his crutches – 'I don't regret a single moment.'

The dessert trolley rattles towards us, the two couples in the restaurant still not talking.

'Sorry, it's a little dead in here, isn't it?' He's almost smiling.

'It's not the most lively of places,' I reply, before both of us laugh, fully relaxed now.

'Why don't they talk?' Edward whispers. 'I don't get it, do you? Why come out to a fancy place and then say nothing?'

'Exactly, and how can you go home and ignore the fact that you've just had dinner and it wasn't exactly a bundle of fun? It's weird. Makes me feel uncomfortable.'

'Sorry, Cass,' he says again, running a hand through his hair. 'We could do a runner?'

That makes me laugh even more. 'I'd like to see you and me making a quick exit.'

'We wouldn't get very far,' he admits.

'Nope. We're staying put I'm afraid. I've just seen the tiramisu.'

As we share a tiramisu, Edward complaining that I gave myself the bigger half, he asks me about my first week at Back Up. As I talk, I'm aware of his intense gaze and all I can think about is what happens after the meal. Will he be inviting me back to his flat for a *coffee*? Edward lives in a ground floor flat in Richmond. What will I say if he asks me? I can't leave Ticket overnight. But if I say no, I'll be giving him the wrong signals, won't I? Can I see him as more than a friend? Maybe it's too early to tell, I should stop worrying. I never used to worry. Is Edward asking himself the same questions?

'Can we have the bill, please,' he asks, fishing his wallet out of the inside pocket of his jacket. 'No, Cass, this is on me,' he insists when I produce my debit card.

'But it's so expensive.'

'Costs an arm and a leg,' Edward jokes. I'm attracted to his dark humour. 'No arguments,' he says, before excusing himself to go to the bathroom.

When he's left our table I catch a glimpse of a black and white photograph in one of the compartments in his wallet.

Tentatively I take a peep. It's a picture of a woman in her twenties, thick wavy hair and heart-shaped mouth. Quickly I place the wallet back on his side of the table, telling myself to stop being nosy. Could she be his sister? No, he said he was an only child.

When Edward returns the bill is presented to us on a small silver platter, accompanied by some dark chocolate mints. I daren't look at his face as he assesses the damage. He swallows hard, as if to say 'ouch'.

'Next time it's on me,' I say when he hands his credit card to the waiter.

'Next time?' He taps his pin number into the machine.

'Yeah, next time, but I'm not sure I can compete with this place,' I say, tucking into a mint. 'It might have to be McDonald's.'

Edward raises an eyebrow.

'Or Pizza Hut,' I say.

'With screaming kids?'

'If you're lucky.'

He grins. 'Cass, I'm going away tomorrow, for two weeks, to Cornwall.'

Oh. That's bad timing. 'How lovely.'

'I was wondering if we could meet up again, when I get back?'

The traffic is busy on a Friday night, lots of people hailing cabs and groups of friends coming out or going into bars.

Edward walks me slowly to my car. The closer we get, the more I sense both of us thinking, 'What happens now?'

We're right outside my car. 'Well, this is me. Thanks so much, that was great.' I wrap my arms around myself, shivering in the cold night air. 'Don't hang about, it takes me ages to sort myself out, you know, to get my chair into the car and—'

Edward leans down to kiss me, possibly just to shut me up. It's a soft, slow kiss. I kiss him back, loving the closeness and warmth of his face, his stubble grazing my cheeks. When finally we pull apart and he says goodnight, I'm disappointed that this is where our evening ends, but when I see the flirtatious look in his eyes, I realise that maybe this is only the beginning.

'I've had a great time tonight.'

'Me too.'

'I'll call you,' he says, before kissing me goodnight once more. 'Until next time.'

'Next time,' I say, watching him walk slowly away.

31

Charlie and I are racing along the Kings Road. We're going to Peter Jones to look for a sofa. Charlie has decided the one in the sitting room has to go. It sinks in the middle like a soufflé gone wrong. I left Ticket behind today; he doesn't like department stores. I'm taking him for a long walk later this afternoon with Edward and Tinkerbell. Edward returned from Cornwall a week ago, and I'm surprised by how much I'm looking forward to seeing him again.

'Slow down, Cass!' Charlie insists, only making me go faster.

'Come on, Grandpa,' I call out to him. 'Keep up.' I lift the front wheels up on to the kerb in one fluid movement and push forward. Charlie has tried doing wheelies in my chair in the sitting room – lifting the front wheels and balancing on the back ones – but was unable to understand why he couldn't do it. I told him that it took me two weeks to master the skill. 'Two whole weeks,' I reiterated. 'It took

Dom a week. It would seriously annoy me if you, Mr Perfect, could pick it up in two seconds.'

We enter through a set of double doors and I'm hit by a blast of warm air. 'Sofas are at the top,' Charlie tells me, heading for the lifts.

I think of Dom's latest email. 'Miranda gets cross with me for going on the escalators. She says I deliberately want to scare the general public.'

'What are you doing?' Charlie says as I position myself at the foot of the escalator, near the cushions and rolls of fabric. If Ticket were here he'd hate me for doing this. He'd plant himself on my lap to protect me.

'Cass, don't risk it,' he says.

'Dom does it.'

'He was a professional biker. You might hurt yourself.'

I shake my head. Why is it that people fail to realise that I'm broken already? In many ways it makes me want to take more risks. What have I got to lose?

'Fine.' Charlie crosses his arms. 'But I'm not taking you to hospital.'

'There's a lift,' a man beside me points out, 'over there.' Then he has the audacity to push me towards it like a baby in a pram. 'Excuse me?' I say, turning to face him and noticing Charlie is trying not to laugh. 'What are you doing?'

'Sorry,' he mutters.

'I'm taking the lift,' Charlie says, expecting me to follow

him. There's a group of women talking by the escalator and I ask them politely if they could move. A few members of staff walk past, along with a mother and a pair of ginger-haired twins wearing identical football jumpers. One of them stops to watch. 'Come on, Max!' the mother says. 'But, Mummy! I want to watch that girl in the chair!'

Charlie is still waiting by the lift, pretending to ignore me. I have to get my front castors on to the step first, then quickly get the back wheels on, grab both rails and . . . OH MY GOD. I'm moving!

'Look, Mum!' I hear Max crying out. 'Wow!'

I'm balancing. Can't look at him. Keep straight ahead. Hold on tight. When I reach the top I turn to Max, still clapping.

'Thank you!' I call down to him.

'Go, dude!' Max dances, before his mother pulls him off towards the exit doors.

Charlie joins me upstairs. 'There's no way you're going down in that. No way,' he says.

'We'll see.'

We test out what seems like the twentieth sofa. 'Make your mind up,' I urge him.

'It needs to be comfortable.'

My mind drifts to Libby and Charlie kissing on the sofa last night. I saw them on my way to the bathroom.

'We've been ages, Charlie.'

'Ticket will be fine.'

It drives me mad that he knows what I'm thinking.

'Let's go for this one.' I'm in front of a modern cream one. 'That'll do.'

'That'll do?'

I let out a sigh.

'He's just a dog, Cass.'

'What did you say?'

'Nothing.'

'He's just a dog?' I repeat like a mother scorned.

'Sorry.' A small smile surfaces.

'I'm hungry,' I say. 'Let's get some lunch, order a sofa and then go.'

After a quick lunch Charlie and I wait for a cab outside. I did think about bringing my car but it's hard to park on a Saturday, even in a disabled slot, and the tube station has no disabled access.

'Come on!' I shout, stretching out my arm towards a taxi with its amber light on. It races past us.

'What are you doing?'

Charlie is covering me with his jacket. 'Charlie!' Next I hear an engine stopping and he's saying that we want to go to Barons Court and then: TA-DAH! The jacket is whisked off and out I come like a rabbit out of a hat. 'Is she coming too?' the driver asks.

I'm about to say something but Charlie doesn't allow me. 'Yes.'

The driver gets out the ramp, huffing and puffing as if he's doing me an enormous favour.

'Why did you do that?' I ask when we are finally seated in the cab and moving.

'What?'

'Hide me under your jacket?'

'It did the trick, didn't it?'

'Right.'

'You didn't mind, did you?'

'It's fine.'

I stare out of the window.

'You were the one so anxious to get home, back to Ticket.'

'Who's just a dog. Oh look, it doesn't matter.'

'Clearly it does.'

'Well done, Charlie! You saved the day getting me into a taxi because I could never have done it on my own! You're my hero. Happy now?'

'No. Not really.'

'You and the driver were talking as if I wasn't there.'

'Fine. Sorry. I won't do it again.'

We sit in stony silence for the next five minutes before glancing at one another at exactly the same time and then quickly looking away, annoyed we've been caught out.

'Cass?'

'What?'

'This is our first lovers' tiff.'

'We're not lovers.'

He rolls his eyes. 'You know what I mean.'

'Just shut up.'

'Won't say another word.' He pretends to zip up his mouth. 'I wasn't trying to be a hero,' he says, only seconds later. 'Look, it could have taken forever and we both wanted to get home. I'm meeting Libby this afternoon and you're . . . well . . . you're anxious about Ticket, who I know isn't just a dog, I really didn't mean it like that.'

'It's not just about Ticket.'

'Right,' he says, sounding irritatingly like my father.

'I'm meeting Edward.'

'Really?'

'Yes, really.'

'Where are you going?'

'Just out,' I say.

He waits for more information.

'We're meeting for a dog walk. He has a chocolate Lab, Tinkerbell.'

'Is it like a double date? You and Edward, Ticket and Tinkerbell?'

'Maybe. Ticket's bought some flowers. And brushed his teeth.'

Charlie smiles.

'Then I think we might see a film or something, maybe go out for a meal. What about you?'

'I think we're playing tennis or something.' He downplays it, like he always downplays any sport he takes part in.

'Then we're meeting a few of Libby's friends in Soho. Tell me more about this Edward guy.'

Charlie must sense my reluctance.

'Do you think it could be serious?' he continues.

'I don't know, maybe. Who knows?' I hesitate. 'How about you and Libby?'

'Yeah. She's great. Good fun.'

We fall silent once more.

'I'm sorry about earlier,' he says. 'I was patronising and I promise it won't happen again.'

'Forget it.' We shake hands. 'Deal?'

'Deal.'

'Cass?'

'Yes?'

'Wear that red top tonight. It really suits you.'

32

Edward and I are out with our dogs in Kensington Gardens, close to the Serpentine Gallery. After returning from Cornwall, he'd called to ask me on another date. 'You don't like swanky restaurants, and nor do I,' he said, 'so how about a dog walk?'

Ticket and I love this park; it gives me a feeling of space and peace, and the straight pathways are easy to navigate in my chair. It's a beautiful day today. The autumn leaves are beginning to change colour.

Edward's in his wheelchair this afternoon since long walks cause him too much pain. As we're talking about his holiday, people can't help but notice us. Some walk on by but then glance over their shoulder. London does throw up a strange mix of people but I guess you don't often see two people in wheelchairs side by side, both with purple-coated dogs. Some smile as they watch Ticket and Tinkerbell playing with one another and chasing the squirrels. Others throw us that 'poor wee things' look. Others simply stare.

'Just wave back,' I say, waving at the woman with a camera round her neck. 'Always throws them off guard.'

'Or do this.' Edward leans over and kisses me, hard on the mouth.

I push him away. 'Edward!' I say, then we both laugh, watching her tentatively wave at us before walking as fast as she can in the opposite direction.

Some people approach us, unafraid of asking questions. 'I feel like I'm with a celeb,' I whisper, when an elderly gentleman tells Edward he's proud of him and what our lads do for this country. 'So often the press only focus on those that have lost their lives, but it's important we support fine young men like you. God bless you.'

Early in the evening, after our walk, Edward is at the bar, ordering drinks. We decided to give the cinema a miss, instead choosing to go to the Curtains Up, round the corner from Charlie's flat. It's a cosy pub with a little theatre in the basement. What I like about it is it's normally busy, people sitting on stools around the bar or relaxing on the comfy leather sofas. There's no sign of couples not talking to one another. Charlie and I occasionally come here if they're playing live music. We often have a drink on Sunday night too, to beat the Sunday night blues. He and Libby rarely spend Sunday night together. I like those nights, just the two of us.

My mobile rings. It's Sarah. 'Take it,' Edward says, returning with the drinks.

'It's fine,' I say, rejecting the call.

'Who was it?' he asks. 'But don't tell me, if it's private.' I sense Edward thinks it could be another man, maybe competition. To put him at his ease I tell him about her. 'She's too tangled up with my old life,' I confess. Sarah is now working at St Mary's Hospital in Marylebone. She wants to specialise in paediatrics. 'I feel guilty shutting her out,' I admit. 'But equally I know she finds it hard, she doesn't know what to say, so we're stuck.'

'Maybe it will take time,' Edward suggests. 'If your friendship is strong enough, you'll find one another again.'

'That's what Charlie says.'

'You talk about him a lot, you know.'

'Do I? Well, you get to know someone pretty well when you live with them.'

'Sure. Anyway, he's right.'

I finish off my beer. 'I don't know, Edward, I feel bad, but the thing is, I've found so much more peace being with Charlie and Frankie, Guy and Dom.' I pause. 'And you. You didn't know the old me.'

Edward nods. 'It can be the same with my friends from the Marines. It's tough. They're doing the job I used to love. But, Cass, you could go back to King's?'

'Shall we order another?' I hold up my empty glass, dodging the question.

At the end of the evening I ask Edward if he'd like to come back to Charlie's flat for a coffee. I'm not sure what

I mean by a coffee, but he kisses me softly on the lips, saying he needs to go home. 'I like you, Cass, that's why I want to take things slow.'

33

I'm in my bedroom getting ready for my evening with Edward. Charlie and Libby are next door, in the sitting room. They're spending more and more time together, so much so that she might as well move in with us. As for Edward and me, since our walk in the park, we've continued to meet regularly over the past month. Last weekend we went to the O2 Arena. Edward had bought tickets to see Katy Perry. I smile, remembering us driving home late at night, me singing 'Last Friday Night' at the top of my voice.

'Don't give up the day job,' Edward had said, glancing at me, humour in his eyes.

I pick up my mobile, in need of advice. 'Nothing's happened yet,' I tell Frankie.

'Nothing?'

'Well, you know we've kissed, we've kissed a lot, but we're taking things slow.'

'Still? I know it's romantic and all that, but can't you speed it up?'

'He's asked me to his place tonight, for dinner.'

'That's great!'

Silence.

'Isn't it? Cass?'

'Yep. Great.'

'You can't be getting cold feet? He sounds perfect. In a way it's quite romantic.'

Through the crack in my door I see Charlie walking past my bedroom.

'This is totally normal,' Frankie reassures me. 'You're bound to be nervous first time.'

'Maybe.'

Charlie pokes his head round the door.

'Frankie, I have to go,' I say, before she insists I take a toothbrush just in case. I hang up quickly.

'Everything OK?' he asks, perching on the end of my bed.

'Fine. What are you up to tonight?'

Charlie tells me he and Libby are going to a birthday party in Tooting. 'To be honest I don't fancy it, I won't know many people but . . . How about you?'

Suddenly I wish we could forget Libby and Edward and spend the evening together. I miss him. I miss us. 'I'm seeing Edward,' I say. 'He's cooking for me, at his place.'

'It's going really well, isn't it?'

I nod. 'I might stay over.' I watch his reaction.

'If you do, will you let me know,' he says, giving nothing away.

'What was the food like, when you were out in Afghanistan?' I ask, over supper, a mushroom risotto. We're in his small kitchen, painted a pistachio green. I take another mouthful. At least I think it's mushroom.

'Ration packs,' he says. 'Boil-in-the-bag. I lost two stone. I looked dreadful, but then we all did, Cass. Our stomachs shrank. On Christmas Day they flew over a chef and we had Christmas dinner, though not many of us could eat the meat, it was too rich, and a can of beer. That can of beer was the best I've ever tasted. Amelia sent out parcels too,' he continues. 'Coffee, chocolate, pork scratchings.' He smiles, as if he's thinking about her.

'Who's Amelia?'

'My ex-girlfriend,' he says, in a tone that implies he doesn't want to talk about her.

'Tell me more, about Afghanistan.'

'It was the worst experience of my life and strangely the best too, if that makes sense.'

I ask him to describe it to me. I want to be able to picture his old life.

'Oh, Cass, it's hard. You see the images on the news, the kids with missing limbs, the dusty tracks, you hear reports about the mines and the soldiers and civilians that have died.' He inhales deeply. 'When you're out there, it's terrifying and exhausting, but also nothing has ever made me feel more alive. If I was pointing a gun at the enemy it was to save my troop and myself. So if you can imagine that, and then coming home, it's been tricky. The adrenalin got me through at first. I was working so hard to recover I didn't have time to feel sorry for myself. But when I was back home, reality sunk in. That's why I got so low.' He stops. 'Do you really want to hear all this?'

I nod. 'It's good to talk about it.'

'I had some counselling, had to get my shit into one sock.'

'Shit into one sock?'

'Sorry.' He almost smiles. 'Means I had to sort my life out. A lot of soldiers do mad things after they return from Afghanistan.'

'Like what?'

He refills my glass of wine. I realise I'm well over the limit to drive home, that I'll have to call a cab, but neither one of us mentions it.

'Speeding, crashing their motorbike, hijacking a car on a motorway. Some turn violent. A lot of us suffered from post-traumatic stress disorder. I didn't want to hurt anyone, but I wanted to hurt myself,' he admits quietly. He runs a hand through his hair. 'I'd walk down a street and expect to be attacked. Any unexpected noise or bang set me off. Mum had to be careful waking me up. If she jolted me, I'd freak out. I never thought I'd be able to go outside and feel safe or live on my own again. When I was in Headley Court there were people worse off than me, double-leg amputees, so I kept on thinking I should be feeling lucky, that I'd got off lightly. Lucky seems such a weird word, but you know what I mean.'

I tell him how Georgina, the abrupt nurse on our ward, had told me, only days after my accident, that I was lucky to have a low-level injury. 'I know what she means now, but back then it didn't make any sense. Was it your idea to get a dog?'

'Mum's. Funny thing is, I've never liked animals much. Got nipped when I was a young boy by some horrible sausage dog called Spike.'

Edward asks me how I found out about Canine Partners. I tell him about Mum and our Friday afternoon drives.

'This isn't lucky,' he says, gesturing to my wheelchair, 'but we are lucky to have support. So many of the lads come from foster or broken homes. If they're injured they have nothing. It's their whole life, and then it's taken away from them in seconds by an IED blast. They have no family at home waiting to pick up the pieces.'

'What happened to you . . . out there?' I ask.

He tells me he was in a WMIK, a Weapons Mounted Installation Kit, explaining that they're basically a stripped-down Landrover with a heavy weapon mounted on the back and a machinegun mounted for the person in the passenger seat. 'We used to drive in and out of contacts in them, often as fire support for the troops on foot who entered and cleared compounds. Our vehicle went over a mine.'

'What happened next? Were you unconscious?'

He nods. 'I don't remember much, Cass. They did the amputation in Camp Bastion and then I was flown back home. All I remember is waking up in a hospital bed, unsure where I was. It was terrifying.'

'When I was at King's, I was in my own bubble,' I say, ashamed. 'I didn't think about brave guys like you.'

'We're not brave, Cass, we're just doing our job.'

After supper Edward gives me a guided tour of his flat. 'It won't take long,' he says. He leaves his bedroom until last.

'So, this is my room,' he says, Ticket and Tinkerbell following behind us. Edward tells them to settle down in the corner. In front of me is a double bed and beside the window is a desk on which sit a computer, books and files.

'What are these for?' I ask, pointing to some miniature medals on a small wooden table. Edward tells me he was in South Armagh, Northern Ireland, in 2002 and Iraq in 2003. I look at some framed photographs, including a picture of the same woman I had seen in the photograph in his wallet.

'Who's this?' I ask, but I think I know.

'Amelia.'

'She's beautiful.'

He doesn't say anything.

'Are you still in touch?'

'No. She left me last year,' he says, a tremor in his voice.

'How long had you been together?'

'Four years.' He bends down to stroke Tinkerbell. 'She's met someone else. The ironic thing is we got through the hard times. She stuck by me through rehab, but then . . . Maybe she left when she thought I was strong enough to cope alone, but I still loved her. I didn't think . . .' he trails off. 'Anyway, I'm over her now.'

'Right,' I say, far from convinced. The last person I'd want in a photograph frame is Sean. 'Do you miss her?'

'No. Cass, do you want to sit . . .'

'Hang on,' I say, picking up another framed photograph, realising I want to delay whatever it is that might happen tonight. Why do I feel this way? Edward is handsome and charming; he's good company and we have so much in common . . . what's stopping me?

'Where are you?' I scan the picture of young lads lined up in rows, wearing green berets.

'There,' he points. 'And that's Dan, next to me. We trained together, at Lympstone. We were so young, about nineteen.'

'And this?' I point to a coloured, hand-drawn map.

'Helmand Province.' Inside the map are signed messages from his friends.

He picks up the photograph of him and Dan standing

252

next to one another in their green berets, two fit young guys with a bright future ahead of them. 'Are you still in touch with him?' I ask.

There's a painful silence and I realise the answer. 'Oh, Edward, I'm so sorry.'

'He was the brother I never had,' he says sadly. 'We always thought we'd be big and strong and yomp up mountains until we were eighty.' He turns away. 'Let's not talk about this any more. Why don't we move . . .' He gestures to the bed.

'Yes,' I say, my heart thumping as I head towards him.

'OUCH!' Edward cries out when I run over his foot.

'I'm so sorry,' I say. 'Oh shit, does it hurt?' Stupid question.

'A bit,' he pretends, his face puckered in pain.

'Shall I take a look at it?'

'No, I'm fine, really,' he says. He laughs and I find myself laughing too with relief, watching as he heaves himself on to the bed. It's my turn next, transferring myself from my wheelchair on to the bed. Tinkerbell rests a paw against the side of the mattress.

'I have competition,' I say. Edward orders Tinkerbell and Ticket to settle down on the fleece rug by the window. When he turns to me, I look away. 'How's your foot?' I ask.

'I'll survive.'

'Oh God, sorry,' I say nervously again, when I can't stop laughing. 'I know it's not funny.'

'It is kind of funny.' He grins.

There's a long silence. Edward lifts my face to his. He kisses me, his arm around my waist, his hand now inside my top. I don't mean to pull away so abruptly. 'Edward, I'm not sure . . .'

'What?'

'I like you, so much.'

'There's a but, isn't there?'

I nod, wishing there weren't. 'I'm sorry.' There's a long silence. 'Maybe I should go?'

'Don't.'

'But . . .'

'Cass, stay.'

When I look at him, I see how much he has lost, especially his best friend, Dan. I see the loneliness in his eyes. I think he's still in love with Amelia. I see a young boy who wanted to be a soldier, a son who has come back home, a son who would have made his dad proud, someone who is braver than I will ever be, and I edge closer to him, noticing tears in his eyes.

'I'm sorry,' he says. 'What a twit, I'm not normally like this. It's being with you, Cass, I can talk to you and . . .'

'Shh.'

I touch his face, wishing I could take all that pain away.

'I still miss her,' finally he admits, quietly.

'I know. Sean and me, we were always together, and then suddenly he wasn't around any more. It's like losing a limb,' .

I say, before realising that wasn't perhaps the best word to use, but Edward doesn't take offence.

'You know, most of us lads, after waking up in the hospital, were much more concerned that we still had our balls.'

We both laugh.

'Stay, Cass. I don't want to be alone tonight.'

'Nor do I,' I say, holding him in my arms.

34

'Where have you *been*?' Charlie asks the following morning when I return to the flat and find him in the kitchen. He's dressed in a pale blue shirt and pair of scruffy jeans, his hair damp from the shower.

'At Edward's.'

'I've been trying to call.'

I can smell bacon.

'Sorry. I think my phone's run out of battery. I'm starving.' I open the fridge.

'I'm making bacon sandwiches,' he says. 'I was worried. I thought you'd been mugged or taken hostage.'

'Oh, Charlie, you knew where I was.'

'I asked you to let me know if you were staying over.'

'It got late. I'd had a couple of drinks and—'

'Right,' he cuts me off, opening the cutlery drawer.

'I'm sorry I didn't call though. I should have done.'

'It's fine. So I'm guessing the evening went well?'

Edward and I had held on to each other, both of us

craving touch, reassurance, and love. We'd stayed up until the early hours of the morning talking about Amelia. I then felt able to be open about my feelings for Charlie, going right back to the beginning, when we'd met in Colorado. Finally we gave in to the dogs whining to come up on to the bed. Tinkerbell rested her head gently over Edward's sore foot; Ticket somehow lay sandwiched in between us. We laughed at how funny we must look. What a sight. Finally we fell asleep in each other's arms. It was a night that neither one of us will forget for a long time. We were two people who had found one another through extreme circumstances, just like I'd made friends with Dom and Guy. 'We see things in similar ways, Cass. I can tell you anything,' he'd said, stroking my hair as we lay in the darkness.

Edward is attracted to me, but he hasn't moved on from Amelia. She broke his heart. I'm attracted to Edward, but I'm in love with this man holding a grill pan in front of me.

'We had a great time,' I say.

'Is it serious between you two?'

I'm about to tell him the truth, but then I hear the sound of the hairdryer blasting from his bedroom. 'Maybe,' I say.

'Morning, Cass!' Libby enters the kitchen, long brown hair tumbling down over her shoulders, and dressed in a tracksuit and sporty Lycra turquoise T-shirt. 'I thought I heard voices.'

Charlie grabs some plates, Libby brushes past him, towards the sink, and they kiss, briefly, before she helps herself to a carrot juice from the fridge. 'I always feel so good after yoga, as if I could float away, do you know what I mean?' She turns to me, stretches out her long graceful arms. 'And how are you, Miss Out All Night Cass?' Her eyes light up.

I feel hungover and in need of a strong coffee, my teeth need brushing and my hair's a mess and I don't need a carrot-drinking-yoga-bunny in front of me . . . Oh but, Cass, it's not her fault she's with Charlie. 'I'm good, thanks. Just need some sleep.'

'You look knackered,' she announces with delight. 'So come on, how was your evening? Charlie was getting all paternal on you, like you were out late on a school night.'

'He sounds incredible,' Libby says, after I've filled her in with Edward's background in the Royal Marines and how he was injured out in Afghanistan. 'What a brave guy.'

I show her a photograph on my mobile of Edward with Tinkerbell. 'Oh look,' she says. 'He is seriously handsome and *what* a cute dog. Charlie, you have to see this!'

'In a sec. Just need to put the rubbish out,' he states, making quite a noise as he lifts the bin lid to retrieve the bulging black sack.

'Ignore him,' Libby says when he's left the room. 'He's been in a stinky mood this morning. Someone got out of the wrong side of the bed. Anyway, back to Edward. Did you . . . did you . . . you know?' she asks as Charlie returns.

I sniff the air. Something's burning.

'Oh shit!' he says, flying towards the oven and without thinking pulling out the grill pan. 'Fuck!' The pan clatters to the ground.

'Ticket, no! Basket!' I say, before taking a look at his hand. 'Put it under some cold water, quick!'

Still cursing, Charlie runs the tap and holds his hand under it. Following my orders Libby then heads to the bathroom to find some Ibuprofen and a dry gauze bandage, or any dressing to wrap around his hand, along with some aloe vera cream, which is in my medicine bag.

'How's it feeling?' I ask him, a couple of minutes later. 'The cold water should lessen the burn. Keep your hand under the tap.'

'It hurts,' he says.

'It will be sore for a bit, Charlie.'

He nods gravely. 'How long?'

'A couple of days.'

'I wouldn't make a very good Royal Marine, would I?'

'No.'

He smiles, as if to say he deserved that.

'I'll dress it for you, but keep it under water for a little longer, OK.'

'So, Dr Brooks, tell me more about last night.'

'Just worry about your hand.'

He moves closer towards me. 'You know, last night, I was—' he turns, looks me in the eye '—jealous.'

'Jealous?'

He nods. 'I know I have no right to be.'

'You don't, Charlie. You have no right at all.'

'Is it serious between you?' he asks again.

'Why do you care?'

'Of course I care.'

'Jealous? You're with Libby,' I remind him, aware of his eyes still fixed on mine.

'Here! I've got some . . . oh . . .' Libby stops.

I move away from him. 'That's great, thanks,' I say, taking the cream and assortment of bandages from her, aware she's looking at me, and then back to Charlie. 'Crisis over,' I say. 'I think our patient will live.'

35

I'm lying in bed, the world peaceful until Ticket barks at the tribal music coming from the sitting room next door. I squeeze my eyes shut, wishing Libby would turn the volume down. It's Sunday morning. Give the chanting a rest. She's a little too health-conscious for me as well. Everything she touches is organic, even wine. I'm surprised she doesn't spray Charlie with something green before touching him. Oh, Cass, it's not her fault she's going out with him, I tell myself again.

Charlie and I haven't mentioned that moment by the sink a couple of weeks ago. We now have first-class degrees in pretending nothing is going on between us. Part of me thinks I should ask him if we can talk, grab a coffee round the corner, clear the air and finally find out where we stand with one another, but each time I race down that track I turn round and limp back home. I have too much to lose. I know we have a connection, an attraction, but Charlie's made his choice. He's going out with Libby and however much she can irritate me, I still like her. Charlie needs to stop playing games, messing with my head. Who the hell does he think he is? He has no right to be jealous. Rich's voice also haunts me. 'He's complicated, Cass. He can't commit. He bottles out.' If only Edward and I had fallen in love.

On my way to the bathroom I catch a glimpse of Libby sitting cross-legged on her yoga mat, hands in the prayer position. 'Morning, Cass,' she says, gracefully stretching herself out like a cat. 'Morning,' I say back, wanting to tell her to eat a doughnut.

When Edward and I meet for a dog walk in Richmond Park, Edward senses I'm not myself. 'I'm sorry I'm being so quiet,' I tell him. 'It's Charlie. I want to move on, I do, but it's hard when we live together. I think Libby could be getting suspicious too, and I don't want that. Maybe I should move out?'

'That's a bit drastic! Besides, it could be hard finding a new place. Why don't you pretend we're still together? It could take the pressure off? Use me.'

'I can't do that,' I say, throwing the ball for Ticket.

'Why not? I don't mind as long as you say I'm the best kisser in town.' He raises an eyebrow.

I smile. 'You are pretty good.'

'It would help me too,' he confides. 'Since I've met you,

Mum's laid off asking questions about my private life, thank God.'

I glance at him, thinking that maybe it isn't such a bad idea after all.

36

When I fibbed to Libby that Edward and I were officially going out, she clapped her hands in glee, as if I'd announced my engagement. 'We must go on lots of double dates,' she'd exclaimed. She has been trying to sort a night out with Charlie, Edward and me for the past fortnight. 'It'll be Christmas before we know it,' she had moaned in email exchanges, when Charlie couldn't do this date because of work, or Edward was away. I'd also thrown in the odd lie to say I was busy too, as no one wants to be available all the time. Besides, I have been working late these past few weeks, organising all the last-minute details of the Sweden skiing course for next January.

During our last dog walk, Edward had asked me to describe Libby, Charlie and now Rich, who had returned from filming abroad again and wanted to come along too.

'Oh, this will be fun. Where do I start?'

'I don't need their whole life story, Cass, keep it brief.'

'OK, I can be brief. Libby first. She's pretty, a yoga freak, ambitious.' I paused, stuck already, deciding I needed to make more of an effort to get to know her.

When it came to Rich, 'Tall, scruffy, workaholic, skinny bean, intellectual, loves history documentaries and *Homeland*.' Something was missing. Finally I said, 'Lonely.' Charlie had told me that he'd been single for a couple of years, not through lack of women interested but through choice. Charlie's sister, Anna, had broken his heart. He also has a poor relationship with his parents. 'Why they had children is anyone's guess,' Charlie had said. 'When he was growing up, all they wanted to do was travel round the world. Rich was an inconvenience.'

'Charlie?' Edward said.

I took in a deep breath. 'He loves photography, great skier, creative, works hard, eccentric in many ways, you know, quite British. But he's kind, really kind, generous, and he makes me laugh. He can be so frustrating too,' I said, not wanting to make him sound perfect. 'It's hard to know what he's thinking, he can drive me insane sometimes, just when I think he's about to—'

'Stop!' Edward looked at me. 'I get the picture.'

Tonight's the night we're meeting at a Greek restaurant on Fulham Road. Charlie, Libby and I are the first to arrive. This place is very much a traditional taverna, Grecian statues and murals adorning the walls. As we wait for Rich and Edward, olives, pickled chillies, hummus and pitta bread are brought to our table. Charlie orders some house wine and a couple of bottles of cold beer.

'Oh look, this must be Edward!' Libby waves at someone.

I turn and see him heading towards us. He's dressed in dark trousers and a deep red jumper, hair freshly washed. I feel a surge of pride as he shakes Libby and Charlie's hand. Then he bends down to kiss me, full on the lips, shocking the life out of me until I remember we're supposed to be dating.

Over a supper of kebabs and salads, we talk work, life, films, flatmates, books, dogs, and Libby wants to know all about how Edward and I had met at Canine Partners.

Libby then asks us what we're all doing over Christmas and New Year. 'Maybe we should plan a party?' she suggests. 'It's only a month away.'

'I don't even want to think about it yet,' says a disgruntled Rich. 'The shop round the corner from me has been stocking mince pies since bloody August.'

'I'm not mad on the *festive season* either,' says Charlie, a sparkle in his eye. 'Too much time with Mum.'

'Oh, you're all such killjoys! I love it!' Libby tells us she's one of five sisters and her family lives in Chobham, Surrey. Her father, Bruce, is a stockbroker, her mother raised the children, and from the sounds of it, it's one big happy family. 'Charlie's being very brave, he's visiting us after Christmas, aren't you, sweetheart?' When she touches his hand I feel that unwelcome pang of jealousy. They're spending the New Year together. I turn away from him, cursing myself that I still feel this way.

'I loathe Christmas,' Rich says. 'The Waltons we ain't. Mum can't be arsed to cook a turkey so we go to some swanky restaurant, stick paper hats on and pull crackers. Dad gets more and more drunk and then asks me when I'm going to bring home a nice girl he can crack on to.'

'Christmas can be hard for Mum and me too,' Edward says, before confiding that he's also an only child and his mother hasn't remarried since his father's death. 'Mum and I usually eat beans on toast and watch the Queen's speech.'

'That makes me think of Guy,' I say, reminding Edward about him and his passion for his little orange friends.

'How is he by the way?' Charlie asks.

'Not great.'

'Poor Guy,' Libby sighs. 'Whenever I'm having a bad day,' she goes on, 'you know, if I don't place a client or if I feel ratty because I've missed my morning yoga, I think of Cass and say to myself, "Man up, Libby! Think of Cass!" You're a real inspiration,' she says to me.

'Anyway,' Rich says, sensing my discomfort. 'You know what? One year we should rent a cottage and have an "I hate Christmas" Christmas. No stupid presents, no board games, not a paper hat in sight, just plenty of booze.'

'I'll be there,' Edward says, raising his beer bottle towards Rich.

'Will you two be spending Christmas together?' Libby asks Edward and me.

'What? I mean, yes, maybe,' I stammer. 'We haven't really spoken about it yet, have we?'

I can't bring myself to say 'sweetheart' or 'honey'. I'm uncomfortable pretending. I should never have agreed to it.

I'm jolted back to reality by Edward placing an arm round my shoulder. 'Mum's longing to meet her,' he says. Charlie catches my eye.

As we look at the pudding menu, Libby tells Edward she used to have a boyfriend in the army.

Charlie pours us all some more wine. 'You didn't tell me that.'

She rolls her eyes at him. 'Number one rule, you never talk about exes.'

'Why did you break up?' he asks.

'Oh, it was a while ago, I was pretty young. I thought the whole idea romantic, handsome man in uniform.' She winks at Edward. 'But then he went to Iraq. If I had a boyfriend out in Afghanistan now, I couldn't cope. I'm not cut out for it, I'm afraid.'

I admire her honesty.

'Well, there's no chance of Charlie going,' says Rich with affection.

'Do you mind talking about your time out there?' Libby asks Edward.

Edward coughs. 'No.'

'I was wondering what happened, you know, how you were injured?'

Again, I like Libby for asking.

He explains that he was based in Kajaki. 'I was out four years ago, Operation Herrick 5. The IED threat wasn't anything like it is now. The vast majority of lads on my tour were injured in fire fights, we had some real scraps with the enemy. We were always aware of legacy though. Anything off the cleared tracks was a threat.'

'You mean landmines left over from the Soviet occupation?' asks Rich.

Edward nods. 'We'd see loads of people and children with missing lower limbs and hands. A lot of kids would play in the village, pick up scraps of metal, turns out to be a grenade that blows off both their arms,' he says, pushing his plate aside. 'That's what's so cruel about them. On the whole they're designed to maim, not kill.'

'Didn't Princess Diana do a lot of work to ban landmines?' I ask. I have a lasting image of her wearing a protective mask, walking through the minefields in Angola.

Edward nods. 'She championed it until her death.'

'I worry about the Afghan war,' says Rich, as the waiter clears our plates. 'I think our armed forces are brave, I do, but I can't imagine how we're ever going to leave that place as a peaceful democratic country.'

'I agree,' Charlie says.

'It's OK, Cass. I'm used to this,' Edward reassures me, when I glance his way.

'Afghanistan has always proved a disaster for countries coming in from the outside,' Rich continues.

'Look at us in the nineteenth century,' says Charlie.

'And then the Russians not so long ago,' Rich follows on, 'and now the Americans and us are bogged down after a decade, getting nowhere.'

'Are you saying we should do nothing about the Taliban?' Libby asks both Charlie and Rich.

'I don't know,' Charlie says. 'Maybe we were right to get involved, but equally . . .' He stops, hesitant to continue.

'It is worth it,' Edward says raising his voice, knowing what Charlie and Rich are driving at. 'No one said it was going to be easy, but someone has to help the Afghans against the Taliban, we have to try and stop them from being a base for terrorism.'

'You're right,' says Charlie, trying to make peace. 'But I get what Rich is saying too. It's a tricky one.'

Rich pours himself a glass of water. 'Listen, I'm not against the army or the Royal Marines, but I find it hard to support this war. Afghanistan is a mess and I'm not sure we're making it any better.'

'I was doing my job,' says Edward, clearly angry now.

'Our commanding officers inspired us to do our very best for our country, they told us it was the right thing to do.'

'Well, of course they would!' Charlie says, his voice heating up. 'Your commanding officers are unlikely to be telling you that it's hopeless—'

'Listen, mate, it's not personal,' Rich says, registering Edward's anger. 'I'm just not sure we have any right—'

'Don't talk to me about "rights"! What about our responsibilities? We're part of NATO, are we just supposed to let the attack on the Twin Towers go unanswered? If we'd pulled out of Afghanistan early it would have made a mockery of those soldiers who had died.'

'Yes,' Charlie says 'but—'

'You sit behind a fucking desk, Charlie. I'm proud of what I did, of what the lads still do. Don't you dare tell me Dan's life was a waste.'

'I'm sorry, Edward, I—'

'Excuse me.' He cuts Charlie off, wrestling to leave the table, banging into a chair on his way out.

'Who's Dan?' Rich whispers.

'Well, that went well,' I say pointedly to Charlie.

The following morning I bump into Charlie outside his bedroom, dressed only in his pyjama bottoms. I'm in my dressing gown, towel and washbag on my lap. I see a lace bra and matching knickers, along with Charlie's jeans, leather belt and Calvin Klein boxers, strewn across the bedroom floor. He shuts the door, scratches his head. 'I was about to put the kettle on.'

'I'm fine. Thanks.'

The bathroom door opens and Libby appears wearing a skimpy towel, her brown hair scooped into a loose bun. She seems completely at home as she kisses Charlie good morning and says, 'Bathroom's free.'

I can't take my eyes away from her slim pretty hand resting against his chest. 'I hope we didn't wake you last night?' she asks with concern, without removing her hand.

'No.'

'Oh good. We tried to keep the noise down, didn't we?' She smiles. 'Is Edward OK? He didn't stay over? We're so sorry if we upset him.' Sharp dig in the ribs. 'Aren't we, Charlie?'

'He's fine. Right, well, I'd better get going,' I say, heading into the bathroom.

As I place the padded white shower board over the bath I hear Libby and Charlie talking. She's asking him to cook some of his special poached eggs, the perfect cure for hangovers, while she does twenty minutes' stretching.

After my shower I rush back into the bedroom, praying not to bump into them again. I have nothing planned today but I need to get out of the house.

Ticket sits patiently as I get dressed on my bed. I wriggle around on my mattress, rolling over on to one buttock, then the next, sliding my trousers up my legs. I hear music coming from the sitting room. Ticket barks at the sound of leaves rustling in a breeze, waves rolling on to the shore. I imagine Libby stretched out on her yoga mat, graceful as she bends to do the downward dog position as I struggle to lift one leg over my knee to get my socks on.

'Where are you off to?' Libby asks, sitting with Charlie at the kitchen table, my efforts at slipping away discreetly having failed.

'Meeting Edward,' I pretend, thinking how easy it is to lie. 'And you?' I watch Charlie reading the paper, aware we have hardly spoken since we exchanged words last night in the restaurant. *I get frustrated, Cass,' Edward had said last night when we left the restaurant together. 'I think people confuse the two conflicts in Afghanistan and Iraq. They don't get why we're there. And I miss Dan. It hurts.'*

'We're going to be lazy, aren't we,' she replies, clutching a mug of coffee in both hands. 'Maybe go for a bike ride, grab some lunch.'

Charlie looks up from his paper. 'Cass, I'm really sorry the way last night ended. Rich and I, we didn't mean to upset him. We had no idea he'd lost his best friend.'

'It's been hard for him.'

'I can imagine. Well, I can't . . . Oh God, you know what I mean. I'd like to call him, say I'm sorry.'

I give Charlie his number. 'We'll see you later,' I say. 'Come on, Ticket, off we go.'

When I'm outside the flat I breathe a sigh of relief. I take out my mobile and call Frankie. 'Are you around?' I ask her the moment she picks up. 'I need your advice.'

'This sounds serious. What about?'

'Charlie,' I say. 'I want to give Internet dating a go.'

'Like you said, Cass, you've got nothing to lose,' Frankie says later that morning, in a café on Putney High Street. 'Loads of people date online. It's no big deal. I'm sorry it didn't work out with Charlie but he isn't the only man on this planet.'

'You're right,' I say, determined not to hang around waiting for him any more. He's happy with Libby. Get over it.

Frankie and I discuss which dating sites I should try. Frankie says she met Tom through a site called the Perfect Pair. 'All you need to do is provide a profile picture and then you can either write something about yourself or a friend can. Why don't I?'

'Great. You could say I'm incredible, talented and beautiful and you can't think why no one has snapped me up yet.'

'Exactly! Tell you what? Why don't you come home with me and we can take a few pictures and sign you up today. Tom's working, so we've got the place to ourselves.'

'Today?'

'Yes. Before you lose your nerve.'

37

I'm sitting in a crowded brasserie, waiting for my date to show up. I examine the menu. I reach down to stroke Ticket. I thought I'd bring him to break the ice. I tap my fingers against the table. It's one date, Cass. No big deal. Besides, he seems a nice enough guy, and he has a sense of humour. He might need one when he meets Ticket and me.

Over the past few weeks I've been chatting online to Julian. I've discovered he works in the pharmaceutical industry. I told him I worked for a charity but would love to travel. He replied saying I sounded like a Miss World contestant. 'Not that I mind that,' he'd added, with a smiley face. I've never been sure about smiley faces, but replied, 'And I want world peace.' We began signing our messages with a kiss when 'kind regards' or 'all the best' sounded too formal.

We're meeting for brunch. Frankie had suggested this place as there are no steps, and it's always busy. 'You don't want somewhere half dead,' she'd said, making me think of my first date with Edward.

I pick up the menu again and decide to make my choice now, not dither when he arrives. Why am I so nervous?

Julian doesn't know I have a spinal cord injury.

When Frankie took photographs of me in a wheelchair I felt uncomfortable and convinced her that no one would see me; they'd only see my chair. I asked her to take a head and shoulders shot instead. I let down my hair and reapplied some make-up to highlight my brown eyes. I explained to a dubious Frankie that it might be a better tactic not to shout immediately, 'Look at me, I'm in a wheelchair!' but to meet my date first, let him see that I'm not anything scary. I'm a normal twenty-something girl who happens to be in a wheelchair, and maybe, just maybe, when he gets to know me, the wheelchair won't seem such a big deal. 'Trust me, Frankie,' I'd said. 'I know what I'm doing.'

I received many replies but I liked the look of Julian most. Tall, dark hair, blue eyes and good dress sense. I realise how much I, too, judge on looks and appearance, but then again, that's all we have to go on initially.

Maybe I should send a text to someone, to look busy?

Now I spot him. He walks straight past the table. Hurriedly I put away my mobile. 'Julian?' I call, heart in my mouth as he turns round. He looks at me and then over my shoulder. 'Julian?' I say again, smiling.

'Cass?' He approaches the table hesitantly.

I think he's about to kiss my cheek, but then he shakes my hand, feebly.

'I grabbed a table. It was getting busy.'

He sits down next to me, glances at my wheelchair, looks back at me with an awkward smile, and then, to cap his confusion, Ticket emerges from underneath the table.

'Oh. This is Ticket.'

'Right.' He strokes him, eyes fixed on his purple coat.

Tell him now. Get it over and done with. I explain briefly that I have spinal cord injury and he's my assistant dog. 'Anyway,' I continue, telling myself to act normal, and not to be paranoid about the disappointed look in his eye. I grab the menu. 'I don't know about you, but I'm starving.' I couldn't eat a thing.

When a waitress comes to our table I ask for the first thing on the menu, eggs Benedict. Julian asks for a coffee.

'You're not having anything to eat?' I ask, telling myself again not to be paranoid that he wants to leave as quickly as possible. He orders a croissant.

When our food arrives, he eats his croissant quietly, avoiding eye contact.

'How's work?' I ask. How's work? God, I'm boring.

'Good.' He wipes crumbs away from the corner of his mouth and looks around the restaurant as if waiting for someone else to join him.

'Did you go to that music gig the other weekend?'

He narrows his eyes, as if he can't remember, when it was all he could talk about over email last week.

'Kasabian, wasn't it?' I continue.

'Oh yeah, it was cool.'

'I went to Glastonbury a couple of years ago.' It makes me think of Sean. 'Have you been?' Oh, Cass, you sound as if you're interviewing him.

'Yeah. A few times.'

I wait for him to ask me a question. I wait for some time.

'You didn't tell me you were in a wheelchair,' he says, finally, fidgeting with his watchstrap.

I'm about to explain, but then catch him eying up the waitress. 'Shall we get the bill?'

Once the date, if you could call it that, is over and done with, I call Guy on his mobile. It goes straight to his voicemail. I decide to call his parents'. His mother picks up the telephone.

'Is that Cass?'

'Hi, Angie. How are you?'

'Not too bad, thanks.' She sounds tired. 'Guy's not here, my love. I've just put him on a train to see Philip.'

Philip is one of Guy's oldest school friends. He lives in Norfolk.

'I wasn't sure he was up to going really, but then again he's been so down in the dumps what with all the hospital appointments and missing so much of college, so maybe Philip can cheer him up. I'll tell him you rang. How are you, my love?'

I put the phone down feeling selfish that I wanted to see

him to make my day better, but I miss him too and hate the idea that he's suffering. At least he's with a good friend and not alone. I call Jamie in Madrid. He doesn't answer. Suddenly I don't feel like talking to anyone. I switch off my mobile and ask Ticket where we should go. I don't feel like heading back to the flat yet.

I park my car on one of the side streets off High Street Kensington, telling myself that there are lots of things I can do on a Sunday on my own. I can window shop, grab a late lunch, read the weekend papers, take Ticket for a walk in Hyde Park later this afternoon, before it gets too dark.

I make my way down the High Street, adorned with Christmas lights and decorations, and notice a sign in the window of a bookshop that says Benjamin Gooding is giving a reading at one thirty this afternoon. I look at my watch and see that I'm just in time. I remember Jamie telling me how much he liked this crime writer. I decide to go in and see if I can buy him a signed copy. There are lots of shoppers browsing and many heading upstairs.

'Excuse me?' I say to a tall woman with tight blonde curls standing behind the till.

'Are you here for Benjamin Gooding?' she asks.

'Yes.'

'It's on the second floor.'

'Great. Is there a lift?'

She looks at me now. 'No, sorry. Can you walk at all?'

I shake my head and stare at the stairs.

'I'm afraid it's not wheelchair accessible. If only you'd called in advance.'

Ticket and I go to Hyde Park. I park my car in our usual spot, close to the Albert Memorial.

It's a cold winter's day and everyone is wrapped up warmly in coats, hats and scarves. As we walk past the Serpentine Gallery, my mind wanders to Charlie. We often come here together on a Sunday afternoon, when Libby has returned to her flat. Charlie laughs at me when I pick up Ticket's poop. 'It's the lowest form of human activity, Cass,' he once said.

'Not if it's your dog it isn't.'

'Well, according to Seinfield, if aliens were looking down on us they'd think that dogs were the leaders on this planet. If you saw two life forms, one making poop, the other scurrying behind with its pooper scooper picking it up after them, who would you assume was in charge?'

I watch a man in front of me turn to his girlfriend, take her by the arm and pull her towards him. She laughs in the warmth of his embrace. It's Sunday, they have all the time in the world.

'I'm never going to have sex again,' Guy had said over supper one night on our ward. 'Apparently Mum has got the living room all ready for me, put in a downstairs loo and all that. Fuck, no chance of a one-night stand then.' He'd laughed dryly. 'Sorry, Princess.'

'Stop saying sorry. I'm twenty-fucking-three, Guy.'

Guy reassessed me with a raise of an eyebrow. 'Well, anyway, imagine me bringing a girl home with Mum's fancy trinkets and bowls of pot-pourri, the grandfather clock chiming every hour, Mum bustling in with bangers and mash on a tray. Won't be able to have sex normally again anyway, as the doc so kindly pointed out, so I guess it doesn't matter.' But every part of the tremble in his voice shouted that it did, almost as much as not being able to walk again.

'Why is some girl going to pick us over able-bodied men?' Guy went on.

'I bet some women think it's a turn-on,' Dom said.

'Oh, please, Perky, give me a break.'

'Miranda's still with me.' Miranda came to the hospital without fail every evening, straight after work, bringing a basket of fruit into the ward. She'd tried to get Guy to eat a mango but he refused.

'Ah, now Miranda's different. You knew her before. Also you can tell she's not the kind of woman who goes for looks or money.'

'Are you saying I'm ugly? And poor?'

As Guy and Dom went on arguing, I talked over them. 'Do you know what Sean used to say?'

Dom and Guy stopped.

'What?' Guy asked.

'He always said he was a "legs man".'

We all looked at one another, before laughing.

＊　　＊　　＊

That evening I'm in bed, reading, when Charlie knocks on the door and opens it a crack. 'Hey. Can I come in?' I haven't seen Charlie since breakfast, when he and Libby had asked me if Edward and I would like to go to the movies with them. Since they still believe I'm dating Edward, I couldn't tell them about my Internet date so had pretended I was seeing Guy.

He sits down on the edge of the bed. 'Thanks for my copy of the *Big Issue*,' he says.

On my way home I'd picked up some eggs from Sainsbury's for supper, and told *Big Issue* man about my lousy date and how worried I was about Guy. 'I'm taking my girls to church tonight,' he said. 'I'll say a few prayers to the good lord for your friend.'

'Guy called this afternoon,' Charlie says.

I swallow hard. 'Did he?' I had seen a missed call from him earlier this evening, when I'd switched on my mobile again. I sent him a text, promising to call tomorrow.

'He sent you his love. He said he'd tried you on your mobile? He was all right and that you must stop worrying about him.'

'Good.' I'm unable to meet his eye.

'He called from a train. He said he was on his way to Norfolk?'

'Um.'

Charlie looks confused. 'Cass? What's wrong?'

'Nothing,' I say on the verge of tears.

'I feel like we haven't spoken for a while. I know it's been a bit weird between us . . . Cass, why did you pretend you were seeing Guy today?'

I put my book down.

Charlie makes himself more comfortable.

'I went on a date.'

'A date? But . . .'

'I'm not with Edward.'

'Oh.'

I pray he won't ask me to explain.

'I'm sorry, Cass.' Charlie senses there's something more going on.

'It's fine, we're still friends, good friends.'

'I'm sorry,' he repeats. 'So how was the date?'

'Oh, Charlie, it was a disaster. He couldn't get out of the restaurant quick enough. Who cares?' I say unconvincingly. 'I'm much more worried about Guy.'

'He sounded fine, Cass, as if he was looking forward to the break.'

I nod, relieved that I've confessed about Edward and that Charlie's being tactful not to question me. 'How was your day?'

'I had to work in the end,' he says. 'Libby wasn't too impressed but I've got a big client meeting tomorrow, in Ascot. I'm pitching for this new phone company.' He pauses. 'Are you sure you're OK?'

'I'm fine,' I lie.

'Try not to worry about Guy,' he says, kissing me goodnight.

I turn off the light and shut my eyes, but my mind is determined not to go to sleep. In the darkness I am taken back to the time when Charlie was helping me on to the ski lift. I hear us laughing on the slopes, Charlie telling me to slow down, both of us collapsing in a heap at the bottom of the mountain. I remember us dancing that night. Letting go of all my inhibitions. Then my mind races to Guy, Dom and me in hospital, Guy eating his baked beans clumsily with a spoon. I see Guy's face, his eyes searching for hope. Then I switch to Edward and me, remembering us holding on to one another that night. I picture Libby the first time she'd walked into the kitchen with Charlie. I recall the physical pain of watching them kiss in the garden. I think of *Big Issue* man saying his prayers tonight. I imagine him camping on the floor to make sure his girls sleep well. Who is saying a prayer for their dad?

'Ticket,' I call out in the dark. I ask him if he'd like to sleep on my bed, a one-off treat. 'You're very lucky you know, I only allow Johnny Depp in my bed,' I say as he jumps up and snuggles beside me. 'Oh, Ticket, what would I do without you?'

I'm relieved Christmas is approaching. I want to see Mum and Dad. I miss Jamie.

I need to go home.

38

Three months later

Spring is approaching and life is good. After six months, I still love my job at Back Up and am planning to go on their multi-activity course this summer. I'm making good friends in the office, especially with Simon who teaches wheelchair skills. Charlotte and I are also becoming close. The thing I enjoy most, however, is not being the new girl any more.

Ticket is three years old and just as handsome as ever in his purple coat. He has become the mascot at Back Up, featuring as a team player on their website. Jamie is home from Madrid and living in Shepherd's Bush. Charlie and Libby appear happy, but that's OK. I'm over him. I'm single and giving Internet dating a rest. Sarah and I have lost touch. I'm sad and I do miss her, but perhaps it was inevitable when we lead such different lives now. Dom is the same old Dom. Even Guy has been on much better form too. I think that's partly due to seeing Philip more this year. Philip and Guy worked together in the City. It seems they did virtually everything together until Philip married and moved out of London. 'I gave him such grief when he became the family man with the Volvo estate and moved to the middle of nowhere,' Guy had said.

It's Sunday and I'm having breakfast with Charlie. I tell him I'm meeting Dom and Guy for a pub lunch in Chiswick.

'Where are you meeting?' Charlie asks, putting another slice of bread into the toaster.

'The Greyhound. But Guy's coming here first. I wanted to go to this other pub in Notting Hill but when I spoke to whoever it was behind the bar, to see if the downstairs loo was accessible, he had to go and measure the width of the door.'

'Useless.'

'I know! It was too narrow. He said he'd never had anyone in a wheelchair come into his pub before, he made us sound like reptiles or something. I wanted to say to him, "So where do you think the likes of us hang out? At home, hidden away under stones? Do we only slither out on special occasions?"'

Charlie laughs, shaking his head. 'Do you want to come along?' I ask him, hoping in a way he'll say no. The truth is I prefer seeing Dom and Guy on my own. I haven't met many of their friends either and Miranda rarely joins us. We like it being just the three of us. We call ourselves the Three Musketeers.

'I can't,' Charlie replies. 'But thanks anyway.'

'Are you seeing Libby?'

'She's visiting her mum. I actually feel like a day out with my camera. Might go for a walk down the South Bank, watch the boats.'

I smile. 'Right, well, I'll see you later. Better get ready.' The phone rings and it's right in front of me so I take it.

'Hello, Cass, it's Mary.'

'Hello, Mrs Bell, er . . . Mary. How are you?'

'Very well, thank you. Is Charlie there?'

My heart lifts when I open the front door. 'Come in, come in,' I say. Ticket bounds up to Guy, wagging his tail. 'I really think you should get a dog.'

'I can't.'

'But you're so good with them and . . .' I shut up when I see his face warning me to stop.

'There's not enough space at Mum and Dad's,' he says more gently now. 'But if I was going to get one, it would be just . . . like . . . you,' he tells Ticket.

We overhear Charlie talking to his mother on the telephone about his thirtieth birthday party next month, in April, which he's hosting at his parents' home. The conversation appears to be heated. Guy and I exchange glances.

Charlie hangs up and joins us, looking tense. 'Your mum giving you grief?' Guy asks.

'All the time.'

'This freak,' he gestures to himself, 'still lives with his.'

'She was going on and on about meeting Libby at my party and I was telling her not to make such a big deal of it. Mum will scare her away.'

'Selective hearing is the way to go, mate.'

'Shall we go?' I ask Guy.

'I'm ready.'

I indicate left into the car park. It's unusually crowded because parking is free on a Sunday. A couple of cars are hovering, waiting for someone to leave. We drive towards the disabled bay, where there are three allocated parking spaces. From a distance we can see one is free. 'Get your tits out,' Guy commands, referring to my blue disabled discs.

'If you've got 'em, flaunt 'em,' I say back.

'Yeah, pop 'em out. Let's see them in their full glory on your windscreen.'

We both laugh. No one makes me laugh the way Guy does, not even Charlie.

We're about to park in our disabled bay when a woman in a silver Mercedes, coming from the opposite direction, zips in before us.

'Wind the window down!' says Guy. 'Beep the horn! Hey!'

She ignores us and before we have time to explain, she's rushing out of the car park, towards the shops.

'Bloody hell!' says Guy, furious. 'Parking is the only fucking advantage of this life-sentence!'

'Bollocks,' I say. 'What shall we do?'

'Let's stay right here. Block her in when she gets back.'

I turn to Guy, liking this plan. 'Ticket, settle down. It's OK.' He lies down again.

We turn the radio on. Guy wants a cigarette. I light it for him and he inhales deeply. 'It's good to see you, Cass.'

'You too.' His skin is clearer, accentuating the colour of his blue eyes.

He reaches for my hand. 'You're a great girl.'

I grin. 'Guy? Are you feeling all right?'

'You are, OK? I shall only say it once.'

'Well, you're a top man. You're looking very handsome today too.'

'I think you should go back to your medicine.'

'What?'

'I reckon you'd make a great doctor. You care about things, about people.'

'I don't know, Guy.'

'I can't go back to the City, but you could be a doctor.' He smiles. 'You'd look cute in your white coat and stethoscope.' He stares out of the window, before he turns to me again with that wry smile. 'I wish we'd met in different circumstances. I would have chatted you up, you know.'

'What would your chat-up line have been?'

'I don't do chat-up lines as such. I would have just been

my charming self. What's going on with you and Charlie, by the way?'

'Nothing's going on.'

'What's with the big sigh then?'

'If I do get together with someone, it won't be Charlie. It's . . . complicated.'

'Why?'

'He has a serious girlfriend for starters.'

Guy brushes that off. 'He didn't seem that keen.'

'That's just Charlie. He's laidback and hates commitment.'

'Don't we all.'

I look at him. 'How about you, Guy? Would you like to meet someone?'

'No chance of that.'

'Why not?'

'I feel sad, Cass, because I've never had a fulfilling relationship like Dom has with Miranda. I took it for granted that I had plenty of time to marry, settle down, have kids, wash the car on a Sunday.'

'You still could. Is it difficult meeting someone when you live with your parents?'

'No, they're great, God, really great. I love them. They've done so much for me.' He bites his lip. 'It's me. I'm not a proper man any more.'

'Don't say that, Guy. You're funny, good looking, clever, you make me laugh.' I run a hand through his dark hair.

'That's nice,' he murmurs. 'Don't stop.' He shuts his eyes while I continue to stroke his hair. Then I touch the side of his face. 'You know, Guy, I haven't been with anyone either, not since the accident. It terrifies me.' I pause. 'Any girl would be lucky to have you. I wish you'd believe that. I wish you could see what I see.'

'Princess, will you hold me?'

'Guy? Are you all right?'

'I just need a hug.' He stubs out his cigarette before I put my arms around him. I can hear him breathing in the smell of my hair. 'Along with Philip, you and Perky are my best mates,' he says. 'I love you, Cass, you know that, don't you?'

I'm about to say I love him too when I see the woman with the Mercedes. 'She's back!' She's carrying two bulging shopping bags. 'Excuse me,' she says without even looking at us, 'can you move?' She digs into her handbag to find her car keys. She whacks her shopping bags into the boot, sits down in the front seat and turns on the engine. She waits. She winds down her window when she sees me winding down mine.

'Hi,' I say. 'Did you know you're parked in a disabled bay?'

She seems confused. 'I was quick. Everyone does it.'

'Why?'

She looks at both Guy and me, unsure why we're making such a fuss, until she sees Ticket wedged between our wheelchairs on the back seat. 'There weren't any other spaces. I was quick,' she repeats.

'You shouldn't park in a disabled space,' I tell her, 'not when—'

'Fine!' she snaps. 'If you could move out of my way, I'll let you in.' She revs the engine. 'I was only nipping to the shop, OK?'

'She was only nipping to the shop, Cass,' Guy repeats, leaning towards my window. 'Well, aren't you lucky you *can* nip. Listen, we're not trying to preach, but come on, think about it. We don't want to park here. We *have* to. We need the wide space for our chairs. We can't walk. You can.'

She adjusts the front mirror. 'I'm sorry,' she says finally, unable to look us in the eye.

Dom, Guy and I sit at the corner table by the window. Guy is ordering another round of drinks. 'Steady on,' Dom says, 'I haven't finished this one yet.'

'Drink up, Perky.'

'So, what have you been up to, Guy?' Dom asks. 'I haven't seen you for ages. You've been screening your calls.'

'Well, I've been very busy, you know.'

Dom sings the lyrics to Vaughn Monroe's song 'Busy Doing Nothing'.

I laugh.

'Fuck off,' Guy says. 'I've been busy with my history course, dictating essays and reading about the Tudor Court.'

I take up my half pint of beer. 'Why are you looking so happy, Dom?' I ask, as if it's a crime.

'Well, I've got some good news. Miranda's having a baby. I'm having a baby!'

'Oh, Dom! I'm so happy for you! A mini Perky!'

'Congratulations, mate,' adds Guy. 'Not about the baby though. You've had sex.'

Dom rolls his eyes.

'I'm joking! You are going to be a *great* dad. He's one lucky kid.'

Dom smiles like a bashful schoolboy. When Guy compliments you, you do feel like the clouds have parted and the sun is shining down on you.

'If it weren't for you I wouldn't have got through hospital,' Guy goes on. 'I wouldn't know you, Cass, and without people like you and Dommie boy here, the world would be a cheerless place.'

Dom looks surprised by such a display of affection.

'I'd like you to be godfather,' Dom says before explaining to me, 'Cass, Miranda has asked her best friend from school but if we have another child, I promise we'll ask you.'

'Oh, Dom, you don't have to explain.' But I'm glad he has.

'Just say yes, Guy,' implores Dom. 'It would be an honour.'

He smiles, tears in his eyes. 'That means the world to me.' He looks at both of us. 'Perhaps I'm not so useless after all.'

* * *

'Where shall we go?' Guy asks after lunch. 'Let's go some-where we've never been before.'

'I haven't been to a lot of places,' I say. 'How about Madame Tussaud's?'

'No,' Guy replies. 'Who wants to see a bunch of fake celebrities? Don't even want to see the real ones. Let's go somewhere special. I've never been to the Tower of London?'

'Nor have I,' Dom says. 'Pathetic when I live in London.'

'Me neither.'

Guy clears his throat. 'Just think, it was the last sight that those executed saw on this earth.'

'Talk about morbid.'

'No it's not, Cass,' says Guy. 'It's where Anne Boleyn was imprisoned and executed, where the Crown Jewels were stolen. Thomas Wentworth, Earl of Strafford, was executed there, betrayed brutally by Charles I. It's fascinating history. Imagine how haunted it must be, all those lost sad spirits wandering the grounds.'

'Great,' I say, easily convinced.

'Access won't be great,' Dom warns.

Guy looks at his watch. 'Let's go anyway, give the staff a challenge. And remember,' he smiles, turning to both Dom and me, 'we are the Three Musketeers.'

39

I'm at work the following morning when I get the call. The moment I hear Dom's voice I know something is terribly wrong.

'It's Guy,' he says. 'His mum . . . she called.'

'Dom, what is it?'

I'm scared by his silence.

'What did she say, Dom?'

'He's dead.'

'What?' I place a hand over my mouth.

Dom is crying now.

'He can't be!' I exclaim, fighting back the tears. 'We only saw him yesterday. He was fine.'

'He . . . he . . . It was a train.' Dom chokes out the words. 'He threw . . . Oh, Cass, he threw himself—'

'Stop!' I say. The office turns silent.

'Do you want a lift home?' I'd asked Guy yesterday.

'No, thanks. I'll jump in a cab.'

'He was on really good form,' Dom had said as we watched

him wave goodbye from the window of the black taxi. 'I think he's turned a corner, don't you?'

I push my chair away from the desk, the phone cord stretched to its limit.

I'm going to be sick. This can't be happening.

'Why didn't he say anything?' says Dom, his voice breaking. 'I could have . . . we could have helped him.'

'Promise me you'll go back to medicine,' Guy had said to me again, later in the afternoon.

'I love you, Cass, you know that, don't you?'

I burst into tears. 'No,' I say, trembling, 'not this time. He was saying goodbye to us.'

Ticket and I leave work early and go home. I call Mum. 'What a surprise, darling.'

'Mum . . .'

'What's wrong? Oh God, what's happened?'

When I tell her, three hours later she is with me in Charlie's flat.

Charlie arrives home that evening with Libby. I hear them talking in the hallway. 'Why don't we see a film tonight?' she suggests.

'I'm pretty whacked,' he says.

Charlie walks into the kitchen and looks surprised when he sees my mother there, popping a shepherd's pie in the oven. He glances from her to me, cautiously kisses Mum on the cheek. 'Is everything OK?'

'Charlie,' she says solemnly.

I'm staring at the kitchen table. 'What's wrong?' he asks. 'Cass? What's happened?'

'It's Guy,' my mother says quietly.

'Guy?'

'He killed himself. Cass found out this afternoon.'

'Oh my God,' he says.

'I'm so sorry,' Libby adds, standing at the door.

Charlie takes her outside into the hallway. 'But she has her mum,' she whispers. 'Let's go. They need their space.'

Minutes later I hear the front door shut but then he's back. He pulls up a chair and sits next to me. 'I'd like to stay, if that's all right? But I can go if you'd prefer.'

'No,' I say, looking up at him. My eyes are puffy and red from crying. 'I'd like you to stay.'

He moves his chair closer to mine. 'Come here,' he says, reaching out an arm.

I rest my head against his shoulder. He strokes my hair.

Mum lays one more knife and fork at the table.

40

Mum, Dad, Jamie, Charlie and I make our way to the front of the church, the sound of the organ filling in the solemn silence. Charlie lifts me out of my chair and helps me to sit between my parents, before taking the wheelchair to the side of the pew. When he comes back he sits next to Jamie. Edward is also here today. 'I want to come, for you, Cass,' he'd said touchingly. Frankie was sad to be away. She's working in India.

I clutch the service sheet, still unable to comprehend that it's for my friend. There is a picture of Guy on the front with his name inscribed underneath: Guy Daniel Pearson. I stare at the image in front of me; it's a face I hardly recognise. His cheeks are fuller and he smiles confidently. However, it's the eyes I am drawn to; they are full of life and hope. His parents are two rows in front of us. His mother, Angie, is wearing a cream jacket with a pale green silk scarf. I want to hug her and tell her how sorry I am. Shortly after Guy had killed himself, his mum told

Dom and me that Guy had written to them. When they'd returned from their Sunday lunch, expecting to find Guy at home, instead they found a letter addressed to them on the kitchen table. He'd left instructions that he wanted no one to wear black at his funeral. He'd also thanked them from the bottom of his heart and asked for their forgiveness. Dom and I realise now why he'd been on such good form. For the first time since the accident he felt in control.

The church is becoming crowded and chairs are now being placed at the end of pews and in the side aisles. I turn to see if I recognise any of the faces but then realise that I'd never met any of Guy's other friends. There's a group of young men standing at the back. I wonder if any of them are the ones from the City who didn't know what to say when he had spilt his espresso in the café.

I see Dom and Miranda arriving and Charlie beckons them over as I'd asked him to save them both a seat. Mum clutches my hand; her skin feels cold.

'Dom,' I say when finally he reaches us, my heart lifting, 'Paul's here.' I gesture to the back of the church. To my surprise, Georgina, our ward nurse, is there with him.

I try desperately to hold it together when the coffin is carried in, knowing that it's Guy lying inside. How can I have spent the day with him only five days ago and yet now be here, saying goodbye, for ever? I stare at the coffin again. Its hard surface is covered with a wreath of white lilies.

The congregation stands to sing the first hymn, 'Dear Lord and Father of mankind, forgive our foolish ways'. Dom and I, alone, remain seated.

After the first reading we'll hear Philip's address. Guy used to talk a lot about his close friend because so much of his childhood and memories included him. He even kept an old passport photograph of the two of them in his wallet, taken when they were teenagers fooling around. They had been inseparable until Philip had married. He is sitting with his wife Lisa and their two young boys. I remember Guy telling me how much he liked Lisa even if she had dragged his best friend off to the country to start a family.

Philip walks to the front. He's solid in build, tall with dark hair, ruggedly handsome like Guy. Guy used to say they were often taken for brothers. He holds his notes and as we wait for him to begin he looks around the church, as if giving himself time to prepare.

'I will never forget what my father said to me just before he died,' he starts. 'That it's not about the length of time you live in this world; it's the quality of the time that counts. We are here today to celebrate Guy's life and there is so much to be thankful for. I have 'een lucky enough to know Guy since the age of five. Th first thing he said to me was that he was going to be a pilot and fly across the whole world. He also told me he was going to marry a belly dancer.' He smiles, as if he can see Guy in front of him now. 'We went to school and college together; we even decided to go into the same career. Guy loved working in the City and climbed the ladder rapidly because he was ambitious. He had this great energy for life. He only had to walk into a room and the mood instantly changed. Guy was never boring. He commanded a room, filling it with warmth, fun and humour.'

Philip turns his notes over before he continues, more strongly, 'Guy excelled in everything but was never arrogant or boastful. He rarely sang his own praises. He loved sport: cricket, tennis, football, rugby, skiing. He was good at them all and completely fearless. I had to pretend I wasn't scared of the black runs or the bungee jumping. I envied his daring spirit. He'd think nothing of approaching the prettiest girl in the room to ask her on a date. He used to tell me I was far too cautious. "Life's too short," was his motto.' He stops, drawing breath. 'Well, Guy's life was far too short. This injury was one of the cruellest things that could have happened to him.'

I press one hand into another, anxious about what he is going to say next. Will he bless the fact that Guy no longer has to endure a life in a wheelchair?

'He told me that the only good thing to come out of his accident was that he'd met two of his closest friends, Cass and Dom.' I look up and catch Philip's eye. 'He talked about you a lot,' he says, looking straight at me, and then to Dom. 'He loved you both. You managed to restore so much of the old Guy, but in the end a light went out in his eyes. He could no longer fight.'

Philip discards his notes. 'Guy was one of the most important people in my life; he was the brother I'd never had; the friend who carried me when I was tired. I wish I could have helped him more. He would be amazed to see so many friends here today. You see, he had no idea of his worth.' Philip looks at Guy's parents. 'He loved you so much for still believing in him as your son. He was grateful for your support. He thought he'd let you down.' Guy's mother shakes her head.

'He called himself a cripple,' he says passionately. '"I'm nothing more than a useless, washed-up cripple." But . . . but . . . we . . .' – Philip's voice breaks – 'we are not saying goodbye to a cripple today. I am saying goodbye to my closest, most loyal friend. I'll miss him. I'm sorry,' he says. He clears his throat and from some place deep within he regains strength to say, finally, 'I am going to run the marathon next year to raise money for Spinal Cord Injury, in memory of him.'

Philip returns to his seat. 'What's wrong, Papa?' asks one of his children.

Mum clutches my hand again. I look across to Charlie, tears in his eyes.

41

Alone in my bedroom, I listen to the ringing tone. My heart is beating fast. I haven't spoken to Sarah for months. I think of us back at King's. We were inseparable during our first year. Some of my best memories were Sarah and I gently mulling over tea together in the campus café between lectures or drinking cheap wine post lectures in the campus bar. Maybe she'll screen the call? Perhaps it's too late for us to pick up the pieces.

'Cass,' she says awkwardly. 'How are you?'

'Fine,' I say without thinking. 'Actually, I'm not fine. I'm not good.'

'Oh. Right.'

I glance at the framed photograph of Guy on my bedside table. 'I'm sorry I haven't been in touch.'

'I've tried to call you, many times.'

'I know.' I'm on the verge of tears.

'Cass, what's wrong?' she asks, sounding more like the Sarah I used to know.

'Are you free?'

'Now?'

'It's important.'

Sarah meets me in the patisserie café close to Barons Court tube station. She's wearing a beige cap, jeans and a baggy jumper. Her thick brown hair is much shorter than when I'd seen her last, cut into a bob.

She kisses me on both sides of the cheek before sitting down next to me.

We order some tea. Neither one of us wants anything to eat.

'I was surprised you called,' she says, stirring sugar into her tea. 'What's happened?'

'Last week, a friend of mine, he . . . He committed suicide.'

She stops stirring. 'I'm so sorry. Who was it?'

'Guy.'

'The friend you made in hospital?'

'Yes.'

'How?'

'He threw himself in front of a train.'

'Oh, Cass, I don't know what to say.'

'That's been our trouble, hasn't it? Not knowing what to say.'

Both of us are quiet.

Sarah inhales deeply. 'With you and me, I didn't know

how to deal with it, I felt so guilty that here I was, carrying on at King's and—'

'It's not your fault,' I interrupt. 'It's mine.'

'No it's not.'

'It's nobody's fault,' I suggest.

Sarah nods tearfully.

'Life's too short,' I say, thinking of Guy. 'I miss you.'

'Me too.'

Sarah and I remain in the café until closing hours, downloading our lives since we last met. I tell her about Guy and our time in hospital together. I tell her about our final lunch. We cry together, for Guy and for our broken friendship. Sarah smiles when I recall Guy's plan in the car park, blocking in the woman with the Mercedes. I fill her in about my job at Back Up. I also mention Charlie's support. 'I couldn't have got through this last week without him.'

'He sounds lovely,' she says. 'You seem close.'

I tell her he's going out with Libby. 'Which is fine.'

Sarah looks at me with affection. 'You're in love with him, aren't you?'

I stop pretending. Sarah knows me too well. We talk about Charlie. It's a relief to admit to myself once more that my feelings haven't gone away. If anything, they have deepened since Guy's death.

Sarah has a boyfriend called Matt. He's a doctor. 'He's a science nerd, just like me. He has ginger hair too,' she whispers.

I smile. 'I can't wait to meet him.'

'You will. Soon.' She stops, thinks. 'Actually, Cass, what are you doing tonight?'

'Tonight?'

'Matt's having a house-warming party.' She must register my hesitancy, as she goes on to say, 'Don't worry if it's too soon after Guy, I'd completely understand.'

'What floor is it on?'

'Second, but I'm sure Matt could lift you. He knows about you,' she says warmly. 'You wouldn't have to explain.'

'I don't know.'

'Listen, I'll go home but if you suddenly feel like coming out, call me.'

'It would be nice to meet him,' I say, warming up to the idea of a few drinks.

'After everything that's happened recently, maybe a night out is exactly what you need.'

When I return home I find Charlie in the sitting room, reading the papers. I tell him about Sarah, and how well our afternoon went. 'I'm going out with her tonight.'

'That's great,' he says.

'I'm going to a party.'

'A party?'

'Don't look so worried.'

'I'm not. So whose party is it?'

I explain it's Sarah's new boyfriend. 'It's good to meet new people,' I tell myself as much as Charlie. 'It'll be fun. How about you?'

'I'm staying in.'

'You're not seeing Libby?'

'No. Cass . . .'

'Right, well, I'd better get ready. Need to call Sarah.'

'Cass?'

I turn.

'Don't go,' he says.

'What?'

'Why don't we rent a film and order some takeaway? Just chat, you know?'

'I think I need a night out.'

Charlie runs a hand through his hair. 'But you look knackered. Are you sure you want to go to some party—'

'Charlie, leave it.'

'You won't know anyone and—'

'I'll know Sarah.'

'Guy's funeral was only a couple of days ago, and—'

'I don't need this right now! I'm allowed a night off, OK! I can't sleep, can't eat, I'm having nightmares, I can't think straight—'

'That's why—'

'I need to go out and forget about him, for one fucking night!'

Ticket barks.

'Keep quiet!' Charlie shouts at him, finally losing his cool. 'I am trying to help Cass! You and me, Ticket, we're on the same side, buddy!'

Ticket hangs his head, slopes off to his basket by the fireplace.

'Ticket, I'm sorry, sweetheart, everything's just fine,' I say, before turning back to Charlie. 'Can I leave Ticket here? With you?'

'Fine. Have a good time.'

'Thanks.' I'm about to say, 'I won't be late,' but decide against it.

42

The taxi pulls up outside a block of flats. Sarah clambers out first and we wait while the ramp is installed. She takes out her mobile, texts Matt. 'He'll be down in a minute,' she reassures me.

'Will you know anyone here?' I ask her, anxiously looking up to the second-floor window, where music is playing.

'A few. Don't worry, it's really casual.'

A tall, attractive man with freckles and ginger hair, wearing jeans and a blue-checked shirt, approaches us, a skip in his stride. 'You must be Cass,' he says. 'Great to meet you! Right.' He flexes his muscles, reminding me of Charlie. 'Are you ready for a fireman's lift?'

I see a room full of strange faces. A man steps over my footrest to lean over and give Sarah a kiss. All I can see is his flies.

'Cass, this is Duncan,' Sarah says. 'Matt's brother.'

He looks down at me briefly, smiles, before asking Sarah if she's going to his gig next Saturday night.

'Duncan's in a band,' she fills me in.

'Oh, great,' I reply, raising my voice to be heard above the music. 'What kind of stuff do you play?'

'You're kind of rock, aren't you?' Sarah answers for him.

'Yep. How about a drink?' he asks her, before saying he has a couple of spare tickets going if she wants them. They're playing at the Andover Arms.

Sarah crouches down. 'What do you want, Cass?'

'Anything, thanks. White wine? So, this band,' I say to Duncan, determined not to feel invisible. 'What are you called?'

'Hang on one sec,' he says, touching my shoulder. 'Paul!'

That's the end of that then, I think, watching Duncan disappear. Sarah weaves her way through the crowd, towards Matt and the booze in the kitchen.

It's so crowded I can't move.

Five minutes later.

I need a drink.

Badly.

Come on, Sarah. How long does it take to pour a glass of wine? I try to edge forward in my chair but I'm stuck, sandwiched between groups of strangers. Someone is approaching me. I think he's about to say hello. I smile, open my mouth to introduce myself . . . but then he shoves my chair out of the way to give the girl behind me a kiss, treating me to another view of flies.

Finally Sarah returns with a glass of wine. I gulp it down, praying for escape. She introduces me to a scriptwriter and his French wife, who tells me about her counselling course. I like them, but the bad news is they have to leave early because they're driving back to Newbury tonight, to get back to their babysitter and two-year-old. When they leave, I make my way to the food table and help myself to a couple of mini cheeseburgers.

The buzzer rings. It sounds like a herd of elephants is coming up the stairs, before more people enter the room with bottles of wine and cans of beer. The place begins to smell of smoke and joints. A further low point occurs when I'm mistaken for an ashtray and cigarette ash is flicked into my hair. Then someone knocks into my chair and sends my mini cheeseburger flying, but not before tomato ketchup has stained my jeans. I shut my eyes, wishing I could rewind to earlier this evening. I could be sitting on the sofa with Ticket and Charlie, enjoying a Thai takeaway and watching a movie. I'm surrounded by people and yet I have never felt so alone.

As I wait outside the bathroom, I work out how to make my getaway. This is when I hate being in a wheelchair with a passion. There's no such thing as slipping away. I'll have to talk to Sarah, wherever she is now, get Matt to lift me . . . call a cab . . .

The buzzer rings again.

'About time,' says a woman in a black dress answering the intercom. She heads towards the front door. I hear someone coming up the stairs.

'Sorry, bad traffic,' he calls to her.

He walks into the room, stops when he sees me. My past is standing in front of me, staring.

Alone, in the bathroom, I rock back and forth, all those memories I'd buried, returning.

'I have a very woolly head.'

'Well, Miss Brooks, I happen to know a great cure for woolly heads. Sex.'

'Sex?'

'Yep, sex.' Sean strokes his chin and adopts a serious expression. 'And plenty of it. In fact, I'm going to write you out a prescription right now.'

Feeling sick, I pour myself a glass of tap water. 'How do you know her?' I'd overheard the girlfriend asking Sean.

'How about a big fat bacon butty?' I wave a hand in front of him.

'I love you, Cass.'

I rummage in my handbag to find my mobile. I call him. The line's engaged.

'Cass!' I hear Sean shout.

I turn round, look up to our flat on the third floor and see a

bare-chested Sean leaning out of the window, waving my wallet.
I'm such an idiot.

'Chuck it down!'

'We need sugar too. And fags.'

'Fine. Throw.'

He hesitates. 'I'll come down.'

'Don't. Get on with your packing! Just throw it!'

Sean hurls my wallet towards me. I jump to catch it. It hits the
side of my hand and flies over my shoulder and on to the road.

Without thinking I run towards it. I hear him shouting.

A car horn blasting.

I stab at the numbers again, tears running down my cheeks.

'What's wrong?' Charlie says immediately.

'Can . . . you . . . come . . .'

'Cass? I can't hear you properly. Where are you?'

I stare at the lock. I can't go back out there. I wrap my arms
around myself for protection. Someone knocks on the door.
'Who's in there?' she calls. 'You've been ages!'

I hear more voices, a crowd gathering outside the bathroom. 'Cass!' I hear Sarah calling. 'Cass! It's me.'

'What's going on? Who is she, Sean?' I hear the girlfriend
ask again. 'Why won't you tell me?'

'She's an old girlfriend, that's all. Come on, let's go.'

Finally I open the door. Sarah rushes forward, says she's
been looking for me everywhere. 'I had no idea he'd be
here,' she says. 'Don't worry, he's going.'

'Wait!' I call after him. Sean and his girlfriend turn round.
'I'm Cass.'

His girlfriend looks blank.

'He probably hasn't told you about me,' I say to her.

'Cass,' Sean warns me. 'Don't. This is between us.'

'We went out together at King's, but then this happened,'
I tell her, gesturing to my wheelchair. 'Sean visited me once
in hospital, then he left a letter by my bedside, ending it.'

'Cass, please. I've grown up a lot since then.'

'Congratulations,' says Sarah.

'Please, can we talk?' Sean asks. 'Alone.'

He locks the bathroom door and sits on the edge of the
bath. 'I'm sorry, Cass. You've got to believe me.'

'Why? You were about to leave, Sean. Run away again.'

He hangs his head low. 'I feel terrible,' he whispers. 'I
still do.'

'So terrible you moved on, pretended it hadn't happened.
It was as if I'd never existed.'

'I felt guilty.'

'Oh I'm sorry. Poor you.'

'Don't you understand? It was my fault. I shouldn't have
thrown your wallet down. If I hadn't—'

'Stop, Sean.' I take in a deep breath. 'I never blamed you.
I needed you. I know we were both young, it was a massive
thing to deal with, but you took the easy option. You buried
me with your guilt. You're a coward.'

'I know, I know. I'm so sorry.'

'It's too late to say you're sorry.'

'Where's Cass?' I hear Charlie say outside. 'Where is she?'

I wipe my eyes. 'I'm in here!' I hear Ticket bark at the sound of my voice. Never before have I been so relieved to know that the two friends I love and trust most in the world are here, right behind this door.

'Cass!' Charlie calls, knocking on the door. 'Open up.'

Sean unlocks it for me.

When we come out into the hallway a few people have gathered. They stare at Ticket, Charlie, Sean and me. Sean leaves abruptly with his girlfriend. Charlie kneels beside my chair. 'I'm here now. I'm taking you home. Ready?'

He puts a hand on my shoulder to steady me before carefully lifting me into his arms. 'Ticket, chair,' he says, 'good boy.' Ticket finds the strap and nudges the wheelchair to the top of the stairs.

'Cass, I'm so sorry,' Sarah says again, breathlessly. 'I had no idea Matt knew his girlfriend. Here, let me give you a hand.' She picks up my wheelchair.

'Don't worry,' I say to her. 'It's not your fault.'

I hold on to Charlie tightly as we head downstairs, Ticket and Sarah close behind us. 'It's all right, Cass, we're taking you home,' he says.

Run, Cass, run. He's chasing me. My limbs are heavy. I have to drag my feet off the ground. I turn a corner and in front of me is a spiralling staircase. His footsteps are getting closer. Sean appears at the top of the staircase. He looks down and laughs at me. 'Come on,' he taunts. 'Run!'

I scream in frustration.

'Cass,' a voice says.

'What?' I shout, before opening my eyes, disorientated. Charlie switches on my bedside lamp and gets into bed with me, wrapping an arm around my waist.

'Is it Guy? The party? Seeing your old boyfriend?' he asks, when my crying has finally subsided.

'I didn't get to say all the things I wanted to say . . .'

'I love you, Cass, you know that, don't you?' I'd pulled away from him when I saw the woman returning with her shopping bags.

'I didn't tell him I loved him . . . or say goodbye properly. He didn't give me a chance, he . . .'

'Cass, Guy knew how much you cared about him, I know he did, just from the way he looked at you.'

'I miss him.'

'I know.'

'Guy did the right thing. The sensible thing.'

'Don't say that.'

'He's the brave one.'

'He is brave, he was brave, but so are you.'

'No. No I'm not. I'm the coward, trying to pretend everything is fine.'

'Cass, you have a great job, you have friends, you have Ticket who is devoted to you.'

'I know,' I say quietly, 'but I'm still in a wheelchair. I'll always be in a wheelchair. Sometimes I don't want to live, Charlie.'

There. I've said it. Sometimes I want oblivion. I want to shut my eyes and never wake up. Never have to do another transfer in the middle of the night, or have another bladder infection, never think about Sean and my old life, the accident. Never feel alone.

He grips my hand.

'When I was in hospital,' I say, 'I couldn't remember what had happened that morning, after I'd stepped out into the road, but it comes back to me, at weird moments.'

'Do you want to talk about it?'

I lie so still in the darkness as I tell him. 'I wasn't screaming out in pain but I had these sensations; I can't describe them. All I can say is that they were sensations I'd never felt before. I remember being dragged under by the car, trying to move my feet but nothing happened. I couldn't feel a thing. I must have been in shock because I felt strangely calm.' The only sound I can hear is Charlie's breathing. 'In the ambulance I had one of those masks on, breathing in some pain relief. It tasted like gas. I think someone asked me my name but I couldn't even say Cass. I think Sean said my name.' I swallow hard. 'I can remember the taste of blood when I tried to talk. There was just this blood.'

Charlie touches my arm.

'All I wanted was someone to phone my mum. After that I think a part of me went into a coma. I was concussed. The next thing I remember is seeing my father in hospital, when he told me I'd never walk again.'

'Oh, Cass.'

I think of the party. 'Sometimes, Charlie, I feel invisible, as if I don't count any more.'

'No, Cass, no! I love your courage, spirit, everything about you. Not a day goes by when I don't think about what you've gone through, what you still go through. You have made me appreciate what *I* have and—'

'I'm glad I make you feel better.'

'Oh God, it's coming out all wrong. I didn't mean it like that. Who knows why we're all on this strange planet and who the hell knows why bad things happen to good people. The only thing I know is my life wouldn't be the same if I didn't have you in it.'

Touched, I say, 'I'm sorry about earlier, for shouting at you. You were right.'

'It doesn't matter.'

We hold on to one another in the darkness, both quiet, until Charlie says, 'Cass, do you remember our skiing? Seeing those incredible views of the mountains? You flying down them like nothing was going to stop you.'

'I was on top of the world.'

'Please don't think life isn't worth living. It is, I promise

318

you.' His arm is around my shoulder now and he strokes it gently. I'm wearing a thin camisole top. His fingers touch my bare skin.

'It must be the scariest possible thing being told you will never walk again,' he says.

I agree, but I never believed something could scare me more: not having Charlie in my life. Knowing that however close we are, we are never going to be more than friends. That there will come a time when he meets someone he will really fall in love with, someone who won't make him scared of commitment. If only he knew that that terrifies me more than he can imagine. All I want is for him to take his hand away from my shoulder; for him to touch me in places that need to be awoken. I want to feel alive again. Never have I felt so old and tired.

'Libby is lucky,' I whisper.

'I'm not with her.'

I think, deep down, I already knew this.

'It's over. I . . .'

'You don't have to explain.'

'I want to. You see, I did like her, but the thing is, Cass . . .' He pauses. 'I didn't love her. It was fun to begin with, I can't deny that, and the sex was great . . .'

I nudge him. 'I don't need all the details.'

'But it felt wrong.'

'Why?' I ask, quietly.

'It began to feel like I was cheating on you.'

43

'How long are you going for?' Charlie asks the following morning, after breakfast.

'A week.' Ticket is holding his lead, agitated by the sight of luggage in the hallway. 'Calm down,' I tell him. 'Of course I'm not leaving you behind, my angel.'

Going home was an impulse decision. I woke up this morning, Charlie asleep beside me, and knew I needed time away from London, to be with Mum and Dad and grieve for Guy. I haven't taken any holiday leave at Back Up. My manager, Charlotte, had also suggested I have some time off.

'The rest will do you good,' Charlie says, 'but I'll miss you . . . both.'

Ticket jumps up and gives Charlie's arm a nudge and lick.

'Did you see that! Oh, Ticket! I feel honoured.'

Ticket bows his head as if to say it's his pleasure and Charlie crouches down to stroke him.

I laugh. 'See, he does love you.'

We both look at one another wanting to say something but not sure what's left to say after staying up talking into the early hours of this morning. 'So . . .' I start.

'So . . .'

'Thanks for being such a good friend, for coming to my rescue last night.'

'It was nothing.'

'Well, it meant everything to me. You're one in a million, Charlie Bell.'

He runs a hand through his hair. I sense he is battling to say something else. I wait, to give him the chance, but when he says nothing I tell him I'd better get going to beat the traffic. I open the front door but he stands in front of me, blocking my way. 'Charlie?' He kneels down and presses his forehead against mine. It happens so quickly. I must be imagining his lips on mine, the smell of his skin, hair, the palm of his hand resting against my cheek.

He picks up my arm and kisses the back of my wrist, his eyes not leaving mine.

He kicks the door shut with his foot and looks at me again, eyes imploring me to stay.

'Charlie, I can't.'

'Why?'

Part of me wants to go home and imagine him. That's where I'm comfortable, in a fantasy that some day we'll be together.

'You're running away.'

My throat is dry.

'Haven't we waited long enough, Cass?'

I tuck a strand of hair behind my ear. I don't know how to say it.

'What's wrong?' he asks.

I put my head into my hands. 'I'm killing the moment, aren't I?' I look up at him.

'Slightly.'

'Charlie, you mean the world to me, you know that, don't you?'

'What's stopping you, then?' he asks gently.

'You know this makes it complicated. I don't want to lose you as a friend.'

He shrugs his shoulders. 'Ha! We were never that good friends anyway.'

I smile. 'I haven't been with anyone, you know, not since . . .'

'I know.' Now it's Charlie who stumbles for the words. 'Is that what you're scared of?'

I nod. 'I won't be able to . . .'

'To what?'

'Feel . . .'

He stops me. 'Cass, this is new for me too.'

'But can you feel this?' Paul had said, his fingers touching the back of my neck.

'I'm scared too, Cass, but . . . you know how I feel about you—'

'Shh,' I say, pressing a finger over his lips, my eyes telling him I'll stay. Charlie takes off my jacket and throws it on to the floor. 'No more running away,' he says as we move closer. I unbutton his shirt, my pace quickening. I lift up my arms. Expertly he gathers my top into his hands, slides it up towards my shoulders and over my head, his touch gentle but exciting and urgent. 'You're beautiful,' he says, when I'm dressed only in my silk bra and jeans. I stroke his cheek. We kiss again, until Charlie whispers, 'Ready?'

I nod.

Carefully he lifts me out of my chair and carries me into his bedroom. 'Hang on! Ticket's in here,' he says. We both laugh nervously. Ticket is staring at us, ears pricked, wondering what's going to happen next. Charlie encourages him to leave the room and to my surprise Ticket leaves without a murmur of protest. 'Good boy,' I hear him say outside. 'You settle down for an hour or so. Good boy.'

'For an hour?' I say, impressed.

'At least.'

'That's promising.'

'Now where were we?'

'Here,' I say as I take his face in my hands. The fear of becoming too close to Charlie, of being hurt again, has paralysed my mind.

I kiss him with all my heart and soon my mind is running free.

'Car,' I tell Ticket later that afternoon. I open the door and he jumps in, taking his royal position in the back seat. Charlie loads my suitcase into the boot and then stands on the pavement ready to wave us goodbye. He knocks on the window; I open it.

'I love you,' he says.

'I love you too.'

When Charlie and I made love a million bright lights went off in my head. I have never felt closer to anyone. What I felt for Sean doesn't compare to how deep my love has grown for Charlie. I feel guilty for feeling this happy when Guy has died but I know he'd be telling me not to be so stupid.

'You've just had sex, Cass, so sing all the way home, Princess,' I can hear him say, as if he were sitting right by my side.

44

I'm in my old bedroom, surrounded by boxes. Earlier I'd asked Dad if he could go up to the loft to bring down all my old university files, books, and loose photographs in old shoeboxes that I'd packed away after the accident, promising myself I'd never look at them again.

I sift through some photographs of Sarah, Sean and me. Some of my happiest memories were during year one and two at King's. I pick out a photo of Sarah. She's in a long black dress that shows off her curves. I remember that night. It was summer and we were about to go to a party to celebrate the end of our first-year exams. There's another picture of the two of us, taken by me. We're way too close to the camera, making our smiles look enormous.

I take out my books and coloured files filled with notes. I pick up *Gray's Anatomy for Students*. It's a shiny, full-colour version of the classic text, a bible for medical students. I open my old and very used *Kumar & Clark's Clinical Medicine* and flick through the pages, look at the pencilled notes in the margin and see myself back in the Greenwood lecture theatre with Sarah. It was our second home during our first two years, a huge auditorium with walls painted an oppressive shade of dark orange, and tiers of battered folding seats with fold-down tables for writing notes. I smile, remembering Sarah invariably falling asleep during lectures. When I think of the thousands of hours I sat in that auditorium, listening and taking notes . . . 'It seems a waste, somehow, a shame to let it go,' Charlie had said to me when I was lying in the bath, that very first time I'd visited his parents' home. 'Don't you miss it, Cass? The adrenalin, the buzz, the people?'

I do recall the excitement when Sarah and I were allowed to help with a delivery for the first time. We could hardly sleep that night; neither one of us had expected it to be so dramatic. I also remember how I'd rushed back to the flat one time, dying to tell Sarah and Sean how I'd just seen an obstetrician deliver a hypoxic baby by emergency cae-sarean, 'And then, oh my God, he had to resuscitate him, and it was incredible,' I was saying, my words tumbling out. 'It was awe-inspiring the way he was so calm. He saved that baby's life.'

I pick up some old cards I'd received after the accident. The first one I open is from Dr Helena Ray. She was one of my favourite doctors in my third year at Chichester Hospital. She was a consultant neurologist, elderly, tweedy, brisk and eccentric. Her patients loved her; you could see it in their eyes and from the way they hung on to her every word. Most had chronic conditions, so she knew them well and treated them as if they were all her dear friends. She challenged the idea that to be a good doctor you must distance yourself from your patients. I read, *If at any stage there is anything I can do to help, please let me know, Cassandra. Find strength in your heart.* One of the things I found most touching about working in my placement hospitals was the courage and optimism of a lot of patients, especially when I could see there was little hope. I think of Jenny at Canine Partners, in hospital for twenty years. These people are fighters, wanting to hang on to life until the bitter end, determined to shake out of it as much as they can.

I pick up my framed picture of my two special donkeys at the sanctuary, Feliz and Branson. This photograph used to be on my dressing table. I decide to put it back there, where it belongs. As I reach the bottom of the shoebox I come across a photograph taken when I was eight years old and about to go to a fancy dress birthday party. I'm posing in front of the fireplace wearing a white and blue nurse's uniform with white knee-length socks, a toy stethoscope round my neck and I'm carrying my first-aid box.

I don't hear my father coming in until he says, 'Cass, supper's nearly ready.' He glances over my shoulder. 'Look at you. I remember that party,' he says nostalgically. 'You told me in the car that your dream was to have superpowers and save the world.' Gently he squeezes my shoulder before leaving the room.

I pick up my telephone. If I'm going to do this, I'll need Sarah's help. As I listen to the dialling tone, all I can hear is Guy's voice when he, Dom and I were on our way to the Tower of London. Looking back now, I see clearly why he'd said it. He knew it was our last time together.

'Promise me you'll think about going back to King's. She should, right Dom? Do what you set out to do, Cass, and each time you come across a difficult patient who swears too much, think of me.'

45

Rich drives me to Charlie's parents' house. We've been invited for Saturday lunch before Charlie's thirtieth birthday party tonight. 'I'm picking Anna up from the airport Friday evening,' Charlie had explained on the telephone last night. 'Then we're driving home to help Mum organise everything before you arrive. Rich is going to give you a lift.' He paused. 'By the way, I don't think it's a great idea telling Mum and Dad about us over the weekend, do you?'

I found I was relieved. I wasn't ready to tell Mrs Bell either.

I gaze out of the window, thinking how much I have missed Charlie in the last week. 'His phone bill must be huge,' Mum had said one evening when my mobile vibrated again, though secretly I could tell she was delighted that finally I had a love life, and especially one with Charlie.

'You and Charlie are together, aren't you?' Rich asks as we follow the signs for Oxford.

'Hmm . . . how do you know?'

'He's been behaving strangely all week, even paid for a whole round of beers the other night. He told me,' he adds. 'Plus you can't stop smiling.'

I smile even more.

'Don't say anything to his mum though, will you?'

'Wouldn't dream of it.'

'She's terrifying, isn't she?'

'Nah, not really, not when you get to know her.'

'Right. What's Anna like?' I watch Rich's reaction, remembering Charlie saying how he was still in love with her.

'Hot.'

'Sometimes you guys are as shallow as puddles.'

'Now that's a compliment. Firstly you said "sometimes", and secondly there's a lot of rainfall in this country and puddles can be deep. So deep that one time on New Year's Eve there was such a flood that my entire car was submerged in water and I had to swim out of the passenger window.'

I laugh. 'Come on, what's she really like? I want all the gossip before we arrive.'

'Well, she's a fashion journalist, has been living in New York for a while but then had a bad split with her boyfriend out there. The guy lived a double life, he had a family.'

'The lying sod.'

'Tell me about it. But I don't think she's ever been that great a judge of character. I mean, we went out together for over a year.' He turns on the stereo. 'Then she brutally dumped me.'

'Rich, how could she?'

'I know, I'm a good catch,' he says, trying to be humorous but the rush of redness to his cheeks gives him away.

'Well, it's her loss.'

'That's exactly what I say to myself. Anyway, we'd be a nightmare together. She's too fiery and outspoken and I'm way too laidback for her. What's that expression?'

'Yin and yang?'

'That's it. I'm yin, she's yang. Yin yang no work,' he says with a bad Chinese accent.

'Sometimes it does.' I tell him about my mother and father. 'Also Edward and I were too similar in a way, too yin and yin, so we realised we were much better off as friends. Maybe you should talk to her?'

'And get my heart trampled on all over again? I don't think so. Honestly, Cass, you have to be careful of those Bells.'

As we drive over the sleeping policemen, my mind wanders back to that very first time Charlie drove me to his parents' home, just over a year ago. I realise how much has happened since then, and how happy I am right now, in this moment. I want to hold on to it for ever, never let it go.

Rich beeps the horn when we arrive in the courtyard. Charlie comes out with his father. He opens the door and kisses me on the cheek. 'How was the journey? I've missed you,' he whispers into my ear.

Charlie lifts my wheelchair off the back seat, along with the detachable wheels, and positions both in front of me. I'm aware of Charlie's dad watching me. 'Very clever the way you do that,' he says. 'It's a neat little chair, isn't it? Can I take your suitcase, Cassandra?'

'Thank you, Mr Bell, and please call me Cass.'

'In that case, please call me Henry,' he says warmly. '"Mr Bell" makes me feel rather old.'

When his father strides on ahead with my suitcase, Charlie kisses me on the lips.

'You two will get caught,' Rich teases as he carries in his black tie suit, which was hanging ironed and pressed in the back of the car.

'Oh my God!' Anna screeches. Rich drops his suit as she flings her arms around his neck.

She's wearing skinny jeans with a baggy bright pink top and her hair is cropped short, with streaks of blonde.

'My sister, Anna,' Charlie says to me, 'if you hadn't guessed.' She looks over Rich's shoulder towards me. 'Shit, sorry!' She steps on the collar of his jacket as she walks towards me. Rich picks his suit up without a murmur of complaint.

'Anna, this is Cass.'

She bends down to give me a kiss on both cheeks. She is beautiful in a tomboy sort of way. No make-up, just raw good looks. Her eyes are huge and so blue you'd think they glowed in the dark, and her short hair accentuates her graceful neck and strong jaw line.

'Where's your dog?' she asks.

'Ah, he's with my friend, Sarah.' Matt loves dogs, so they were going to take him to Hampstead Heath tomorrow for a walk and picnic.

'Shame! I was dying to meet the little fella! I'm starving!' She tugs on Rich's arm.

Charlie touches my shoulder and when Anna turns to tell us to hurry up he withdraws his hand immediately.

After lunch we all go for a walk around the grounds, except for Mrs Bell. Rich and Anna walk on ahead, whereas Henry stops frequently. He tells me that each tree he has planted has been labelled carefully because otherwise, when he dies, no one will know what on earth it is. 'Each one has a special meaning for me,' he says. 'For instance, I planted this when Charlie was born. It's a *Metasequoia glyptostroboides*.'

'I'm not even going to try to repeat that,' I say.

'Dad knows all the Latin names,' says Charlie.

'It's a Dawn Redwood.'

'Phew. I can remember that.'

'It must be about forty foot tall now,' Henry says. 'It's a quick-growing conifer and the leaves are pink in the spring and turn green later on.'

'How exciting to see the colours change.'

'It's magical. Come, have a look at this one. It's a *Liquidambar styraciflua*.'

'Now you're just showing off, Henry.'

He stamps over a few thistles and nettles to get to it. 'The leaf is pretty, don't you think? It's like a maple. There are so many varieties, this is a Lane Roberts.'

'Does this one's leaves change colour too?'

'Oh yes, in the autumn the colour is fantastic. The leaves go from a yellow to red to burgundy. It's incredible.'

'I think it's my favourite one so far,' I say. 'It's beautiful.'

He cuts off a leaf and hands it to me.

After tea Mrs Bell shows me to my bedroom. 'Now, Cassandra, I hope you'll be comfortable.'

'Yes, this is lovely,' I say looking around the room with an en suite bathroom. There are fresh flowers on the dressing table, along with a slim glass vase holding my liquidambar leaf that Henry touchingly left for me.

'Good. You must be tired. Do have a rest before the party.' I breathe a sigh of relief when she shuts the door.

'Charlie, what are you doing?' I hear her asking him outside.

'Just checking on Cass.'

'She's resting. Can you give me a hand?'

'In a minute.' Pause. 'I'll be down in a sec, Mum,' he says. I hear the floorboards creaking as finally she walks away.

Charlie comes in and lies down on my bed. I join him. 'Come here,' he says, wrapping his arms around me.

'This feels good,' I say. 'I've missed you.'

Lying in each other's arms we talk briefly about my decision to try and go back to King's. I tell him how my tutor is putting forward my case to the governing body and if I'm accepted, I'll return this autumn. 'I'm so proud of you,' he says, running his hand down my back. We stop kissing when we hear footsteps outside my bedroom door. 'It's quite fun having a secret, isn't it?' Charlie whispers, placing a hand over my mouth to stop me from laughing.

When it's quiet I whisper, 'Are you nervous about telling your mum?'

'No.'

'Are you sure? I mean, it's fine not saying anything this weekend, but if you're having any doubts . . .'

'Why would I be having doubts? Are you having any?'

Anna bursts in without knocking and Charlie moves away, almost falling off the bed. He stands up, his hair unkempt, and says stiffly, as if he were a butler, 'So, if there's anything else you need, give me a shout.'

'Absolutely,' I say, acting equally badly. 'Will do.'

'Wow!' Anna exclaims, pushing him out of the way. 'Is this what you're wearing tonight, Cass?'

Hanging on my wardrobe is a golden Vivienne Westwood top that used to belong to Mum. 'I love her work,' she sighs, touching the silk. 'So timeless.'

Then she walks over to the bed and sits down next to me, crossing her long lean legs, a gesture that suggests she could stay for some time. 'See ya, Charlie.' She waves at him. 'Scoot. Girly chat.' She turns to me. 'So, Cass, what do you do?'

I tell her I've just handed in my notice at Back Up. I was sad to leave and felt guilty that I hadn't worked a full year, but Charlotte was understanding, and we'd discussed how I could still volunteer and come on some of the courses. Charlie and I have talked about returning to Colorado.

'Charlie said you were in a car accident. It must be so tough, I don't know how you do it.'

'Do what?'

'Be in a wheelchair. You're really brave.'

'Isn't being brave throwing yourself into a house that's on fire? You see, I don't have a choice.'

'That's true,' she says, surprised to have been challenged. She starts to hum, looking around the room. 'How about boyfriends? Dating anyone at the moment?'

'Er, no, not really.'

'Not really,' she repeats. 'Interesting.' She smiles, showing off snow-white teeth.

'Well,' I say casually, 'there is someone I like but it's early days, you know. How about you? I'd love to go to New York. I've been to Colorado – that's how I met Charlie.'

Immediately I regret mentioning his name because it brings her back to the path she wanted to be on.

'He's pretty special, my brother, isn't he?'

I nod.

'What's it like living with him? He's so messy, isn't he?

Does he leave his smelly socks lying round the place?'

'Sometimes!' I laugh. 'Ticket chews them. He's not brilliant at washing up either.'

'An important phone call has to be made, right? Or a sudden migraine?'

'Exactly.' I begin to relax. 'And I tell you what else he does.'

'Go on.'

'When he eats he bites against the whole of the fork and it really irritates me.'

'Oh God, that's a family habit, we all do that!'

'And he doesn't chuck away empty cereal boxes.' I laugh affectionately, remembering our last argument about the empty pack of Shreddies. 'But he's lovely. The other day I was in real trouble and he dropped everything to help me out. He's a good friend.'

'Yeah, he is. He loves to come to everyone's rescue.' She pauses before she says, 'I think people can take advantage quite easily.'

I breathe deeply, unsure where this conversation is heading now.

'Did you meet Libby?' she asks.

'She was lovely.'

'Do you know why it didn't work out?'

'No.' I fiddle with the embroidered flowers on the bedspread. 'Charlie said something about it not feeling right.' I can feel her penetrating stare.

ALICE PETERSON

'We all really liked Jo, his ex. Maybe it's got something to do with her?'

'I don't know. Maybe.' I look at my watch, but she doesn't take the hint.

'So come on, is the guy you like coming tonight? Some of Charlie's friends are seriously cute, I wouldn't blame you.'

'Anna, sorry, I really need to start getting ready.'

'We've got ages yet,' she says with no intention of leaving.

Charlie opens the door. 'Anna, Mum needs you.'

'What for?'

'She didn't say.'

'We'll finish this chat later,' she says to me, reluctantly leaving the room.

When she goes I lie down and shut my eyes. 'I felt like I was being interrogated, Charlie. Why the hell didn't you tell me she was a prison warden in a former life?'

We eat in the dining room. Mrs Bell has cooked beef Wellington for twenty guests, and after the main course the men move two places to their left and I am now sitting next to Charlie. He touches my thigh under the table. I can't feel it but I know his hand is there. I expect Anna to climb under the table and investigate. Get the handcuffs out. Worse still, the truncheon.

At midnight Anna carries in a chocolate cake and we sing 'Happy Birthday'. When his parents finally go to bed

338

more wine is poured and the party gets louder. There's music and dancing, and by the early hours of the morning, when all my inhibitions have gone, I can't resist giving him a proper birthday kiss.

46

I wake up the following morning and slide my arm across the bed but he's not there. I frown heavily when I see that Charlie left my wheelchair at the opposite side of the room. I hear Rich crashing around next door and knock against the wall, repeatedly. Thankfully Charlie's parents are on the other side of the house.

Finally Rich appears, dressed in his jeans, looking hungover. 'I feel dreadful,' he moans.

'Me too. I can't move.'

'I know. Why do we drink so much? Oh God, you really can't move.'

I laugh feebly, holding my head in my hands. 'Can you bring my chair over?'

'Sure.'

When Ticket and I are apart, I realise just how much he does for me.

An hour later Rich carries me downstairs. 'Where is

everyone?' he grumbles when we enter an empty kitchen. We look for Charlie and finally hear voices coming from the sitting room. The door is slightly ajar. Rich is about to go in, but I pull him back, certain I heard Anna say my name.

'You know who I'm talking about,' she says.

I lean in closer.

'It's none of your business,' Charlie replies. 'Or yours, Mum.'

'Darling, we're concerned, that's all.'

'Are you?' Anna presses.

'Yes. Yes I am.'

'Well, I wish you'd just told us,' Mrs Bell says, 'instead of creeping round the house like teenagers.'

'I didn't want to tell you yet because you get too involved. Look at what happened with Jo. *You* went out with her, Mum, not me.'

'That's a bit over the top, Charlie. I'm not trying to interfere. . .'

I wait for the 'but'.

'. . . but have you really thought this through?'

'What do you mean?'

'She's younger than you.'

'She's twenty-five. There's eight years between you and Dad.'

'Well, yes, but . . .'

'But what?'

There's a long painful silence.

'I know what you're thinking,' he says, 'both of you.' I can tell Charlie is struggling to keep calm. I hear footsteps approaching the door. Rich tries to pull me away.

Mrs Bell raises her voice. 'Charlie! Wait! We *must* talk about this. Are you in love with her?'

'I don't know, Mum! Christ, what is this!'

'You realise, don't you, that you will have to look after her for the rest of your life?'

I flinch.

'What's the prognosis?' Mrs Bell persists.

'Prognosis? What are you talking about?'

'Can she have children?' Anna asks.

Rich is pacing behind me.

'I don't know!' Charlie snaps. 'We've only been going out for a few weeks, Mum. Funnily enough we haven't visited the family planning clinic yet.'

'Well, I think you do need to give it some thought.'

'What if she can't?' Anna supports her mother.

'Can you have children?' he asks her.

'Charlie! What kind of question is that?' Anna laughs nervously. 'Yes,' she adds.

'How do you know?'

'You're being ridiculous now.'

'Well, you can't take it for granted, Anna. No one knows until they try. It's not a God-given right.'

'But I'm not – you know.'

'Not in a wheelchair?' Charlie finishes off for her.

Rich is standing over me. 'Cass, please can we go,' he whispers urgently.

But I can't move.

'Charlie,' Anna says. 'We're concerned because we love you.'

'We're worried that you're being sucked in,' Mrs Bell continues. 'You feel sorry for her, and I do too. It's a tragic thing to happen to anybody.'

'Mum, just stop.'

'And then her poor friend committing suicide, it's awful, but you can't always be there for her. She's vulnerable, darling, but the girl is clearly in love with you and I don't want you to feel trapped.'

'I don't believe this!' Charlie shouts now. 'Do you think it was my dream to go out with someone like Cass? Did I have posters in my bedroom of women in wheelchairs?'

Rich puts his head into his hands. '*Please.* Let's go.'

'I know she's vulnerable, Mum. That's why it's taken me this long to admit my feelings!'

'But will Cass mind you doing all the things she can't do?' his mother carries on. 'You haven't even talked to her about it, have you?'

'How can I? You make it sound so easy! Of course I'm worried, I'm fucking terrified, Mum.'

A tear runs down my eye. Rich begs me to leave now.

'If I could, I'd be with Jo or Libby in a second. Life would

343

be a whole lot easier. I'd far rather go out with someone who wasn't like Cass, Mum! I don't want to feel like this. It would be a hell of a lot less complicated . . . but—'

'Well, I'm not stopping you,' I say, finally opening the door.

Silence descends across the room.

'I heard everything,' I say, Rich standing by my side.

'Cass, I was angry, I didn't mean, well, I meant it but, oh God . . . See what you've done!' he shouts at his mother and Anna. Neither can look at me. They stand helplessly by the fireplace, looking down at their feet.

'Mrs Bell, just to put you straight, I can have children. I've spoken to my doctor about it.'

'Oh good, good,' she mutters with a pained smile.

'The only problem I have is people assume I can't have them.' I clear my throat. 'And, Anna, I'm not sure you have any right to lecture Charlie on relationships.'

Charlie approaches, but I back away. 'But you —' I look at him, my voice breaking – 'all my worst fears, everything I hate about myself, the fear I hold you back, well, now I know how you feel.' I wheel myself out of the room as fast as I can, move down the hall, past the squatting Buddha—

'Wait!' Charlie calls out, catching up with me. 'Where are you going? I'm so sorry, Cass. Can we talk?'

'Oh God!' I scream, looking towards the stairs.

'Here. Let me help,' Charlie says.

'Just go, leave me alone!'

'Cass, please . . .' he begs.

'Go, Charlie.' Rich intervenes, resting a firm hand on his friend's arm.

He walks out of the front door, slamming it behind him.

'What on earth is going on?' asks Henry, coming inside, dressed in his gardening hat and wellington boots.

When I am packed I ask Rich if we can escape quickly, without any goodbyes. I don't want to sign the visitors' book. 'No, you have to find Charlie,' he pleads. 'Cass, I'm not driving you home until you've talked to him.'

'I can't face him, not yet.'

'Please. He's my best friend.'

Rich and I find Charlie sitting by the lake, throwing a stick into the water, staring ahead. Instinctively he turns and stands up.

Rich discreetly leaves us alone.

'Cass,' he says, trying to touch my shoulder, but I move away. 'I'm so sorry. I feel terrible.'

'You were being honest. Do you think I'll hold you back?'

He shakes his head.

We are quiet, until finally he says, 'Cass, there is this part of me that's scared.'

'Me too, Charlie.'

'I'm nervous of hurting you if things don't work.'

'But I'm no different to any other girl.'

'That's not true,' he says, and deep down I know I can't argue with that.

I look at Charlie, try to picture my own image in a silver frame, mounted in his parents' sitting room, on top of the grand piano. 'This isn't going to work, is it?'

'Don't say that.'

'Your family will never accept me.'

'They will.'

'Charlie.' I shake my head, telling him to stop fooling himself. 'I think we need a break.'

'No.'

'But those things you said, that you don't want to be in love with me, that life would be so much easier if you were with Libby or Jo—'

'Don't,' he cuts me off, not wanting to be reminded.

'We can't pretend, go back to how things were. Everything's changed between us.'

'But we're letting Mum and Anna win, can't you see that?'

'It's not about anyone winning. I love you, Charlie, and I know how much you do for me, but I'd hate it if you started to resent me. I'd never forgive myself.'

'I won't.'

'I think we should have time apart,' I say quietly again. 'I'm going to move out, back to my parents'.'

Charlie throws another stick into the water. 'Time apart? For how long?'

'I'll be gone by tomorrow night.'

47

Ticket positions himself in front of me and I wipe the corners of his eyes with damp cotton wool pads and when I'm finished he licks my hand twice. 'I need to give you a good brush today too, don't I?' I say to him. 'Wasn't Kim pleased with us?' Kim from Canine Partners visited last week to check up on Ticket's progress. She recorded his weight, tested the condition of his coat and I assured her I only shampooed him when he rolled in something unmentionable on his walks. 'We passed with flying colours. And we've got such an exciting day ahead, haven't we?'

Today we're taking the train to London to see all our Canine Partner friends for a reunion lunch. Softly spoken Jenny has arranged it all and we're meeting at Westfield Shopping Centre. There's a stretch of easy access restaurants along the Southern Terrace.

'Westfield won't know what's hit them,' Mum says, as she drives us to the station.

*   *   *

When I'm on the train I think about everything that has happened in the last two weeks, since I left Charlie. We haven't been in touch. I shouldn't be surprised that he hasn't called because I said we both needed time apart, space to think. *'You need to work out what you want, Charlie.'* Rich has been in contact and we've become close. He's made it clear he supports us both, but wants to be sure I'm OK. If Anna weren't so intent on interrogating everyone else, she'd realise that she was a fool to let him go. I wonder what Charlie is doing right now. He'll be at work, of course, but will he be out tonight with his friends thinking that life is much easier without Cass and Ticket? Does he suspect his mother and Anna were right after all? Is this time apart a chance for him to break free from the spell I have put him under?

'I'm nervous of hurting you if things don't work.'

I look out of the window at the world passing by. I'm not angry any more. I understand why he said the things he said. I only wish I hadn't heard it in that way.

Studying has been a great distraction. After careful consideration King's has allowed me to sit my final two years, and not only that but they will help me find suitable accommodation. I hadn't realised how much it had meant to me until Mum handed me an official-looking letter. I ripped it open, Mum hovering over me, saying repeatedly, 'So?' When I shrieked with joy, Ticket jumped on to my lap and Mum threw her arms around us.

I have been reading all my old notes and textbooks, to make sure I'm up to speed to begin year four this autumn. Returning to my past will haunt me. I'll picture the old Cass running into the auditorium, late for lectures. I'll see the old carefree Cass with Sean.

When I'd told Frankie I was feeling both anxious and excited about King's, she described her first day back at school after her injury. 'It was hard, Cass. When you're seventeen you want to blend into the crowd, not be a spectacle. I'd look out of the window to the sports field where I used to play hockey. I remembered how I used to run down the corridors to avoid bumping into the teachers I didn't like. But it got easier, and by the end it felt like a massive achievement. If I could survive school, I could survive anything.'

Frankie is right. Nothing is going to stop me any more. If I can do this, I can do anything, even live without Charlie.

A ticket conductor walks through our carriage; he slots my ticket into his machine.

Yet, one of the first people I'd wanted to call was Charlie. It felt so strange not being in contact. I phoned Dom and Jamie. I told Guy. I talk to him at odd moments of the day and as crazy as this sounds I feel as if he can hear me. I also rang Sarah immediately and she came to stay last weekend, to celebrate. After a couple of glasses of wine we ended up talking about Charlie. 'I miss him,' I said. 'Maybe I should call?'

She was shaking her head. 'No! Don't you dare give in, Cass! You'll regret it tomorrow.'

I nodded. 'I hate it when you're right,' I added, putting my telephone away.

I tell Ticket we're approaching Paddington. However strange it feels to be in London, and not to see Charlie, I tell myself to put him out of my mind. It's Ticket's special day today.

When Ticket sees Cilla he jiggles and wags his tail. Then he spots Captain, his fur so golden and wearing the smartest red-studded collar, and the three of them jiggle some more, almost as if they're dancing and reliving their puppy days. When Pandora and Tinkerbell come along it's all too much. Tails can't stop wagging. It's like the best school reunion, ever!

Over lunch, we talk about the training course, laughing at how Alex had smuggled gin into the room that night after Edward and I had had a bad video session. We're all sorry not to see Tom and his partner Leo. Tom was the one with cerebral palsy, studying in Leeds. Tom wasn't well today, but Jenny tells us she's kept in touch with him via email. 'He's doing a skydive for Canine Partners,' she says, 'so we must all sponsor him.'

'Email?' I say, finding that more surprising than Tom's skydive, recalling how terrified Jenny had been of computers and social networking.

She laughs. 'I know I telephoned you all to arrange today, I'm still old-fashioned like that, but look!' She digs into her handbag and out comes a Blackberry. 'I've been on a computer course,' she claims proudly, 'and I can text.'

'You'll be on Twitter next,' I say.

We all clap and cheer when Jenny also tells us she and Captain will be torchbearers for the Olympics this summer. Out of thousands of nominations, they were selected.

Trevor is looking healthy and fit, and often doesn't need his wheelchair. He tells us Pandora is the best four-legged personal trainer. 'She's much more fun than going to the gym.' He has begun to go to church again. Pandora sits quietly with him. 'She did, mind you, let out one giant yawn in the middle of the sermon last week, so she's now a real hit in the congregation!' His eyes are alive, which reminds me of what Stuart Harris had said to me that very first day at the Canine Partner Centre. *'When I see applicants for the first time there's something dead in their eyes.'*

Next up is Alex. 'I haven't met no one, Cilla can't work miracles, but I'm not lonely no more. She's my life.'

Edward goes on to tell us his news. He's met someone. 'She's my physio,' he says. 'You see, my social life is pretty much built around the hospital.' He also tells us that he's beginning to give talks at schools about his experiences, along with giving a Canine Partner demonstration at Tedworth House, the Personal Recovery and Assessment Centre (PRAC) for wounded, sick and injured servicemen and women. He's thinking about returning to college, maybe to do a business course. 'And Tinkerbell and I are hoping to take part in the closing ceremony of the Paralympics,' he says.

'Wow, Medalman,' says Alex. 'I'll be watching you on the box! Bet your mum is dead proud.'

'How about you, Cass?' Jenny asks.

'Wow, I don't know how to beat all that,' I exclaim. For a moment I think of Charlie, and wish I could tell them all about him. 'Well, I'm still single too, Alex, but the really good news is I've decided to go back to medicine. I'm going back to King's this autumn.' I wag a finger at them all. 'So pretty soon you'll be calling me doctor.'

They cheer and laugh and we all agree to make this an annual event for the dogs, and for us.

Before we leave, Edward pulls me aside. 'That's great news about King's,' he says, 'but what about Charlie?'

48

I'm mashing up some chicken meat with biscuits, Ticket sitting by the kitchen door, waiting patiently to be fed, when my mobile rings. I don't recognise the number on the screen. I'm tempted to let it go to voicemail, but then again . . . 'Hello?'

'Hi, Cass. It's Anna.'

I wish I'd let it go to voicemail.

'How are you?' she asks.

'Fine,' I say cautiously.

'I should think I'm the last person you want to speak to right now.'

When she pauses, I don't correct her.

'I was wondering if we could meet up?'

'Meet up,' I repeat, giving myself time to think how to respond. 'I don't think so.'

'Please, Cass.'

'I'm not living in London at the moment.'

'I know. Charlie told me.'

Hearing his name feels strange.

'I can drive to your parents this weekend?'

'Can't we just talk? On the phone?'

'No. I need to see you. Please give me a chance to explain.'

Jamie is down for the weekend, and we're having breakfast together. He still lives in Shepherd's Bush but now works in a marketing company that sells sports clothes and gym equipment. He has a girlfriend called Harriet. She's a veterinary nurse. I haven't met her yet, but I can tell he's happy, especially when her name is dropped into virtually every sentence. 'I still want to travel. Harriet likes to travel too. But not at the moment, not when Harriet and I have just got together.' He smiles, shyly. 'You know what I mean?'

I shake my head. 'No. I'm a disaster in that area.'

'You and Charlie will work it out.'

'Pass the milk, would you?'

Jamie slides the jug across the table. 'So why's his bonkers sister driving all this way to see you? Mum said we had to be out of the house or something.'

I decide to tell Jamie everything. 'Jeez,' he says at the end, 'you heard all that.'

'Exactly. I'm dreading seeing her.'

'It'll be all right. I hope she's bringing one mega box of chocolates to say sorry,' he adds.

When Anna arrives, Ticket greets her in the drive. 'Aren't you handsome,' she says.

As I watch her stroking him, I'm overwhelmed by her presence. She is stunning. Her cropped hair is now dyed back from blonde to its original brunette and she looks chic even in cropped jeans and a simple navy jacket.

'What a lovely home,' she remarks, following me into the kitchen. She looks out of the window to the view of horses in a field. 'It's beautiful countryside down here.'

I turn on the kettle. Anna talks about her journey from London and how she got stuck behind a tractor for what seemed like hours.

'Have your parents lived here a long time?' she asks, when I hand her a mug of tea.

'Since I was sixteen.'

'Charlie and I worry about Mum and Dad, you know, that they're getting old and the house is too big for them, but . . .'

'Would you like to sit down,' I suggest.

She takes off her jacket and pulls out a chair.

When I join her, she now comments on the grey day. As she continues to moan about the British weather, all I can think of is: when are you going to get to the point? I gulp down some tea, burning the roof of my mouth. 'Anna . . .' I say, stopping her mid-flow.

'No, wait, Cass. Sorry, I'm rambling. I'm nervous,' she confesses, fidgeting with the strap of her handbag. 'You know why I'm here.'

'Not really,' I admit, 'although I know it's not to talk about the weather. Does Charlie know you're here?'

'No! He'd kill me. Please don't tell him, Cass.'

I twist my hair round and round, waiting for her to say whatever she's come here to say. It takes some time.

'I should have come sooner,' she says finally. 'I haven't stopped thinking about what I said. I can't imagine what it must have been like hearing us arguing over you.'

'It wasn't nice.'

'I'm so sorry. I don't know what else to say except Mum and me, we didn't mean to hurt you.' She chews her thumbnail, taps her foot against the stone floor. 'Seriously, Cass, I can't defend myself except . . . I do love Charlie and want him to be happy.'

'That's all I want too,' I say, raising my voice. I stop playing with my hair; I try to compose myself as I ask, 'How is he?'

'Terrible,' she says. 'He's staying late at the office most nights, eating takeaway at his desk. Rich is worried about him. So am I. He still won't talk to Mum.'

'I think what upset me more than anything was your mum suggesting that I was holding Charlie back, sort of trapping him.'

'Stop!' Anna says. 'What Rich said was true. We behaved badly. I was prejudiced, and Mum and I hadn't given you a chance or really seen you and Charlie together. I'd swanned back from New York and had no business to poke my nose into your relationship with my brother.'

I can almost hear Rich saying that.

'I'm selfish and vain and ignorant and have never had to deal with anything serious or had to show any kind of strength, and you are a million times the person I am.' She looks at me with genuine remorse. 'The list goes on, according to Rich.'

'You care about what he thinks, don't you?'

'Yes.'

'I don't blame you. He's lovely.' I'm touched by how much Rich has been a true friend to me despite the long history he has with Anna and his strong bond with their family.

She leans towards me. 'I want to put things right. I don't want to be that person Rich described. Do you think you can ever forgive me, that maybe we could become friends?'

'I was about to take Ticket for a walk. Would you like to join us?'

She smiles. 'I'd love to.'

49

I take a break from studying at the kitchen table. I hear the familiar sound of hooves. I look out of the window, wave at Emily riding past. On our walk yesterday, Anna had asked me if I'd call Charlie. 'He misses you.'

'I miss him too, but it's complicated.'

'That's what Rich keeps on saying. Charlie doesn't want to hurt you again, but Cass, clearly he loves you and you love him.'

'So he hasn't called then?' Mum says, entering the kitchen.

I look away from the telephone. 'Who?'

'Charlie Chaplin.'

'No.'

'Sorry, darling.' She turns the kettle on. 'I've just been talking to Mrs Henderson.' Mrs Henderson has become a close friend and neighbour of Mum and Dad's. She was the one who asked me to type her memoirs. I wrote her a postcard from Colorado, telling her what her wages had paid for. 'She's in a right old twit because her basin's blocked.'

'Oh, great.'

'I told her Michael would go round later with his plunger and sort it all out.'

'Great.'

'And I'm going to jump off a cliff right now. With Ticket.'

'Uh-huh.'

Mum sits down next to me, scratches her arm. 'Cassandra Brooks, you haven't heard a word I've said.' Pause. 'Cassandra!' Mum prods my arm.

'Ouch! What?'

'You're in the clouds again and it doesn't take a rocket scientist to work out why.'

'I was . . . er . . . thinking about lunch. I'm starving.'

'Sometimes you are so like me,' Mum says, crossing her arms with resignation. 'You act all tough and pretend nothing's wrong, but inside it's a whole different story. Everyone thinks I wear the trousers in this family.'

I raise an eyebrow.

'It took me a long time to admit I needed your father, that it's OK to be vulnerable. I know you miss him like mad, I know you love him.'

'I didn't think time apart would be this hard,' I confess, wondering how people survived during the world wars. Edward tells me I was right to break up with him.

Mum nods. 'You did the right thing though.'

Here we go again. 'Did I?'

'You stood up for yourself. That takes courage.'

'Yeah, but maybe I've lost him.'

'Cass, you had to have this time apart,' she says. 'What's that saying?' She pauses. 'If you love someone, set them free. If they come back, they're yours.'

In the afternoon Ticket and I go for a walk. On our way home, my mobile rings. When his name appears on my screen, I freeze.

'How are you?' he says.

'I'm good, thanks.' My heart is thumping. 'How are you?'

'I'm good too.'

There's an abnormally long silence between us.

'I've wanted to call for some time,' Charlie says. 'There are things I need to say. Can we meet up?'

50

Sarah and I go to an exhibition at the V&A on Saturday morning. We then attempt to go clothes shopping in High Street Kensington, but quickly give up as it's too crowded with aggressive shoppers and mums pushing twins in giant buggies. We end up having lunch in a crowded wine bar instead. We talk about my returning to King's. Sarah fills me in on year four and five, those sleepless nights close to exams, and sore backs after lugging heavy library books home. 'Oh but, Cass, it's worth it,' she assures me. 'Gibraltar was one of the friendliest places I've ever been to, such a strange little "British" paradise where everybody speaks this mix-up of Spanish and English, and the weather was glorious except that thanks to the rock the sun sets on one side of the territory at five in the afternoon, and then there's this strange cloud that settles over everything when the wind blows east . . .'

I push my plate aside, distracted.

'Are you listening?' she says, sounding like my mum.

'Sorry. What were you saying?'

Sarah looks at me with disapproval. 'Never mind. I saw that.'

'What?'

'Giving Ticket your lunch. No man is worth starving for. Besides –' Sarah gestures to the menu – 'it's a rip-off this place. About a pound a mouthful.'

'I'm nervous.'

'Oh, Cass, don't be. This is good. One of you had to make the first move, and I'm glad it was Charlie.'

I'm outside the Serpentine Gallery. I'm developing Dad's habit of arriving early. My mobile vibrates and for a moment I dread that it's Charlie cancelling. 'Good luck,' Sarah texts. 'Thinking of you. Call me later. X'

As I wait with Ticket, I think about the time when Charlie had taken me on our scooter ride through the mountains. I smile, picturing us fooling around on his parents' lawn, Charlie carrying me in his arms, pretending to be a horse in the Grand National. Then I see us at the sink, when he'd burned his hand.

I think about the way Charlie hadn't hesitated to pick me up from Sarah's boyfriend's party, when he could have easily said, 'I told you so.' But that isn't Charlie's style. Carefully he'd carried me downstairs, Ticket behind us. *It's all right, Cass, we're taking you home.*

When I see him approaching, carrying his old leather

rucksack, Ticket rushes towards him, wagging his tail. 'Hello, Ticket!' I watch Charlie stroking him, grateful how Ticket always breaks the ice. He looks up and we both smile. 'Cass,' he says, taking my hand, 'it's so good to see you.'

'You too.'

'Shall we walk?' he says.

Charlie asks me how I feel about returning to King's. 'Good,' I say. 'And how have you been?' I ask, when all I want to do is talk about us.

'I've signed up for a photography course.' He glances at me, warmth in his eyes.

'Maybe you'll become the new Mario Testino,' I say.

'I doubt it.'

'You're very talented, Charlie.'

As we head towards the Serpentine Lake, Charlie digs his hands deep into his pockets. 'The house feels quiet without you and Ticket,' he says, staring ahead.

I've missed you. Why can't I say that?

'You were right,' he continues. 'We needed time apart. What I said that morning, about life being easier if I was with Jo . . . I didn't even realise I felt that way, until I'd said it. Does that make sense?'

'I think so.'

'I'm sorry.'

'It's OK,' I say, fighting back the tears, fearing it's over between us.

He turns to me. 'You see, the thing is our family has led pretty sheltered lives. I'm not saying we've had nothing to deal with, but . . . well, all Mum has had to put up with is a rebellious daughter and a useless son. I'm not making any excuses for her, or for myself, but Mum didn't set out to hurt you.' He pauses. 'Nor did I.'

'I know that, Charlie. I do, but—'

'Cass, wait. Let me finish. I know I said I'd rather go out with someone who wasn't in a wheelchair. That might sound hurtful, and I'm sorry, it just came out that way because I was angry.' He kneels down beside me. 'I wish you could walk and run and do all those things that most of us take for granted.' He gestures to an ancient-looking man practising some kind of Tai Chi under a tree, a group of cyclists riding past, a woman jogging with her dog alongside her. 'Sometimes I get so angry that I can't do more, that . . . I'm still not making any sense, am I?'

I shake my head.

He unties his rucksack, where he normally keeps his camera, and hands me a small parcel wrapped in brown paper.

'What's this?'

'Open it.'

Charlie watches as I unwrap it. The sound of paper rustling brings Ticket by my side, thinking it could be treats. 'A first-aid box?' I say, even more confused now.

'Carry on.'

I open the box. The first thing I see is a Starbucks card.

'I figured when you're a student again, it might come in handy.'

I pick up a photograph of Charlie in between his mother and Anna, with a small dart attached to it. I look up at him and smile. Beneath that is a photograph of me in Colorado, skiing without my reins. 'Earplugs?' I say.

'When I'm annoying you, or snoring.' He raises an eyebrow.

There's a bag of mint fresh treats for Ticket.

Finally, there's an envelope. I open it, aware of Charlie so close to me. 'Dear Cass,' he writes. 'I miss not eating spaghetti with you at our local and I miss my copy of the *Big Issue*. But most of all, I miss you.'

'Oh, Charlie,' I say.

'That morning, when you walked in with Rich,' he says, 'you didn't hear what I was going to say next. You missed the "but" part.'

'So tell me now,' I ask gently.

'I was going to say how much I loved you and that I hadn't felt this way about anyone before.'

I watch as he digs something out of his jacket pocket. He hands me my old keys to his house. I wipe my eyes with the sleeve of my cardigan. 'Please come home, Cass.'

I throw my arms around him.

'Don't cry, Cass,' he says tearfully, holding on to me.

'I can't help it.'

'Is that a yes?' he asks, brushing a strand of hair away from my eyes. 'You'll come home?'

'Yes,' I say. 'A million times, yes.'

51

Two weeks before Christmas

Dear Cass, I read at the kitchen table. *Happy Christmas! All our love, Dom, Miranda, and Lucas Guy. PS. We're all sleep deprived but doing well and little LG would love to see you soon to show off his impressive vocal cords. Love to Charlie too – hope all is Ticketyboo between you (sorry, dreadful joke).*

Charlie enters the room as I open the next envelope. 'It's like a card shop in here,' he mutters, heading straight for the coffee machine. 'By the way, we need to get going pretty soon.' He looks at his watch; it's early on a Saturday morning. 'You know what Mum gets like if we're late for lunch.'

'Oh my God!' I say. 'Frankie and Tom have bought a dog!'

Tom and I went round Battersea Dogs Home and fell in love with her. She's a bit of this, bit of that, but she's perfect and we're calling her Bean, because she jumps up all the time. I'll have to train her in the New Year not to pull me out of my wheelchair! Lots of trips to the park with Ticket in 2013!

'That's great,' Charlie says, the coffee machine gurgling.

Captain and I are off to my sister's in Cornwall, writes Jenny. *I hope it snows, because Captain has a whale of a time, we love building snowmen.*

Happy Xmas! Cilla sends her love to Ticket. Thanks for visiting me last month with Medalman.

'She means Edward,' I say, when Charlie sits down next to me and reads the card. 'Have you packed?' He asks.

'Yep. All I need to do is get your mum some flowers or something, then I'm ready,' I say, gathering my handbag and Ticket's lead.

'I thought you'd bought Mum the scarf?'

'This is a tiny extra. Give me twenty minutes.'

Charlie grins. 'That means at least thirty.'

'Hello, my friend! Where have you been?' *Big Issue* man asks me outside Sainsbury's, stroking Ticket. He's wearing a dodgy woolly Christmas reindeer hat that he tells me was a present from his two girls.

'Well, where have *you* been? I haven't seen you in months!'

'I asked you first,' he says with a broad smile.

I fill *Big Issue* man in on everything that's been going on in my life in the past eight months, including my break-up with Charlie and moving back to Dorset.

'But we're back together,' I say. 'In fact I'm going down to stay with his parents this weekend, before Christmas.' I gesture to the box of Belgian chocolates in my shopping bag.

'It sounds like a soap opera, man!' He laughs. 'But seriously, I'm well pleased for you. You deserve to be happy, my friend.'

'Your turn now,' I say, aware a queue is forming behind me.

'I've been on a different patch, not nearly so friendly as here but someone took this spot for a while.' He shrugs his shoulders. 'Also been sorting out my kids. I've been talking to the council, to see if we can get a bigger flat. It got too cramped so Mum's been looking after them, but I want to have them back at home full-time. I miss them, man.'

'I'm sorry,' I say. 'It must be hard.'

He nods. 'I've been taking my girls to church every Sunday. I've been saying a few prayers to the good Lord.'

Quite a crowd are now lining up behind me. 'You have fans. You should be on stage. You should sing,' I say, remembering his version of Louis Armstrong's 'Wonderful World'.

'You think? I haven't thought about that.'

I buy two copies of the *Big Issue*. 'Well, maybe you should. Happy Christmas . . .' I pause, realising after all this time I don't know his name.

'Patrick,' he says. 'Happy Christmas to you too, my friend.'

It's Sunday morning and Charlie and I are in bed. 'We need to get up,' I say sleepily.

'In a minute,' he says, wrapping his arms around my waist and kissing me. 'I wish we could stay in bed all day.'

'So do I. But your mum might have something to say about that. And Ticket.'

'Just ten minutes longer then?'

We kiss again. 'Ten minutes couldn't hurt,' I say.

After our time is up, 'Another five minutes,' he suggests. Charlie lifts my face to his. 'I've never been so happy,' he tells me.

'Nor have I.'

'How's the studying going, Cass?' Mary asks me in the kitchen over breakfast, pouring the coffee. I catch her stroking Ticket under the table, and feeding him a toast crust.

'Oh it's great. I *love* being back at King's. I'm planning to travel to Africa at the end of the summer term, to work in a bush hospital.'

I tell Mary we have to organise a two-month placement during the holidays. It will be a challenge travelling and working abroad, but I'm ready for it.

'The hardest part will be leaving Ticket and Charlie,' I confess. 'But we can't wait to go to Colorado again.'

Charlie and I are joining the Back Up course next year. It will be our first holiday together, as a couple.

Mary is about to ask me another question but Charlie rushes in, gumboots still on and wearing dirty jeans. His mother tells him to take the boots off. 'He's such a mucky pup,' she adds.

I take his hand. 'What's up?'

'Dad wants your help over something,' he says breathlessly.

'My help?'

'Just come outside, it's important. You too, Mum.'

'Hey! What about me?' Anna says, gulping down her coffee.

We grab our coats from the back hall. Mary wraps a scarf around me because she knows how cold I get. Anna pulls on some sheepskin-lined boots over her pyjama bottoms. 'Come on, Ticket,' I say, as Charlie leads me down to the lake. 'What's going on?' I ask him.

Henry is standing by a deep hole with a spade, a bag of compost and a small baby tree. It must be about four foot high. 'Oh good, Cass,' he says, 'you're here. I want you to help me plant this.'

'Right,' I say with surprise, looking over to Charlie who nods reassuringly. 'Sure.'

'It's a liquidambar,' Henry continues. 'I remember you saying it was your favourite; that you loved the way the leaves changed colour. I thought you would like to plant it in memory of your friend, Guy.'

Tears rush to my eyes as both Charlie and Mary come to my side. Mary holds the tree. 'Make sure you get it straight,' Henry instructs.

Charlie helps me spade in some of the soil over the roots. When it's well covered, gently he treads it down and we fill up the remainder with the soil. 'This is for you, Guy,' I tell him. 'Wherever you are, I hope you're happy now.' And finally I am able to tell him what I never managed to say the last time we were together. 'I love you.'

Henry puts an arm around my shoulder and I thank him so much.

We all make our way back to the house, Ticket running on ahead.

ACKNOWLEDGEMENTS

There are many people I'd like to thank.

Firstly, Canine Partners, a charity that helps disabled people to enjoy greater independence and a better quality of life through the help of specially trained dogs. A moving article about a Canine Partner inspired me to find out more, and when I visited the centre to watch puppy training, I was hooked! I am in awe of these dogs that so transform the lives of people with disability. I'd like especially to thank Jenny Moir, who advised me about the training and how the process works. *By My Side* sticks as closely as possible to reality – but I was allowed a little artistic licence.

I'd also like to thank Nina Bondarenko. Nina started the Canine Partners Training Programme in 1992 and told me about the residential courses. She is so knowledgeable about dogs and their behaviour.

Canine Partners put me in touch with the following partnerships: Eileen and Sailor, Susi and Lex, James and Nemo, Judy and Kermit, and finally Jon and Varick. I was moved by the incredible bonds they shared with their dogs.

I'd particularly like to mention Jon Flint and Varick. Jon took so much trouble to tell me about his time in the Royal Marines and his experiences in Afghanistan, along with what life has been like since returning home after his injury. I met Varick, the most handsome flatcoat retriever, and was touched to see how much he has changed both Jon's and his wife, Sarah-Marie's, lives.

Another partnership is Susi and Lex. Horses were always Susi's passion and she was determined to ride again after her spinal cord injury. I watched Lex, her beloved golden Labrador, running along beside her, ready to be called for help if she was ever in trouble. Lex, sadly, died at the age of twelve but he will always be remembered. He was Susi's best friend, and without him she would have been lost.

To learn more about the charity please take a look at their website: www.caninepartners.co.uk

The second charity I'd like to thank is the Back-Up Trust—who like to be referred to as Back Up. Back Up is a national charity that has helped thousands of people of all ages and backgrounds rebuild their confidence and independence after a devastating spinal cord injury. Many thanks go to the CEO, Louise Wright, who told me about the courses Back Up run across the country and abroad, and who advised me on many aspects of this novel. To find out more about Back Up, please go to their website: www.backuptrust.org.uk

There are other people I'd like thank for helping me in so many different ways: Christopher Walker, army chaplain, and Ian Wylie, Royal Artillery, Afghan veteran. Sue Annesley and Peregrine Pollen. Many thanks also go to Kate – a fourth-year medical student, for telling me about her degree.

I'd like to thank my editor, Jane Wood at Quercus. Jane challenges me to bring out the best in my writing, and I love working with her. I'd also like to thank all the lovely team at Quercus.

To Charlotte Robertson, my agent, for always being supportive and getting behind this book. I very much value her support and friendship.

To Mum & Dad, as always – for being the best parents and for looking after me so well when I need to meet deadlines!

Finally, *By My Side* could not have been written without Sarah Orr, to whom the book is dedicated. Following her C7 spinal cord injury aged sixteen, Sarah returned to school. When I met her for the first time back in 2006 she was studying for a Masters in Human Rights. She told me about her experiences backpacking across the world. I discovered she went on a skiing course and worked for Back Up. She had also undertaken an independent tour of the twelve spinal injury units throughout the UK and Ireland to share her backpacking experiences with newly spinally injured individuals and healthcare staff.

More recently, Sarah has had experience developing peer

support networks and other rehabilitation and support-related services and opportunities for people with spinal cord injuries in the UK, New Zealand, and a number of developing countries in Africa.

Sarah is an inspiration. Her life is tough in every way. Spinal cord injury is unrelenting but she has determination, spirit, humour, stubbornness, talent, grace and beauty. She also has endless patience! I have tested her to the limit with my never-ending questions and wanting to dig deep to find out what it's really like to be in a wheelchair. It has been an honour to work with her and to become her friend.